THE ENEMY FACE OFF

HOCKEYMANCES BOOK 3

ASH KELLY

AUTHOR NOTE

Dear reader,

Thank you for picking up a copy of this book!

Your comfort and enjoyment are my top priorities, so before you start reading, I'd like to tell you what you can expect from *THE ENEMY FACE OFF*.

- A hockey romance with a few (minor) fictionalized season details.
- A contemporary closed-door romance with on-page kisses and off-page intimacy discussed. This is **not** a Christian romance.
- All language is PG, typical of what you'd expect on prime-time TV.
- It's mainly lighthearted, but some serious issues are mentioned. Skip the section below if no trigger warnings are needed.
- *Death of a former partner*

- *Child abandonment and adoption*
- *Past bad treatment (including fat shaming) in a relationship*
- *Former bully (minor character)*

Please make an informed decision about whether this book is right for you.

I hope you enjoy Beth and Milo's story!

Ash, xo

ABOUT THE BOOK

Payne by name, pain by nature...

Milo Payne is the grumpiest goalie in the NHL. He's also annoyingly attractive with his broad shoulders, stubbled jaw, and piercing green eyes.

Not that I care.

He may be used to women falling at his feet, but I refuse to be one of them. I'm a *shelf*-diagnosed, snarky booktrovert who's only a sap for romance on the page, not in real life. I've been treated like dirt by guys before—I won't let it happen again.

But suddenly, Milo is everywhere I turn. On my early morning walks. Hanging out with my friends. Moving in next door.

It's irritating...and okay, maybe a little fun to have someone to exchange barbs with.

Because under his gruff exterior, he's surprisingly quick-witted, smart, and kind. A dream guy...if I were looking for that sort of thing, *which I definitely am not.*

Then I discover why he's moved to Comfort Bay, and slowly, the stone walls I've built around my heart start tumbling down.

Milo and I started off as enemies, but will we end up as something else?

The Enemy Face Off is a closed-door pro hockey romance between an anti-love bookworm and a grumpy goalie. You can expect plenty of banter, fast-talking friends, the most unromantic (yet totally romantic) first kiss ever, kiss coupons, a man bun on a mission, and a heartwarming happily-ever-after.

*It's the third book in the **Hockeymances** series, and while it can be read as a standalone, for maximum enjoyment, you may like to read books 1 and 2 first.*

It comes with Ash's PG-passion "All heart, no heat" guarantee!

The Enemy Face Off is PERFECT if you love:

- Pro hockey sports romance
- Enemies to lovers
- Suddenly a single dad
- He loves her teasing him
- An us-ship
- Small town
- Chosen family

- Closed-door romance: no cheating, no cursing, just kisses

1

Beth

Early morning walk people are the best.

There, I said it.

And I stand by it.

Whether it was strolling along the scenic Elizabeth River in Norfolk, Virginia, hiking the trails of Brackenridge Park in San Antonio, Texas, enjoying the serene Cape Fear Botanical Garden in Fayetteville, North Carolina, or any other places we moved to during my childhood, my theory about humanity was affirmed time and time again—the best people start their day with an early morning walk.

How else do you explain a *shelf*-diagnosed, snarky booktrovert like me, whose idea of heaven is being curled up in a dark room with the thermostat set to a chilly sixty degrees, a nonstop supply of books on hand, and who *hates* the outdoors at any other time of the day, strolling through Comfort Bay with a big smile on her face, saying things like, "I saw your garden yesterday. Those marigolds are beautiful this year!" as I pass Mrs. Maynard. Or thanking Dusty Bennett for the strawberries he brought into the bookstore last week, "They were so sweet!" Or smiling ear-to-ear when Mrs. Huxley grabs me by the arm, double checks to make sure no one is within earshot, and with a devilish smile on her sweet seventy-four-year-old face, whispers, "Thanks for the recommendation on that hockey romance novel, I'm really enjoying it."

I'm not a smile-when-I-see-someone person.

I don't take much of an interest in other people's lives beyond the polite surface level stuff. And I certainly don't spend time doing outdoorsy things in nature, like hiking.

With one notable exception.

Yep, that's right.

On my early morning walk.

They've been a regular part of my morning routine, like brushing my teeth and scrolling through Bookstagram, for as long as I can remember. Mom's an early morning walker, too. I joined her one day when I was a little girl and have never looked back.

I do it every single day when it's not raining, which, in Monterey County, California, is hardly ever.

When I do occasionally miss a walk, I'm sluggish all day. It takes my brain way too long to think of my trademark quips. I often find myself chasing after a customer with a clever retort five minutes too late, only to find them gone and my witty comeback wasted. I'm kidding, of course...I'd never run.

I've even managed to rope my closest girlfriends into joining me. My goal was to have a weekly group walk, but with Evie not exactly being a morning person—plus her life being consumed by her hockey stadium, Hannah spending every spare second of her summer with Culver, her best friend, *cough cough*, and with Summer living in LA and busy with dad-caring duties when she's back in town on weekends, it really only leaves Amiel, who, much like me most of the time, isn't an outdoorsy, exercisey kind of gal, either.

But we do manage a group walk every once in a while, which is enough for me.

I spot Elise Daniels, who I know from senior class, coming toward me. I pass on my concern to her. "I hope your mom is feeling better. Let her know I'm thinking of her."

"Thanks, Beth. I will. Have a great day."

"You, too, Elise."

And see, the thing is, a little friendly exchange wouldn't happen on a walk at any other time.

Trust me.

I've tested my theory out by walking at other times of the

day—on my lunch break, after work, even at sunset—and for whatever reason, people are just different.

Not as friendly.

Not as likely to stop and chitchat for a few moments.

Not as willing to smile and say hello and wish you a good day.

I think once people get their caffeine hit, log on to social media, and start dealing with whatever they're dealing with in their lives, they change. They get bogged down by the everydayness of things.

That's why walking first thing in the morning is so great. People aren't bombarded and overwhelmed with everything and are just...nice.

It's refreshing.

I take a deep breath and savor this magical time of day. The sun is just beginning to rise, casting a soft, golden light that gently illuminates the empty streets and buildings of Comfort Bay, the place I've called home since Dad left the military and he, Mom, and my three sisters settled here.

Sometimes I hike up to Cuddle Cove Cliff to watch the sun come up, but most days, I like to wander around town and watch as it slowly comes to life.

I wave to Doyle as he unlocks the door to his grocery store and begins arranging the display, quickly scurrying away when he brings up the Festival of Living Pictures taking place later in the summer. Yeah. I won't be doing that. My community spirit vaporizes the second I step through my front door and kick off my sneakers.

I wander past the bakery and stop for a second, inhaling the inviting smell of freshly baked bread and pastries wafting through the air. I tap on the glass, and Amiel smiles. She finishes sliding a tray of colorful cupcakes, beautifully decorated with icing and sprinkles, into the cabinet then lifts a gloved hand and waves.

"Save you one?" she mouths.

I shake my head. "No thanks."

With a wave, I take off again.

I wish I could sample Amiel's exceptional creations more often—she is one seriously talented baker—but throughout my entire childhood, I was the obese girl with thick glasses who wore a Hello Kitty T-shirt and would get teased at every new school I started for being the obese girl with thick glasses who wore a Hello Kitty T-shirt.

My weight is now in a healthy range. I eat well. I walk every day. And I do allow myself the occasional treat. But the fear of returning to the girl I used to be is never too far from the back of my mind. I'm not consumed by it, but I am careful with what I eat.

I crouch down and get treated to an affectionate flurry of affection, by which I mean a furious licking by Bella, the cutest, most excitable golden retriever I've ever met. Her owner, Felix Logan, is a nice guy. We exchange a few words before he pulls Bella off me, explaining, "I should get going. I'm heading down to LA for an audition."

"Ooh, for anything exciting?"

"Nah. It's a laundry commercial."

"I love doing laundry." I lie with a smile. "Break a leg."

"Thanks, Beth."

I set off again.

Felix and his girlfriend make an adorable couple. So do Evie and Fraser, and so will Hannah and Culver when they finally get their act together and see what's right in front of them.

I let out a sigh that comes out a little more wistful than I intended.

Me?

I'm fine without love in my life.

No, really. *I am.*

I get all the romance I need from the books I devour. Which, admittedly, sounds a little sad.

But when it comes to men, there's a reason why I have my expectation bar set to just an inch above the ground. I've been treated like dirt in the past, so believe me, it's better to be alone than with someone who disrespects you and doesn't value you. Been there, bought the T-shirt, have no intention of ever repeating that again.

Besides, reading as much romance as I have has taught me one thing loud and clear—total package men only exist in the pages of books, not in real life.

Well, except for Fraser.

And Culver's pretty great, too.

And so is Bear for Summer when *she* finally realizes he's head over heels in love with her.

Okay. Let me backtrack here.

Total package men do exist, they just never pop up in my life.

And that's...fine.

The day is beginning to get brighter, and the streets are coming alive with activity. Bear's diner is busy, kids are hanging out in the gazebo waiting for the school bus, and the early morning calm is giving way to the hustle and bustle of the new day.

That's my cue to retreat and go home.

Another successful walk completed.

Well, almost completed.

I'm not in the clear yet, and I don't want to jinx it.

Because, you see, there has been one little wrinkle in my early morning walks recently.

And by *little wrinkle*, I mean a certain grumpy NHL-playing goalie with broad shoulders, a stubbled jaw, and piercing green eyes that do absolutely nothing for me, who I've seen out jogging these past few days and potentially blowing up my entire theory about early morning walkers being the best humans.

Because Milo Payne is most certainly not one of the best humans. He's moody. Grouchy. Arrogant. Oh, and he sports a man bun.

A man bun.

As someone who has faced a great deal of scrutiny over my appearance—especially in my plus-size years—I'm the last person to judge anyone else for theirs, but I can't help how I feel, and there's just something about man buns that makes me shudder. It's like a guy wearing flip-flops when he's not at the beach. It's plain wrong.

I scan the area, but nope, there's no six-foot-something, yummy, broad-shouldered, stubbled-jawed, piercing green-eyed, man-bunned pro hockey player to be found.

Good.

So why does my heart sink a little?

I've been out in the fresh air too long, that's why. All this smiling and talking and interacting with people has messed up my anti-love radar. I need to get home, shower, and scrub all this small-town niceness off of me.

I round the corner onto my street and *bam*—a moving wall plows into me. I'm saved from crashing into the sidewalk by a pair of strong arms gripping me tightly.

I shake my head out, recovering from the shock.

When I look up, I'm greeted by a pair of piercing green eyes. A stubbled jaw. And with the sunlight illuminating him from behind, a haloed man bun.

"Are you okay, Beth?"

I haven't heard him speak a lot, but I'd recognize that deep timbre of his voice anywhere. And for a split second, I thought I heard a trace of concern in his tone. It matches the intense gaze in his eyes as he studies my face.

He's probably just worried I'll sue him for mowing me down.

"I'm fine," I say, brushing his hands off me.

He releases his grip but keeps his hands hovering a few inches away from me as I straighten, like he's keeping them there as a backup in case I stumble.

No. It's not that. It can't be that. It's probably so I don't sue him for further damages.

"I'm *fine*," I repeat once I'm steady on my feet and swat his hands away from me.

"All I was doing was trying to help you," he grumbles, his tone defensive.

"I don't need your help, thank you very much. Chivalry is dead, in case you haven't heard."

I tilt my head up, and boy, those green eyes are enough to almost make me lose my balance again. They're a striking shade of green, an emerald hue flecked with tiny gold specks that catch in the light.

Butterflies dance in my stomach.

One of my older sisters, Schapelle, is a romance author, and she would have a field day describing those eyes.

Me, a cynical anti-love bookworm, knows better than to get sucked in by a guy with mesmerizing eyes. Those ones are always the biggest trouble.

The dancing butterflies are wasting their time.

"But you're okay?" he checks.

"Yes, I am." I zip my hoodie up a little. "Don't worry. I won't sue you."

A line forms between his eyebrows. "Sue me? For what?"

"For barreling into me."

"We rounded the corner at the exact same moment. I don't think anyone's at fault here."

I fold my arms across my chest. "Of course you'd say that."

"What's that supposed to mea—you know what, nevermind. You're not injured. That's what matters."

I huff out a noise that's somewhere between annoyed and hopefully a tiny bit sexy.

Wait. What?

I am *not* trying to sound sexy in front of Milo...am I?

Gosh, maybe I have a concussion.

"Look," he says. "No one was hurt. Can we try and be positive here?"

"Okay, fine. I'm positive this is all your fault."

Ah, Snarky Beth has fully booted up and is back online. Good. I'm going to need her. First order of business? Eliminate that pesky *wanting to sound sexy* virus that has infiltrated my system.

The muscle in Milo's jaw twitches, and his eyes darken. His massive shoulders heave up and down with every breath he takes, staring at me like...like I don't know what.

He's the goalie for the LA Swifts, the same team Fraser and Culver play for. Fraser and Culver are your typical, all-around nice guys.

But Milo?

He's known as the NHL's resident grumpy goalie. Not to mention he has a reputation for being a bit of a player.

I'm not into hockey—or sports in general—so I wouldn't know if that reputation is accurate. But a little harmless online sleuthing confirmed he's got a thing for pretty girls who seem clueless and probably hang on his every word, thinking he's the greatest guy ever.

I've only met him once. He showed up at Hannah's karaoke

night a few weeks ago and, as I suspected, he's cocky. Just not exactly in the way I thought he'd be.

He's got swagger, sure, but it came across more as quiet arrogance rather than some over-the-top alpha display. He didn't say much, mostly sticking with Fraser and Culver, and he never sang. He seemed content to stay in the background rather than be the center of attention.

And if I'm not mistaken, his gaze drifted to me a few times during the evening. I made sure to look away quickly, not wanting to give him the satisfaction. If he thinks he can just blink at a woman and she'll fall under his spell, I wanted to be the one to prove him wrong.

So what if his resting grump face was kinda cute—man bun aside, of course.

Or if I found myself stealing glances at him, too, for some weird reason.

Or if I may have wondered a few times since that night whether he's genuinely grouchy or simply the quiet type who gets labeled that way.

Not that any of it matters.

I'm sure Milo hasn't thought about me since karaoke. He can have any girl he wants—why would he be interested in someone like me?

"I don't have time for this," I say, pushing past him. "I have a bookstore to open."

"Wait." His deep voice cuts through the morning air, and it does something to my feet because I immediately freeze on the spot.

He jogs up until he's in front of me, blocking my way. "You're blocking my way."

He backs off and sweeps his hand to the side, pointing to the sidewalk. "There. I'm not blocking you. You're free to leave whenever you want."

"Good. In that case, I'm going."

"But..."

I drop my gaze to my feet.

Come on, guys, this is your cue to do the thing I just said I'm going to do and skedaddle.

But nope, they stubbornly refuse to listen to me. It's probably their punishment for me using the term *skedaddle* and nothing to do with wanting to hear what Milo has to say.

I blow out a frustrated breath and look up at Milo with those incredible eyes, that sexy stubbled jawline, and that supremely annoying man bun. "But what?"

He stares at me for a few long seconds, his eyebrows knitted together.

I have no idea what's going through his mind, but I am *completely* unprepared for what he eventually says.

"Why don't you like me?"

2

Milo

There. I said it.

Puck's in her possession now.

I take another half step back, being respectful and not wanting to crowd her in—when a woman asks for space, you give it, no questions asked—and study Beth's face as she formulates a response.

It'll probably be some sharp, witty barb designed to cut me down, which I should not find as much of a turn on as I do, because what is wrong with me?

The answer to that question is a lot, but since I don't have time to unpack all of that right now, I focus on what's right in front of me—making some progress on the Beth Moore front.

Assuming she bites.

She stamps her foot, her cheeks puffing out in frustration.

"What do you mean, *why don't I like you*?"

She bit...

I play with the puck for a moment before passing it back to her.

"You completely iced me when we met at karaoke," I say, referring to the group karaoke Culver invited me along to a few weeks back. Beth and I barely exchanged a few words the whole night, and whenever our eyes met, she'd look away so fast it's a wonder she didn't get a crick in her neck.

"I did not *ice* you," she says the word with disdain, like even the faintest hockey reference is too much for her to stomach. "I...don't know you, that's all."

"Well, you could try talking and getting to know me."

"Oh. That's what you want, is it?" She comes in nice and close to me, eliminating the gap I'd created between us. "For me to fawn all over the big, burly hockey player? To bat my eyelashes and hope against hope that you pick me over all the other desperate puck bunnies clamoring for a little bit of your..." She backs off a fraction, and her eyes roam slowly down my body. "...little bit?"

I blink.

Did she just insult my manhood?

Right.

That's it.

My feelings for this woman have torpedoed from liking her to...to full-blown infatuation.

Who *is* she, and why haven't I been able to get her out of my mind since the night we met?

I wish I knew more about her than the few scraps of information I've managed to scrounge together.

All I know is that she's friends with Fraser's girlfriend Evie and Culver's best friend and soon-to-be girlfriend—because come on, it's so obvious—Hannah. She works in a bookstore and is a total bookworm. Big surprise. She's feisty, smart, and not afraid to serve it to anyone, least of all me.

And she's the most beautiful woman I've ever laid eyes on.

The sleek shine of her jet-black bob perfectly frames her pale, flawless face, accentuating her large, expressive hazel eyes, and her full red lips look so soft, so inviting, so irresistibly kissable. When they're not otherwise occupied firing quips at me, that is.

She's wearing teal-green athletic shorts, a fitted, charcoal-gray hoodie over a white T-shirt, and running shoes. An outfit that's meant to be sporty, but wearing it, Beth looks nothing short of mesmerizing. The material clings to her curves in all the right ways and seeing the smooth skin of her legs does something to me.

"Cat got your tongue, hey?" Beth guesses with a self-satisfied smirk, but my silence has nothing to do with being unable to come up with a reply—contrary to what she probably thinks, I actually do have some brain cells—and everything to do with being completely and utterly captivated by her.

And, okay, checking her out slightly.

The sad truth is, she's right.

Not about my manhood. She's *very* wrong about that.

But her comment about the puck bunnies.

I'm not saying that all women are looking to hook up with hockey players so they can tick them off like items on a grocery list, but I am saying that I've attracted more than my fair share of those who have.

I don't know why.

I'm naturally a quiet person. I only open up to people once I feel comfortable around them. That usually takes me some time. Even around my teammates who are the closest people I have in my life, I still come across a little...gruff. Guarded. Scowly, but that's just my face.

I would've thought my grumpy, less-than-inviting demeanor would be a warning sign to women, some sort of red flag for them to stay away. But nope, it seems the grouchier and more aloof I appear, the more the media incorrectly depicts me as a player, the more some women are drawn to it.

Well, apart from one woman who's currently glaring at me, waiting for me to talk.

"I don't want you to fawn all over me, Beth." I speak in a lower tone than I normally do. "But I would like a chance for you to...get to know me."

Her large eyes narrow into a squint. "And why would I want to get to know you?"

"Because, well, isn't that what people do? Get to know each other and maybe become friends?"

"I have enough friends." She shoots the puck back a tad more aggressively than needed.

"You can never have too many friends, though, right?"

I attempt a smile, but it's been a while since I've cracked one, and my cheek muscles have no idea what to do. There's a good-to-high probability I currently look like a confused chipmunk.

Beth scrunches her nose. "What are you doing?"

"Smiling," I answer, then without moving my lips too much, add, "Is it working?"

"I'll just say it's a good thing there are no kids here, or they'd be running away in fear."

My attempt at a smile is replaced by a genuine laugh.

For a second—for *less* than a second—Beth's demeanor shifts and she softens, but then she zips her hoodie all the way up and is back to frowning at me.

"What's wrong now?" I ask. "I've stopped smiling."

"Nothing." Her eyes narrow even more, and I swear it's like she's got X-ray vision and is peering into my soul. "You're just... nothing."

"I'm nothing?"

"No. I paused between the words *just* and *nothing*. On the page, it would have been written as *just ellipsis nothing*."

"On the page?" I lift my chin. "You really love books, don't you?"

She slow claps. "Well deduced. I work in a bookstore, so yes, I like books. I'll save you the hassle and let you know that Hannah, who works in a flower shop, likes flowers, and Amiel, who works in a bakery, likes pastries."

"Let me see if I'm getting this right, because you know"—I tap my head—"Ape for brain here. But first, you belittle my manhood, and now you're questioning my intelligence?"

"Correct." Beth rocks on her feet. "On both counts."

Ooh, I like this girl.

I *really* like this girl.

And if this is how she wants to play, then game on!

"All right." I plant my hands on my hips. "What's the plural of cul de sac?"

"Excuse me?"

"Need me to speak slower to help you understand?"

She huffs out another cute sound before responding. "Cul de sacs, duh."

"Errr!" I make the sound a game show buzzer makes for an incorrect answer. "I'm sorry, but you're wrong."

"What? No I'm not."

"You are. The plural of cul de sac is culs de sac."

"But that *sounds* wrong."

"And yet, it's correct."

As she whips out her phone, I widen my stance to even out our height difference.

"What are you doing?" she asks.

"I want to get the close-up view for when you see you're wrong. I have a feeling I'm going to enjoy it. Also..." I point to the sidewalk again, "plenty of space for you to navigate around me with your head bowed in shame for your loser walk."

Her eyes fire up at the insult. "Oh, I am not the one who will be doing a loser walk, my friend."

"Ah, so we're friends?"

Another adorable little noise. "Shut up."

She purses her lips and focuses on her phone. "That can't be right," she mutters, scrolling more and more aggressively. "Give me a minute."

"Take all the time you need, *friend.*"

It's not going to help her.

She may think I'm just another dumb pro athlete, but I actually do like to read—psychological and domestic thrillers are my genres—and English was always my best subject in school.

She finally gives up.

Clearing her throat, she says something that sounds like, "*Youwereright*," but she says it so quickly I can barely distinguish the words.

I point to my temple again. "Man. Words. Too fast. No understand."

She smiles.

Then catches herself smiling.

Then tries to school her features into a neutral expression as she repeats, slower this time, "You were right."

Now, if it were anyone else, like say, my teammates, I'd use this occasion to gloat and rub it in her face.

But this isn't a *goofing off with my teammates in the locker room* situation. This is a *I'm finally having a conversation with the girl who's inexplicably been on my mind since the second I saw her* situation.

The non-neanderthal part of my brain kicks in, and I decide to play it smart.

"You were right, too," I tell her, kicking a few loose stones on the sidewalk. "About the puck bunnies. It happens. Quite a lot. But I'm not that kind of guy. That's not what I'm looking for."

"Really?" There's a battle going on in her eyes, like whether she's trying to decide whether to believe me or not. "Because if you were a hockey bro who traveled from city to city and slept with a different woman at each place, you'd 'fess up to that? *Orrr*...would you feed me some line about how you're..." She puts on a deep voice, trying to imitate me, '*I'm not that kind of guy. That's not what I'm looking for.*'"

"Sheesh. Now my voice is under fire."

"I think you can handle it."

"You don't know that. I could be a real sensitive guy with real sensitive guy feelings."

She chuckles. "I highly doubt you're going to be losing any sleep over this."

I open my mouth but stop myself in the nick of time from blurting out something stupid like I have already lost sleep over her.

Ever since that karaoke night when she completely ignored me, I haven't been able to get her out of my head. It makes no sense. She barely acknowledged me, all the signs point to her not having the slightest interest in me, and yet, I can't stop thinking about her. This has never happened to me before.

I've brought it up with Fraser and Culver at our off-season training, casually checking if Beth has said anything about me. They always say that she hasn't. So, either she hasn't mentioned me at all to her girlfriends, or she has, and the guys simply don't know about it. As much as I don't want it to be, I have a feeling it's the former.

Maybe I really haven't registered on her radar at all?

Which *should* be fine.

I *should* be able to walk away from someone I've hardly spoken to and know almost nothing about.

So why am I standing here, scrambling to find ways to prolong my time with her for as long as I can?

I shove my hands into my track pants pockets. "So, what historical figure are you going to Fraser's party next week as?" I ask, since it's the only thing I can come up with.

"Not telling."

"Right. Well, I left ordering my costume too late, so I'm stuck going as—"

"Milo, hi." I stop talking and spin around to see my realtor, Willow Wilkins, approaching. She's tall, blonde, and I have no idea how she manages to walk on those crazy high stilettos, but somehow she does. "I thought I recognized that strong back of yours."

Another sound comes from Beth. Less cute this time. More grunty.

"Beth, this is—"

"I know Willow," she cuts me off and directs a glare at Willow that makes me think these two have history. "I really need to get going. Milo, it's been...something. And Willow, I love your shoes. Bye."

And with that, Beth takes off.

"I'll see you at Fraser's party!" I call out after her.

"I'll ignore you there, too," she shouts back without turning around.

I grin to myself.

I wouldn't expect anything else.

3

Beth

Maybe I was a little too harsh on Milo last week.

Ugh. Why can't I get that stupid thought out of my head? It's been buzzing around my subconscious like a swarm of flies around roadkill.

Okay. That's a disturbing image. Sorry.

I've recently branched out from my usual sweet romcoms and read three dystopian romances back-to-back. They're clearly affecting me.

Much like a certain grumpy goalie I can't seem to get out of my head after he—or okay, *we*—bumped into each other on the street.

What can I say? I was thrown off-balance, both figuratively and literally, and I may have rebooted into Snarky Beth mode a little too fast. A little too...aggressively.

I mean, I insulted his manhood, made jokes about his smile scaring children away, and insinuated he was a dummy.

He proved me wrong on that one, and I will never look at the term *cul de sac* the same way again.

In fact, he kind of proved me wrong on all counts.

Not that his expression wasn't a bit...unusual when he tried to smile, but maybe he was nervous?

And not that I can verify my dig about his, uh, manhood, but when I served it to him, he didn't cower or back down.

Importantly, he also didn't get mean or cruel.

He simply volleyed back in a smart, funny, and genuine way.

Maybe a genuine way.

I'm not that kind of guy. That's not what I'm looking for.

Look, I'll give him props for saying the right thing. He even sounded like he meant it. So why couldn't I believe him?

Because guys have said one thing to my face, then another thing behind my back before.

And that's a special type of pain.

That's betrayal.

And yeah, maybe I haven't entirely gotten over the way Liam and Dylan treated me. Maybe I've built up a sky-high wall around my heart to protect myself from getting hurt. But until I *really* know a guy, I'm not giving him my trust ever again.

I've been fooled twice, I am *not* going to be fooled a third time.

If that means I come across a little...harsh, then tough. So be it.

I scratch my arm, not liking how that makes me feel. I may be snarky and sarcastic, but I'm never outright mean.

Unless it's to Willow Wilkins.

She made my senior year at Comfort Bay High a nightmare, mocking me about my weight relentlessly, so she deserves all the stink eye I throw at her.

But I do owe Milo an apology.

It's the right thing to do. So if our paths happen to cross tonight, then I'll quickly slip one in, and we can move on.

I scan the ballroom.

Not that I'm purposely on the lookout for him. I'm just taking in the scene at Fraser's historical romance-themed party.

I've hung out with the girls, which was nice since I've hardly seen them all summer.

I had a memorable meeting with Evie's boss who, like me, came dressed as Marie Antoinette. Unlike me, the majority of her cleavage was pushed up and spilling out the top of her corset. But hey, if you've got it, flaunt it. And believe me, she had *plenty* of it.

Then Fraser took to the stage to reveal the real reason for throwing this party. I may have shed a tear or two at his beautiful proposal to Evie.

Amiel and I joined the lineup, and we've just finished congratulating the newly engaged couple, which means... operation ATGG (Avoid The Grumpy Goalie) can recommence.

"You know, for a person who says she's trying to dodge a certain someone, you seem overly concerned in trying to find him," Amiel observes, bringing her champagne flute to her mouth in an attempt to hide her wry grin.

I ignore the underlying point she's making and take in the newest member of the Fast-Talking Five, and the person who, in a short space of time, has become my closest friend.

I don't make friends easily.

Since meeting Evie and Hannah in high school when my family moved to Comfort Bay, and Summer joining our posse a year after we graduated, I haven't made any new friends. Being a military kid and moving all the time meant I never developed friend-making skills. What was the point of getting close to anyone if we were bound to move anyway?

Not to mention, my personality is something of an acquired taste.

Characters in books make complete sense to me. I can see their strengths as well as their faults. Even when I don't agree with their actions, I at least understand their underlying motivation.

Humans in real life confuse me.

I'm a perpetual disappointment to my mother, but the apple of my dad's eye. I've got two twin sisters, Schapelle and Tenley, who are five years older than me. Schapelle and I click because we're both huge book nerds, but Tenley and I don't have much in common. My youngest sister Allie and I fight like cats and dogs even though we love each other like crazy.

And men?

Do not even get me started on men. They're not just from another planet, they're from another universe.

But with Amiel, it was friendship love at first sight.

She comes across as a little shy and reserved at first, but when you get to know her, she's witty, smart, super loyal, has the best taste in books, and makes the most wickedly delicious, salted caramel cupcakes I've ever had. They're so good, they've become my go-to when I feel like indulging occasionally.

She looks stunning tonight, a Greek goddess draped in a white toga-style dress with gold accents and accessorized with golden sandals, a leafy crown, a few pieces of chic jewelry, and a plastic apple in her hair. She's bronzed her skin and is positively glowing.

She lifts a brow, waiting for a response.

"I'm trying to find Milo so that I can avoid him," I explain, my eyes raking over all the people dressed in elaborate historical costumes, with one *Flintstones*-inspired exception.

"Okay. Whatever you say." Her grin grows into a smile. "I think I just saw him step outside."

"You know what," I say, casually setting my drink on a nearby table. "Think I need some fresh air. And while I'm outside, breathing in all the fresh air, I'll make sure he's there. So that I can avoid him, of course."

"Whatever you say."

A small giggle escapes her, which I ignore, and make my way to the doors that lead out to the terrace.

Amiel was right. Milo is there, leaning against the railing, facing away from me, with those impressively wide shoulders lit up by a streak of moonlight.

From what I've been able to gather from the quick glances I stole his way during the evening so far—all to keep my distance from him, obviously—he's come as a Renaissance poet. An unconventional choice, but I like it. It's unexpected.

His costume is a burgundy velvet doublet, a ruffled collar, a beret that hides his man bun—bonus points for that—and ivory-white tights.

Very tight ivory-white tights.

So tight that even from the other side of the ballroom I could clearly make out his massive quads.

Can't say I've ever really been impressed by a guy's thighs before.

Until tonight.

So yeah, I can admit Milo is an attractive guy...if you go for that whole well-built, muscular, pro athlete vibe, which I definitely do not. I've never watched a hockey match—or is it game?—in my life, and I have no intention of starting anytime soon.

I've tried to push him out of my mind since that karaoke night, but he keeps finding his way back in. It's strange because not only is Milo not my type, but no guy has really caught my eye since things ended with Liam and that was over four years ago. I've only been interested in boyfriends of the book boyfriend variety since.

Not that I'm interested in Milo. He's just suddenly on my mind.

Hannah's recent news that he's been house hunting in town isn't helping. That explains why I've been running into him—and trying to avoid him—on my early morning walks, and why my old bully, now Comfort Bay's star realtor Willow Wilkins, recognized him on the street.

Which makes me wonder why?

Why would a super-rich and famous athlete want to settle down in a small town he has no ties to?

Maybe I'll ask after my apology.

I take a few steps toward him.

He's standing in the far corner, away from everyone, and as I get nearer, I notice he's on his phone.

I stop walking when I start catching snippets of his conversation.

"That's not good enough...Uh-huh...Uh-huh...No. I don't care. Do your damn job. That's why I pay you the big bucks, Gary...Not my problem. Get it sorted. *Now*!"

I inch back a few steps.

He ends the call without saying goodbye, and I don't know what to do. Should I keep backing away and pretend I never overheard anything and then continue ignoring him, or should I go up to him, get my apology out of the way as fast as I can, and then continue ignoring him?

Before I can make up my mind, Milo spins around. His brow furrows as he marches toward me.

My throat suddenly goes very dry, but I manage to eke out a, "Hey, Mil—"

"I'm sorry, but no, Beth," he cuts me off gruffly. "I'm not in the mood for a round of verbal sparring right now."

My throat suddenly rehydrates, and I regain my full voice, "Nice to see you, too, *jerk*."

"Whatever," he mutters before storming inside.

I stand there in disbelief.

I can't believe *I* came out to apologize to *him* for being rude. He doesn't deserve my apology. Not when he's Mr. Rudey McRudeyson himself.

"Not in the mood, my butt," I angrily grumble to myself as I stomp back indoors, rage surging through me.

"Whoa. What happened?" Amiel asks the second she sees me. "Why do you have steam coming out of your ears?"

"Take a wild guess."

"Milo?"

"Yeah. Milo. We talked. Or rather, I *tried* to talk to him but he's a stuck up you-know-what and brushed past me with a pathetic, *'I'm not in the mood for a round of verbal sparring.'*"

I reach for my drink and down a hefty gulp as I wait for Amiel to respond.

I would have accepted any of the following replies from her:

Oh, I'm so sorry he said that to you, or...

You were right all along, Beth, he really is a grump, or...

Let's find his car and cover it in cake.

But instead, that wry grin is back on her face.

I tap my fingers against my forearm. "What?"

"I can't believe you're not seeing it."

"Seeing what?"

"Uh, hello. What trope are you and Milo currently playing out?"

"No. *No no*. No, no, no. Do *not* even go there."

"Oh, I'm going there. Just like we went there with Hannah earlier this summer about Culver and her going from friends to lovers."

"That was different."

"How was that different?"

"It wasn't me," I mutter, taking another gulp.

Amiel giggles. "True. But the only *actual* difference between your situation and Hannah's is simply the trope involved. Hers with Culver is friends to lovers. Yours with Milo is enemies to lovers."

I fold my arms across my chest. Or try to. This darn corset

is so tight that even basic movements are a struggle. "Mark my words, Amiel. I will *never* be that man's lover."

"But—"

"But nothing. Trust me, I am well aware of how this trope plays out. But Milo Payne is exactly that—a pain. And I will not be falling in love with him. I've crossed paths with him exactly three times. The first time, I brushed him off at karaoke because I refused to be another one of his easy wins. The second time he barreled into me and almost killed me." A slight exaggeration, but who's got time for fact checking? "And now he's validated my low-key online snooping. He's rude and entitled all because he's some big hotshot hockey star." I take a breath. I'm all riled up, and I hate that he has such an effect on me. "Are you ready to go? I know you have an early start tomorrow."

"Sure." Amiel keeps her eyes on me for a moment, and I can tell she's thinking things. Thankfully, she keeps her thoughts to herself. "Let's say goodbye to the girls."

We try to find our friends but Hannah—along with Culver—is MIA, and Evie and Fraser are still dealing with well-wishers. We manage to locate Summer hanging out with Evie's sisters, Harper and Laney, so we pull her in for a quick hug and to tell her we're leaving.

Five minutes later, we're in my car.

I'm still fuming.

And hating this tight, restrictive outfit more than ever. Thankfully, it's only a ten-minute drive to Amiel's place on the outskirts of Comfort Bay, so I'll survive. But once I get home, I am ripping it off me and swearing off corsets for life. My heart goes out to the poor women who had to wear them daily.

"Thanks again for the ride," Amiel says.

I smile at her. "Don't mention it."

She's confided in me a little about what brought her to

Comfort Bay, and by the sounds of it, that ex of hers is a real piece of work. I know she's struggling financially, so a fifty buck Uber ride is an expense she could do without at the moment. It's also why she's working all the shifts she can get at the bakery.

"How are you feeling?" she asks.

"Hot and bothered," I reply, referring to my outfit. The smile rising on her lips suggests she took it to mean something else. Or rather, *someone* else. "Don't start with me."

"I wasn't going to say anything."

"Your smile says it all."

"Fine. I'm looking out the window so you can't see my smile."

As I continue driving, I regret not taking off my rococo heels and wearing a pair of flats like I did on the way to the party. The shoes are restrictive and slippery, and I don't think it's safe for me to be driving while wearing them.

Unfortunately, there's construction on the side of the road, so the second lane is closed and there's nowhere for me to pull over. At least it's not busy out, and I'm only doing thirty miles an hour.

With one hand firmly on the steering wheel and my eyes glued straight ahead of me, I lean down and try to unfasten the strap on my right shoe at least. The stupid thing is stuck, so I have to fiddle with it.

I attempt to loosen it.

Once. Nothing.

Twice. Ooh, it budges a little.

Thrice. Nope. I lose it.

Darn. I was so close to getting it off.

I glance down for a nanosecond to see what the problem is, and I manage to detach it.

My celebration is short-lived because as soon as I look up,

red tail lights fill the windscreen. I slam on the brakes, but it's too late. I nudge the bumper bar of the car stopped in front of me.

"Are you okay?" I ask Amiel.

"Yeah. Fine. Sorry, I should have been looking."

"No. *I* should have been looking. I'm the one driving. This is my fault."

"What do we do now?" Amiel asks, glancing at me nervously.

Before I can answer, the driver's side door of the car in front of us opens.

A man gets out.

A man wearing a beret and with broad shoulders I'd recognize anywhere.

Oh no.

I slink down in my seat.

Of all the people in the world I could have rear-ended, why did it have to be him?

4

Milo

Well isn't this terrific. Just when I thought tonight couldn't get any worse...

As I stride over to the car that hit me, I remind myself to cool it.

It's late.

It's dark.

The road is deserted.

The last thing I want to do is inadvertently scare the driver. My face has the ability to do that, apparently.

An image of Beth flashes in my mind.

I was rude to her tonight.

Even all the layers of makeup she had on couldn't mask the way her expression changed when I charged past her. I didn't mean to snap at her, and I can't even remember what I said exactly, but I'm pretty sure it wasn't nice.

My only excuse is that I'd just been told I was *still* in fatherhood limbo.

This whole paternity testing slash adoption process has been dragging on for three months now, and it's starting to take a toll on me.

I may not have known I was a father until recently, but now that I do, every day I don't spend with my daughter—and potentially my son—feels like an eternity.

Josie, who's five, and Jonah, who's two and a half, are currently living with their maternal grandparents in LA, so at least I know they're safe, well cared for, and loved. They're not bouncing around the system from foster home to foster home the way I did.

But still...they should be with me.

I go to run my fingers through my hair, only to be met with

felted wool. I yank the stupid beret off my head and go to shove it into my back pocket, only to remember I'm not wearing pants but ridiculously tight tights because I left ordering my costume to the last minute—other things on my mind lately—and this was the last available outfit in my size.

Okay. Just relax, man.

I take a long, calming breath and tell myself that while whoever is behind the wheel may not have the best driving skills, they could be hurt. Although I doubt that. They barely nudged my rental.

It's probably someone on their phone, driving distracted.

I approach the car, and the window rolls down.

My jaw drops. "You have got to be kidding me."

"Do I look like I'm laughing?"

The door opens, and Beth struggles to get out of the car.

I want to help her out since her outfit looks as restrictive as it does incredible, but she may not be receptive to offers of help from me at the moment.

I cast my eyes down and notice she's only wearing one shoe.

"Are you hurt?" I ask, when she's finally standing in front of me, and then, because I can't help myself, add, "Or wait, am I not allowed to ask that since chivalry is supposedly dead?"

"What crawled up your butt tonight?" She swats me across the chest with the shoe she's not wearing. "You're even crankier than usual."

I'm taken aback.

Not that she hit me with her shoe—I barely felt it—but that she's paid enough attention to me to realize I'm more cranky tonight than my usual cranky.

Could that be a good thing? A sign that maybe she likes me?

Of course not, you moron. It's a sign that she's mad at you and thinks you're a grouch like everyone does.

The smart thing to do would be for me to shut up. Actually, an even smarter thing to do would be to apologize first *then* shut up.

So of course, my mouth does the exact opposite and baits her. "I suppose you're going to say this is my fault, too?"

The passenger side door suddenly swings open, startling me.

A woman dressed as a Greek goddess gets out. I recognize her from karaoke night. Amanda? Emilia?

I may not remember her name but that doesn't stop me from asking, "Are you okay?"

"I'm fine." She glances towards Beth. "Listen, since no one is hurt, I'm going to leave you two..."

She trails off, and Beth tilts her head to the side. "How will you get home, Amiel?"

Headlights flash across Beth's face as an SUV pulls up on the other side of the road.

"I ordered a ride."

"Are you able to affo—"

"It's not that far. It's fine." Her eyes flick briefly to me then back to Beth. "I'll leave you two to it."

That's the second time she's said that.

Beth makes a noise like she's annoyed at her friend for bailing, or maybe, if I'm reading between the lines, she could be annoyed at something else.

Yeah, being stuck alone with you, doofus.

Amiel gives a small wave before climbing into the SUV.

"Text me when you get home," Beth shouts before the door closes.

"I will!"

Amiel takes off.

Beth looks between her car and my rental, then swings her gaze to meet mine. I brace for an incoming onslaught of how this is somehow my fault because I slammed on my brakes too suddenly or one of my tail lights is out.

But instead, she speaks in a calm voice. "I'm sorry. This accident is my fault. Let's exchange insurance details."

"Um, okay..."

She narrows her eyes. "Why aren't you moving?"

"I'm waiting for the punchline. The jab. The gotcha moment."

"In that case, you'll be waiting a while. I'm an adult, and I can admit fault when I'm to blame for something. I ran into you because my stupid shoe was bugging me." She waves it in front of me. "The clasp was stuck, I got distracted, and here we are."

"And to think, I had it in my head you were a real-life Cinderella."

What is the matter with me? Why am I saying *all* the wrong things to her tonight?

The faintest glimmer of a smile appears on her face. "I've been called a lot of things, but never Cinderella."

Headlights beam in the distance, and I can see a car approaching. Due to the road construction, there's only one lane open, and our cars are currently blocking it.

"Are you okay to drive?" I ask.

"I am."

"In that case, let's meet at the diner to exchange insurance information." She opens her mouth—safe to say, it's probably to object—so I throw in, "Don't worry, I'll have you back before midnight."

～

Fifteen minutes later, we're seated in a booth at Bear's diner. He doesn't say or smile a lot. I like him.

It crossed my mind as I was pulling up, that Beth and I might look a little out of place in a Marie Antoinette and Renaissance poet's costume. But when we stepped inside, we found half of Comfort Bay, fresh from Fraser's party, stopping by on their way home. The place is filled with all sorts of historic characters, getting served by Bear wearing a flannel shirt and backward baseball cap.

Beth takes a sip of her strawberry milkshake then asks, "So, why are you in an extra salty mood tonight?"

"Why do you want to know?"

"Why are you answering a question with a question?"

I cut my slice of boysenberry pie in half and slide my plate toward the middle of the table. "Want some?"

"No, thanks."

"I'll get you another fork."

"It's not that. I mean, it is that. Boy germs are the worst."

"Very true."

"But I'm not hungry. Thanks though."

I take a bite of pie, and as I chew, mull over a response to her question.

No one knows what I've been going through these past few months, not even my teammates, who are the closest thing to family that I've got. Who are the *only* family I've got. Without them, I'm all alone in life. Been that way since the state intervened and took me from my parents when I was seven.

But I can't tell Beth about the phone call with my lawyer that got me all riled up earlier. Why burden her with my problems when she low-key—or, more likely, mid-key—hates me?

I take another bite of pie, wash it down with a healthy chug of chocolate milkshake, and answer her question without really answering her question. "I got some bad news tonight."

"I figured. I overheard you on the phone."

"You were listening in on my private conversation?"

"No. I happened to overhear bits and pieces of it. I didn't do it on purpose. I actually came out to the terrace to apologize."

"Apologize in advance for your plot to crash into me later in the evening?"

That draws a smile out of her. "No. For being rude to you when you—when maybe *we*—bumped into one another on the street."

"Oh. I see."

"I reflected on my behavior, and I was a little...harsh with you. I'm sorry about that."

I'm speechless.

I'm not used to people owning their stuff. I guess when you've been exposed to a lifetime of foster parents who blame everything and everyone else for their woes—the government, their bosses, other family members—rather than take one iota of accountability for their own crummy lives, it's...refreshing.

"I'm sorry, too," I say. "I was rude to you on the terrace. I just had..."

"Some bad news?"

"Yeah. But that's no excuse to speak to you the way I did."

"Thank you for saying that." She lowers her head, bringing her full pink lips to an inch above her straw. Her gaze stays down as she says, "Because you should know, I don't verbally spar with just anyone, Milo."

Ah, that's right. I said something stupid about not being in the mood to verbally spar with her. I remember now.

Man, I'm an idiot.

I'd verbally spar with her any time, any day. Our run-in last week has been playing on loop in my mind. I loved every second of it.

I clear my throat. "I apologize for saying that because I enjoy verbally sparring with you. A lot."

She makes a satisfied noise, like she feels the same way but doesn't want to give me the satisfaction of saying she feels the same way.

"So..." I decide to push my luck, because what have I got to lose besides my dignity and self-respect? "Does this mean that we're friends?"

I smile at her, and it comes more easily than it has in a long time. She holds my gaze for a few seconds, and no children are running away screaming. Both good signs.

"I wouldn't go that far," she finally says, a playful sparkle lighting up her hazel eyes. "We're more like friends...*ish*."

5

Beth

"Brrr, it's chilly this morning," Hannah says.

"It is," I agree, zipping up my jacket all the way to my neck.

Okay, so it's not as cold as plenty of other places I've lived around the country, but as a West Coast girl for the past eight or so years, temps in the mid-fifties in early October are officially classified as cold.

"I'm so glad we're doing this," Summer says.

"And that the sidewalks are wide enough to accommodate all five of us," Amiel quips.

I smile, but it's a sad smile.

This is the last time Amiel, Evie, Hannah, Summer, and I will be physically together in one place like this. Hannah and Culver fly off to Italy next week to begin the next chapter of their lives, and who knows when they'll be back? They certainly don't. They're happy to go with the flow and see where life takes them.

I'm happy they're together, and not only because it proved Amiel and I were right about them going from friends to lovers. I just wish they weren't starting off their couple life all the way over in Europe.

I wrap my arm around Evie's puffy jacket. "I assume your silence is because you're still booting up as much as it is about the sadness of this being our last early morning group walk together."

She pulls the coffee cup from her lips. How she manages to walk like that I'll never know, but she's got it down to a fine art. "Correct. My sadness is battling with my need for caffeine, which I need to fuel my sadness. It's a vicious cycle I hope to break after my second cup."

Because of course, one extra-large, triple-shot monstrosity isn't enough for her, she's ordered two.

"Guys, you're making it sound like I'm leaving for the moon or something," Hannah says. "We'll still be in touch. We've got our WhatsApp group to message each other."

"But time zones," I grumble.

"Yes, they suck, but we'll figure out a day and time that works for all of us. Maybe we can schedule a weekly video call?"

"I'd love that," Summer says with a smile.

"Same," Amiel agrees while Evie bobs her head, signaling it's a yes from her but that her need for caffeine is still in the lead.

"Just make sure you have a good internet connection," I say. "Can you imagine trying to have our normal, million-mile-a-minute conversation with slow Wi-Fi? It'd never work."

Amiel giggles. "That would be hilarious and frustrating at the same time."

"I hate the way I look on camera at the best of times," Summer says. "And I especially hate it when the screen freezes and I look like a giant blob."

"You're gorgeous," I tell her. "You could never look like a blob."

"Beth's in a complimentary mood this morning," Hannah says to Evie but conveniently loud enough for the whole group to hear. "I wonder why that could be."

And with that, she ignites what could very well be our last round of in-person fast-talking.

Me: "I'm not biting."
Hannah: "I don't need you to bite. I have three other girls all ready, willing, and very eager to discuss your Milo situation."

Me: "Ha. Joke's on you. There is no Milo situation to discuss. I haven't seen or heard from him since Fraser's party."

Summer: "So the insurance companies are handling everything with your fender bender?"

Me: "Correct."

Hannah: "I'm not letting you off the hook that easily, missy. Remember at the start of summer how you and Amiel were convinced that Culver and I would become more than friends?"

Me: "I have no recollection of that whatsoever."

Hannah: "Sure, sure. Well, I've been speaking to a certain someone..."

Amiel: "It's purely a coincidence that I'm switching places and moving away from Beth."

Hannah: "...and it turns out that in romance-novel land, people who pretend to hate each other end up loving each other."

Me: "Too bad we live in Comfort Bay and not in romance-novel land. And who says I'm pretending to hate Milo?"

That earns me a win—a rare beat of silence. But my victory fades quickly. They're quiet from exchanging grins and eye rolls—and in Evie's case, finishing her first coffee—not because I made my point.

Evie: "I'm ready to join in the conversation. I can't miss out on the opportunity to rib Little Miss Anti-Love here."

Me: "Why is everyone ganging up on me?"

Evie: "Because I want you to have what me and Fraser do. Or what Hannah and Culver have. True love is a wonderful thing."

Me: "True love is a scary and daunting thing."

Hannah: "That's what makes it so wonderful."

Me: "Not when you get hurt."

"Hey." Hannah gently takes my hand. "Not all men are like your exes. You just had bad luck."

"Sure. But twice?" I ask, meeting her gaze.

She nods emphatically. "Look, it happens. I'm sorry that's been your experience, but hopefully, things will be different next time with—"

"Let's talk about something else." I pull my fingers from her grip and clap, cutting her off before she can bring up Milo again.

I don't even know what I feel about him, or why I'm thinking about him so much. I'm perfectly happy living in blissful ignorance for as long as I can. Men have only ever caused me pain, so if I'm going to fall for someone, it can't be a guy like Milo. I need the next guy to be a good one.

Me: "I'm changing the topic and not even bothering to try and fit it into a neat segue. Summer, how are you doing?"
Hannah: "So not done with this. We're circling back to you later."
Me: "Fine. Later. Summer?"
Summer: "I agree with Hannah about circling back later. But I'm doing well."
Evie: "Define well."
Summer: "Work is good, and Dad's condition isn't getting worse, so we're all happy about that."
Amiel: "Any news on the love life front?"
Summer: "That would be a big no."
Me: "So nothing has progressed with you and Bear?"
Summer: "Also, no. And unless you want to circle back to yourself way sooner than you'd like, can we drop it? Please."
Amiel: "At least you have someone interested in you."
Summer: "I don't even know if he is interested."
Amiel, Evie, Hannah, me: "*HE'S INTERESTED!*"

Summer: "Whatever. I'm moving the circle along. What about you, Amiel? Are you seeing anyone?"

Me: "Are you even ready to date again?"

Amiel: "No and no. I'm still dealing with the mess my ex left me with. That's not to say I'd mind if someone looked at me the way Bear looks at Summer. It's nice to be wanted, you know?"

Hannah: "It is. And you will find someone, Amiel. When the time is right and when you're ready."

Amiel: "Thanks. How are you feeling about Italy? Excited?"

Hannah: "Oh, my goodness. Sooo excited."

Summer: "What are you going to do over there?"

Hannah: "Not sure yet. I'm going to try and keep my hot girl summer vibe going and not make too many plans, because for the first time in my life, I don't have to."

Me: "That sounds great. A little scary, but great."

Hannah: "It is a little scary, I'll admit. But I'm not alone. I've got Culver, and he's rented a gorgeous chateau in Positano."

Evie: "Where is that?"

Hannah: "Southern Italy. It's a picturesque small town right on the ocean."

Me: "Sounds a little like the Italian version of Comfort Bay."

Hannah: "Huh. You know what? I never thought of it like that, but you're right."

Amiel: "Is that why you chose it?"

Hannah: "No. Culver has family there. That was the reason. I might do an art class, and he might take cooking lessons, but again, nothing is set in stone."

Me: "Live your best life, girl. No one deserves it more than you do."

Hannah: "Oh, believe me, I intend to."

This circle hasn't returned to me yet, and I intend to keep it that way for as long as I can.

Me: "And how come you're looking so happy, Evie?"

Evie: "Uh, because I'm caffeinated."

Me: "I don't mean right now, but in general. You've been bummed ever since the season started and Fraser hit the road again."

Evie: "He has a few days off, so he's back."

I let that sink in.

Me: "So...Wait. If Fraser has time off, then the whole team has time off, right?"

Evie: "Correct."

Me: "So, uh, what's Milo doing on the break?"

Evie: "How would I know?"

Me: "It's a hockey question, and you know hockey."

Evie: "No. It's a hockey *player* question, and there's only one hockey player I'm interested in."

Me: "Right. Of course."

Aware that the girls are looking at me and no doubt thinking *things*, I need to move on and move on quickly.

Me: "In that case, I do have an actual hockey question for you."

Summer: "Nice recovery, Beth."

Me: "Thanks. Evie, what happens in a face off?"

Evie, frowning: "That actually is a hockey question."

Me: "I did warn you."

Evie: "But it's a hockey question from *you*. You, who's never watched a second of a hockey game in your life. You don't even follow anything hockey related on TikTok."

Me: "I, uh, may have been flicking through the channels a few nights ago."

Evie, grinning: "This wouldn't have been a few nights ago when the LA Swifts were playing in Chicago?"
Me: "Maybe."
Evie: "I see. Milo had a great game that night."

Heat crawls up my neck, but I do my best to act unaffected.

Me: "Oh, did he? What position does he play again? With all the players wearing the same costume, it's hard to tell them apart."
Evie: "Firstly, they're called uniforms, not costumes, and you know full well Milo is a goalie, easily recognized by the fact that he's the one, you know, guarding the goal."
Me: "*Ohhh*. That's what he was doing. I thought he was alone because the other players didn't like him being a big grouch and all."

Even though I hardly know him, I'm starting to see that may not be entirely true.

Okay, so he looks and acts grouchy a lot of the time, but I've caught a few glimpses of him when he's been mellow—borderline funny, even—so I know there's more lurking under the surface than just his gruff exterior.

Possibly.

Maybe.

Not that I'm spending a significant amount of time psychoanalyzing what he may be like under the surface.

Or what his body might look like under that costu—uniform.

But I can't deny the image of his muscular legs in those white tights is stubbornly emblazoned in my memory bank. He had no business making something so wrong look so irresistibly good.

Evie: "*Riiight*. Why don't we watch a game together, and I can explain face offs and a whole bunch of other stuff to you?"

Me: "Yeah, okay. But I'm not committing to anything."

Evie, laughing: "Of course you aren't."

Summer: "How's the stadium going, Evie?"

Evie: "The final touches should be completed by the end of the month, which means we'll be able to open to the public then."

Summer: "Did you manage to get two junior teams set up?"

Evie, sighing: "No. Just the one team. The requirements for a para team are a lot more complex. For now, I'm only able to offer training, but I hope to register them in the league for next season."

Me: "Hey, don't be disheartened. You're doing an amazing thing."

Evie: "I guess. Ooh, speaking of amazing things, I have some exciting news, you guys. Fraser and I have set a date."

We all stop walking and crowd in around her.

Hannah: "When?"

Evie: "The week between Christmas and New Years."

We all squeal and bundle in for a group hug, jumping up and down in the middle of the sidewalk.

Amiel: "Oh my gosh, that's so exciting."

Summer: "That's so soon."

Evie: "It is. But we're keeping it simple. Guest list is under two hundred."

Me: "That's your idea of simple?"

Evie: "If our mothers had their way, we'd be looking at royal-wedding numbers. We have an amazing wedding planner who is the best and is taking care of everything, so yeah...keep that week free."

Summer: "Consider it free."

Evie, turning to Hannah: "Will you guys be able to make it?"

Hannah: "Of course. We'll probably be back in the US for Christmas with our families anyway."

Evie: "That's what we thought, that most people would be here or at least nearby. It's hard trying to get two hundred people in the same place at the same time."

Amiel: "I bet."

Evie: "Plus-ones are welcome, of course. And Beth?"

Me: "Yeah."

Evie: "Milo will be coming, too. Maybe you could drive up the mountain together?"

Me: "I don't think so, but nice try, girl."

Evie: "And I do know."

Me: "Huh?"

Evie: "About Milo, and what he's doing on his mini break."

Me: "Oh, okay."

There's a pause in the conversation, like she's waiting for me to ask for more information while I'm hoping she offers it up without me having to.

After a few moments, I relent.

Me: "Okay, you win. What is Milo up to on his break?"

Evie: "I'm so glad you asked. He's currently in LA, but he'll be here in Comfort Bay tomorrow."

Me: "Why?"

Evie: "Fraser mentioned he found a house he likes online and wanted to see it for himself."

Me: "So he's definitely buying a house here then?"

Evie: "Looks like it."

Hannah: "Isn't the place next door to you for sale?"
Me, scoffing: "It is. But I seriously doubt a rich hockey player who could afford one of those huge mansions on the hillside overlooking the ocean would be interested in a modest bungalow in a suburban cul de sac."

Just saying the term *cul de sac* transports me back in time, and a warm shiver rushes through me.

I remember his smile at the diner that night, after our minor accident, when he asked if we were friends.

And it wasn't a *hide your kids* scary smile. It was warm and genuine, and it felt like peeking behind a curtain and getting a glimpse of a whole new, hidden side of him.

But we're just occasional verbal sparring partners, nothing more.

Very occasional sparring partners since the guy is away traveling and doing his hockey thing while I live my simple, bookish life here in sleepy Comfort Bay.

Hannah: "You're probably right. But it's a funny thought. You and Milo being neighbors."
Me: "No, it's not. It's a terrible thought."

A terrible, *terrible* thought.

6

Milo

I knock on the front door of the mid-century modern house in a nice LA suburb and wait. My hands clench and unclench, trying to steady my nervous energy.

It's not every day you meet your children for the first time.

The door opens, and Mike and Robyn Malone greet me. They're in their early sixties, and from the countless emails we've exchanged, they seem nice. Genuine. Like maybe we can find a way to navigate this super complicated and potentially fraught process ourselves.

Meeting like this, informally and without the need for social workers or court-appointed monitors, is a good start.

"Welcome, Milo," Mike says. He's stocky, with a head of silver hair thinning just a bit on top. His bright blue eyes twinkle as he looks at me with a welcoming smile.

"It's good to finally meet you," I say, stepping into their entryway. "Here. I bought these." I stick out my arm, and Robyn takes the bouquet from me. I don't know what the etiquette is for an occasion like this, but I figured flowers couldn't hurt.

She accepts them with a smile. "Thank you. They're beautiful." Soft, curly gray hair frames her face, and her warm brown eyes reflect her gentle, caring presence.

They really seem like ideal grandparents, and I'm glad Josie and Jonah have been in their care while we work things out.

"I know we have a few things to discuss," Mike says. "But the children are waiting in the living room."

"They're excited to meet you," Robyn adds.

"I am, too." I suck in a deep breath. "A little nervous, but excited."

"That's perfectly understandable." Robyn smiles and pats me on the arm. "This is a big moment. For all of us."

I force a smile as they usher me toward the living room, tension swirling in my gut with every step.

I've never given much thought to parenthood. My sole focus has always been hockey. It's been the one constant in my life, the only thing I could rely on. But now that paternity has been confirmed, I have to step up.

Honestly, I'm not just a little nervous—I'm petrified. I want to be a good dad more than anything. But how? How can I be a good father when I have no role model to base myself on?

Parenting is hard. I've read countless books and scoured the internet, devouring everything I can on the subject. But at the end of the day, there's no magic manual that teaches you how to be a good dad.

My throat tightens, and I pray I'm up to the task. I have to be. Two little kids are depending on me.

We enter the living room, and my stomach tingles with a fluttering sensation as my eyes land on Josie and Jonah.

Josie is sitting on the couch, keeping a watchful eye on her brother who's on the floor. She's the most beautiful little girl I've ever seen, with tousled dark blonde hair, rosy cheeks, and blue eyes that sparkle with curiosity. Jonah bears a striking resemblance to her. Same wide smile, same big blue eyes, hair slightly lighter and curlier.

"Josie, Jonah, we'd like to introduce you to someone," Mike says. "This is Milo. Your father."

Josie stays seated on the couch, but Jonah drops the blocks he was playing with and pushes to his feet. With a combination of determination and wobbliness, he toddles over to me, arms stretched out for balance.

"Hewwo," he says, tapping my leg.

I crouch down. "Hey, Jonah. Nice to meet you." I wince—

did I really just say *nice to meet you* to a toddler? "What are you building over there?"

"I got house! See?"

"I'd love to see. Right after I say hello to your sister."

"Oh-tay," he says, and man, he is too cute for words.

I get up and Robyn joins me as I walk over to Josie. "She's a little shy at first," she whispers. "Takes her a little while to warm up to people."

"I can relate," I mutter back, then take a seat on the couch. "Hey, Josie. How are you?"

"Good, thank you."

She's wearing a dress with colorful patterns and sandals, her feet dangling off the couch. She holds onto Robyn's hand but keeps her bright blue eyes fixed on me the entire time.

Not sure how to break the ice, I go with, "Do you like hockey? Or sports?"

She shakes her head and looks away. "No," she says quietly. "I don't."

Okay. That didn't work.

"What about books?" I ask, hoping for more luck. "Do you like to read?"

"Oh, yes," Robyn answers for her, rubbing Josie's arm. "Tell Mil—" Our eyes meet, and we exchange an awkward smile. Robyn tries again. "Tell your father about the book we bought yesterday."

"*Green Eggs and Ham*," Josie says softly.

"Oh. So you like to cook?" She and Robyn look at me funny. "That's the name of a cookbook, right?"

Josie looks up at her grandmother, and I hear Mike chuckle from the other side of the room. What am I missing here?

Josie starts laughing as Robyn explains that *Green Eggs and Ham* is a Dr. Seuss book.

"Oh, I knew that," I say, waving my hand in the air even though I have no idea who this doctor is or why he's writing a cookbook that my five-year-old daughter is reading.

But the ice has been broken, and that's all that matters.

I go over to help Jonah build his house. Well, I try to. He's more interested in knocking down whatever he starts rather than finishing it.

Josie sits on the floor, a few feet away from us, watching me intently.

I glance her way now and then, wanting her to feel included without overwhelming her.

She catches me looking and her cheeks turn red. "Do you like my dress?" she asks, bashfully.

"I do. It's very pretty."

"Pwitty! Pwitty!" Jonah raises his arms above his head.

"See, even your brother agrees."

That brings a small smile to her face. I sit, playing with Jonah and his blocks, while striking up a conversation with Josie about the other books she's reading.

After ten or so minutes, a young woman enters the room.

"This is Grace, our nanny," Mike explains.

"Hi, it's great to meet you." She looks me up and down, smiling widely. "I'm a huge fan of the LA Swifts. And you."

"Thank you," I reply politely and try not to bristle. This is definitely not the time for flirting.

"Would you mind taking Josie and Jonah outside, please?" Robyn asks Grace.

"Of course." She takes Jonah into her arms, aims another sultry smile at me, then leaves with the kids.

"You guys have a nanny?" I ask, settling into an armchair as Robyn and Mike sit on the sofa opposite me.

"We do," Mike answers. "She's part-time, but let's face it,

we're not spring chickens anymore and kids have a lot of energy."

"Yeah. I bet."

"Oh, I'm sorry," Robyn says. "I haven't offered you anything to drink. Would you like some water? Coffee? Something stronger."

"No. That's fine. Thank you. I have a house inspection tomorrow, so I can't stay long."

They exchange a discreet look. I mentioned in our emails that I'm planning to settle in Comfort Bay, and I get the sense they're not too keen on the idea. It's a three-hour drive from LA, and I get it. It's not across the country, but it's also not just a few suburbs away like they're used to.

"It's really not that far," I explain. "And I want you to see Josie and Jonah as much as you like."

Robyn leans forward, her expression hopeful. "Really?"

"Absolutely. Of course. You are, and will always be, their grandparents. I don't want to come between that. I have no family myself, which is why I know how important it is. Please don't think that by moving to Comfort Bay, I'm trying to take them away from you."

"If you don't mind me asking, why are you moving there?" Mike asks. "It's not your hometown, is it?"

"No. It's not. But a few of my teammates live there. And it's a beautiful place. A quintessential small American town with tree-lined streets, charming front porches, a local diner on the corner, and a town gazebo. It's close to the water, and only a short drive to the mountains. Everyone knows each other by name, and it's a real close-knit community. I want Josie and Jonah to have a safe and happy childhood, and I think it'll be a great place for them to grow up. And both of you are always welcome to visit. Any time. I mean it."

"Thank you, Milo." I can hear the gratitude in Robyn's

voice. "That really means a lot to us. We've been so worried that—well, never mind. It's just good that you're being so nice and decent about this. It's been a hard few months for us."

I can't even begin to imagine. "I'm sorry for your loss."

"Thank you," Mike says, his eyes watering at the mention of the loss of his daughter.

Not knowing whether to say more about Isla or move on, I opt to move on. "So, everything seems to be going well with the paperwork."

Mike wipes the corner of his eye and nods. "Yes. It is. Even though it's taken a while."

"It sure has."

I'm *almost* officially a father of two.

Josie's paperwork is finalized and custody will be transferred to me in the next two weeks. That part was relatively simple since I am her biological father.

The process with Jonah is a whole other story and the reason for the lengthy holdup. After an exhaustive search, his biological father couldn't be tracked down.

I faced two options—take Josie and leave Jonah with his grandparents or take them both.

The decision was a no-brainer.

Siblings belong together, and there's no way I would tear them apart.

The adoption process for Jonah is well underway. If it all goes to plan, I'll be issued a temporary custody order for him at the same time as finalizing Josie's custody.

"I should probably get going," I say, keen to hit the road and try to beat rush hour. "Mind if I say goodbye to Josie and Jonah?"

"Oh, not at all," Robyn answers.

As the three of us get up, Mike says, "Thank you for doing this, Milo."

I instantly know what he's referring to. "Keeping them together is the right thing to do."

"Maybe. But not all men would make the same decision. I want you to know how much I"—he looks at his wife and she gives a small nod—"how much we both respect you. We're here for you. Anything you need, whether it's help with the kids or advice, just let us know."

"I will."

We step out into the backyard. Grace is supervising the kids who are sitting side by side in a small sandbox. Josie is showing Jonah how to use a bucket to mold a castle, while he clumsily packs sand and laughs when it tumbles down.

I didn't think twice about taking Jonah, as well as Josie. It really was a no-brainer. But I have to confess, a part of me was worried that I wouldn't feel the same way about him as I would for Josie.

But from the moment I laid eyes on the little guy in the living room, I experienced a pull in my gut like I've never had before. Whether I'm related to him by blood or not, I knew then and there that I'd love them both equally as my own.

"And good luck with the house hunting tomorrow," Robyn says. "I hope you find your dream home."

"Yeah," I say, staring at my kids playing in the backyard. "I think I have."

"Are you sure *this* is the house you're looking for?"

The disdain in Willow Wilkins' voice is obvious, and I bite my tongue so I don't snap at her.

She's been showing me properties around Comfort Bay since the summer, usually ones on what's been dubbed Millionaire's Mile. It's an exclusive enclave in the hills overlooking the Pacific Ocean, where prices *start* at ten million.

It's not that I can't afford a place like that. I've been smart with money and contract negotiations my entire career and have a healthy sum stashed away in savings and investments.

But I don't want to raise my kids in a mega mansion.

I want somewhere that's small and cozy and feels like home, not like it belongs in an architectural magazine. A place where we can play basketball in the driveway or squirt each other with water guns in the backyard on hot summer days, creating simple childhood memories they can treasure forever.

This house has caused friction between Willow and me, since her commission just took a hefty cut. But she's apparently the best realtor in the county, and with the season starting and plans to take custody of Josie and Jonah, I've been too busy to find another agent. So I guess I'm just going to have to grin and bear it.

"It's perfect. I'll take it," I say to Willow once we've completed the walkthrough.

Sure, it's not much—just a three-bed, one-bath bungalow on a quiet cul-de-sac a few blocks from Main Street. But it feels homey and safe, and it's the kind of place I can picture us living in. I can always hire a contractor to add another bathroom or more space later.

"But you haven't even looked outside."

I peer out the kitchen window at the decent-sized backyard. It's fully fenced with a few palm trees scattered along the back fence line. There's even plenty of space for a large deck and a pool in the future.

"Looks good to me," I say.

Willow's phone buzzes. "Sorry. I need to take this. Go have a look outside. It's quite close to the neighbor, especially on the left side. You might want to see if that works for you."

"All right," I say, stepping outside as she takes the call.

I want to check out this neighbor situation and see how close it really is. One thing I really value is my privacy.

I walk up to the fence line and glance over. "Holy moly," I mutter under my breath, and it has nothing to do with the proximity to the neighboring house—Willow was exaggerating, it's a fine distance apart—it's *who* my soon-to-be new neighbor is.

"Those evil stepsisters got you doing all the chores again?" I call out.

Beth stops hanging a shirt on the clothesline and spins on her heel, freezing when she sees me—apart from her eyebrows, which shoot up high to her forehead. Even in simple, striped black-and-white joggers and a black long-sleeved shirt, she looks amazing.

"What are you doing here?" She drops the clothespins into the basket and moves toward me. "Are you stalking me?"

"You got me. Good thing I chose pro hockey over a career in the secret service."

"Well, then, what are you doing here?" she repeats, folding her arms over her chest as I try to gauge what mood she's in.

Playful or peeved off?

It's a fine line, and one I haven't mastered reading yet.

I cross my fingers and hope she's up for some verbal sparring.

We haven't seen each other since the night of Fraser's party, which was way too long ago. I'd been hoping to use our little fender bender as an excuse to reach out to her, but the insurance companies have been annoyingly efficient, so I haven't had a reason to contact her about anything.

"Looks like we're not only friends...*ish*, but now also"—I raise both hands and curl my index and middle fingers as I say, "'neighbors...ish.'"

She walks right up to the fence line and hooks her fingers along the top of it. "Don't ever say that again, with or without air quotes. In fact, don't use air quotes at all."

Her words have bite, but the small grin she's trying to suppress gives her away.

Looks like we're in for another round of sparring.

Giddyup!

"Seriously, though..." She aims those multicolored eyes straight at me, and a slow-warming heat spreads throughout my entire body. "You're not actually thinking about buying this place, are you?"

"I am."

"Why?"

"It's got great bones. Decent-size block. It's in a good school district."

"All houses in Comfort Bay are in the same school district."

I lock eyes with her. "And I've always wanted to live on a *cul de sac.*"

Color rises on her cheeks. "You're never going to let me live that down, are you?"

"Live what down?" I reply innocently.

She shakes her head, her black strands moving from side to side. "You're good. I'll give you that."

I shrug. Then smirk. "Yeah, I know."

"And arrogant."

"Not arrogant." Our eyes meet again, and the heat pulsing through me kicks up a few levels. "I just know where my talents lie."

She takes a breath then backs away from the fence. "Well, I don't think real estate is one of them. Why aren't you buying one of the mansions on the hill overlooking the water?"

My smirk grows. "I love it when you're completely wrong."

She zooms back up to the fence, our faces inches apart. "What am I wrong about?"

I don't move back as I answer, "You're wrong about thinking I'd want to live in a place like that. That's not me, Beth. I'm not flashy. I don't need a massive house with ten garages. Or fancy cars. Or any of that superficial, stereotypical rich-person stuff." I lower my voice and lean in closer to her. "I came from nothing. I have no one to rely on in this world except for myself. I'm actually quite careful with how I spend my money."

Too much information? Yeah, definitely. Why the heck did I just blurt all that out?

"Oh." She blinks a few times but doesn't back away. "I'm sorry. I shouldn't have assumed." And then, with the same sincerity in her voice, she adds, "I just don't want to see you humiliated."

I'm confused. "Humiliated?"

She nods. "I may not like you in the traditional sense of wanting to spend time with you, but I also don't want you publicly humiliated. Don't you see, Milo? This is all a setup."

She looks and sounds so serious that I'm convinced she's being genuine.

"What's a setup?" I ask.

"All of it." She tips her chin over my shoulder. "This house isn't really for sale."

Huh?

I get the first inkling she's playing with me because I *know* this place is for sale. I found the listing online myself.

And now the fool-ee becomes the fool-er.

I play along, my expression remaining earnest. "It isn't?"

"It's not. Don't look now, but there are hidden cameras everywhere. In the trees. In the plants on the porch. Scattered throughout the inside of the house. It's for a new reality TV show Evie's sister Harper is producing. A cross between *America's Funniest Home Videos* and *Punk'd*."

I let out a low whistle. "Man, that's something else."

"I know. I feel so bad for you. Not even Willow is real."

"She's not a real person?"

"She's not a real realtor. Come on. Did you really think Willow Wilkins was a real name? She's an actress. Everything about her is fake. Her name. Her teeth. Her hair. Her tan. Her breasts."

I let out a low whistle. "She does have fantastic breasts."

Beth's eyes widen in surprise. "You've noticed them?"

"Oh, yeah. How could I not?" Now it's *my* turn to have some fun at her expense. "They're amazing. Oh, and they feel spectacular."

Her head falls forward and she latches onto the top of the fence. "You've *felt* them?"

"I have. It's incredible how lifelike silicone can feel nowadays."

She opens her mouth, closes her eyes, and turns to the side. "You...you had me there for a minute."

I sure did.

This round goes to me.

"Question is, why did you care so much whether I touched them or not?"

"I didn't."

"Yes, you did."

"No, I didn't."

"Yes! You *did*."

"No! I *didn't*."

"Milo!" Willow calls out from the back door. "Everything okay?"

"Fine," I yell over my shoulder. "Just saying hello to my new neighbor."

Beth makes a sound, but I can't tell whether it's one of pleasure or irritation. Possibly both?

"Do you need me to come over?" Willow yells. "I would, but my heels on this lawn..."

"No. It's fine." I let out a sigh. I'll be glad when this is all over and done with and I won't have to spend any more time with the woman. "I'll only be a minute."

I turn back to face Beth. Her expression is set somewhere between annoyed and exasperated. So, the usual for whenever she's around me then.

"If we're going to be neighbors, you can at least tell me the real reason why you're buying this place." She looks up at me, and I don't know what it is, but there's something about her that just hits differently. Even with the very limited interactions we've had, no other woman has ever made me feel the way she does.

And because she's unlike anyone I've ever met, I do something I've never done before.

I open up to her.

"All right. On one condition."

"What?"

"You don't tell anyone."

"Who would I tell?"

"Your friends. Family. The media."

"I have better things to talk about with my friends and family than you. And I would never go to the media." She pauses for a beat, and I can't tell what's coming next, whether it's something sincere or a burning tease. "You're not that interesting. Fraser, sure. Culver, too. But you?...Nah."

I shouldn't smile, but I can't help it.

Despite not wanting word of my impending fatherhood to come out publicly until I'm ready—and not really knowing

Beth that well—I do what I always do. I go with my gut. And my gut is telling me I can trust her with this.

"Fine. I'll tell you why I'm buying this place."

She lifts on her toes. "I'm all ears."

"They're not that big," I quip.

She rolls her eyes. "Get to the part where you tell me the juicy goss faster please."

"I recently found out I'm a father."

Her eyes go round, and she rocks back. "You're a...father?"

"Go ahead. Make some crack about how unbelievable it is that a woman would even sleep with me, or how terrible it is for the human race that my genes are being passed down to the next generation."

"No. It's not—I would never...I just didn't know you were seeing anyone."

"I'm not," I reply firmly. "Josie is five."

"*Five*? But you said you became a father recently."

"No. I said I *found out* I became a father recently." I blow out a heavy breath. "It's a long story."

"Milo!" Willow calls out again. "I have another appointment. We should get going."

"Okay," I yell back, without taking my eyes off Beth. I hate leaving after dropping this bomb on her, but she asked, so I answered. "Please keep this to yourself."

"Of course." She reaches up and slides her hand over the top of mine, giving it a squeeze. Warmth flares in my chest at the touch. "I won't tell a soul."

7

Beth

I'm scarfing down my salad in the break room *slash* storage space *slash* admin office at the back of the store.

It's three days before Christmas, and Comfort Bay is a flurry of activity.

Twinkling lights are strung across lampposts and storefronts as shoppers—a mix of locals as well as the usual influx of seasonal tourists—crowd the sidewalks, scurrying about from store to store, carrying shopping bags filled with gifts, local crafts, and holiday treats.

A group of carolers are positioned a few doors down from the bookstore, and their songs filter into the bookstore as people bustle in and out.

We've been doing a brisk trade all week, too, and as if that weren't enough, we've set up a craft activities station for kids, so the store is busy *and* noisy.

I take a big bite of my salad and continue what's become my usual lunchtime activity—scrolling through a message thread that started with Milo over two months ago.

Oh, yeah, we've been texting since the day after his house inspection. He got my number off Fraser and messaged the next day.

Because we're neighbors, and it's important to be on good texting terms with your neighbors, right?

The bombshell Milo revealed during his property viewing has been ricocheting in my head ever since he dropped it. It's been hard, almost impossible, not to think about it—and about him—especially since he did buy the house and has moved in next door to me.

Not that I see much of the guy. With the hockey season in full swing, he's barely been home.

I haven't met the kids in person, either, but I have seen photos. *Plenty* of photos. They're adorable.

Milo has filled me in on some of the details of the situation, revealing he has full custody of Josie and temporary custody of Jonah, and also mentioning that he's on good terms with the kids' grandparents. He hasn't said much beyond that, and I haven't asked for more, even though I'm curious.

How does he feel about becoming an instant father?

What's the story with the kids' mom?

And how on earth is he coping, juggling his hectic pro hockey schedule with the responsibilities of fatherhood?

He has hired a nanny to travel with him and help him out as he plays.

A male nanny.

And yeah, I may or may not have let out a huge sigh of relief when he texted me that.

I'm re-reading the message thread from the very start that began with, **Hey neighbor...ish**, and includes frequent detours into book recommendations, me teasing him about his man bun, him asking about my day, and of course, a ton of photos of the kids, because I want to be a really good neighbor.

That's all it is.

Really.

Okay, let's say that—*hypothetically*—I did want something more to develop between us. There is zero chance of it ever happening.

One, Milo is adjusting to fatherhood as a pro athlete. In between training, traveling, and taking care of his kids, he simply doesn't have the time to add a girlfriend into the mix. His focus needs to be on his kids, and I would never want to get in the way of that.

Two, there's the not-so-insignificant matter of being unsure whether we even like each other. Yes, we exchange neighborly texts, and yes, he told me about the kids before telling anyone else he knew—he released a statement to the media a few weeks later—but so what? That doesn't mean he likes me in that way.

I don't even know if he likes me *at all*. I don't treat him the way I suspect most other women do. I don't fawn over him. I tease him pretty much all the time. And there's a fine line between bantering with each other and mildly peeving one another off. I'm sure he'll get sick of it—and me—soon enough.

And three, even if Milo were ready to date, *and* I had written and notarized confirmation that he liked me, there's another not-so-insignificant roadblock in my way—me.

I'm not exactly the easiest person to deal with. I have major trust issues, and even though I may have lost a lot of weight since high school, I still have insecurities about my body. Those feelings didn't just disappear when the weight came off, unfortunately.

I don't know if I'm ready, or even capable, of being emotionally vulnerable in that way with a guy. The two exes who hurt me preyed on my body issues, and I haven't healed from that pain. I've buried it deep down inside, raised my walls, and kept all men at arm's length ever since.

Milo's the first guy who I've let slip past my defenses, even if it's only a tiny bit. I'm not sure if I'm ready to let him in anymore.

I'm fine with how things between us currently stand.

I am.

Really.

"Why are you sitting alone in the dark re-reading for the millionth time messages from the guy you claim is only your neighbor?" my boss Courtland asks, flicking on the overhead light.

My eyes squint as I adjust the brightness. "I wasn't sitting alone in the dark, I had a lamp on. It's called creating a cozy atmosphere."

He surveys the tight quarters packed with books, folders, and cleaning supplies, and then turns to me, sitting at the tiny table in the middle of it all.

"This isn't cozy. This is one step away from becoming a crazy cat lady." I shoot him a pointed stare. He raises his hands in the air. "As a proud crazy cat dude, I'm totally allowed to say that."

"Fair enough."

Courtland is Babette's second—or is it third?—cousin, and she *is* the official crazy cat lady of Comfort Bay. Must be something that runs in that family's gene pool.

"Listen, I won't keep you from..." His eyes slide to my phone. "*That*. I came in to ask if you wouldn't mind staying back tonight?"

"Sure. That's fine."

"Awesome. I'm going to be scheduling author visits for next year, and you mentioned last time you'd like to be involved."

"I did. That sounds great. Ooh, I'm so excited."

"Me, too." He leans against the table and arches a brow. "I'm really hoping we can get Lori Connors."

"Who?" I feign ignorance, and he pins me with a clearly unamused look.

Lori Connors is the author name of my older sister Schapelle, who writes heartwarming romcoms with '90s throwback vibes but that feel very current. Courtland is her number one fan, and it's cool to see a guy who loves reading romance. I'd heard rumors they existed, but I'd never met one in real life.

"You'll be seeing her at Christmas, right? Maybe you can

put in a good word. I assume she'll be doing a tour for her fall release."

I adore Schapelle. Despite being five years older than me —she turned twenty-nine last month—we're super close. Being book nerds helps, but unlike me, she's also stylish, confident, and beautiful, with a kind and humble personality to boot. She's basically my idol.

We have a silent agreement that I won't bug her about her author life, but Courtland's a sweet guy, and I know how much it would mean for him to have a big-name author like her visit our humble little bookshop.

I pop a cherry tomato into my mouth. "I'll see what I can do."

"Your droll tone fills me with so much confidence." He goes to leave, then stops. "Oh, and you've still got five minutes left on your break, so you can jump on your phone the second I leave."

"I am not going to do that. And lower those eyebrows, mister, you're going to pull a forehead muscle."

He smiles then leaves, and the *second* he's gone, I'm reaching for my phone. With less than five minutes until I have to be back on the floor, I can't revisit all of our messages, so I return to what's possibly my favorite convo.

It's one of our earliest.

Milo: *You're going to think I'm an idiot...well, more of an idiot, but after our little chat at the fence line, I went online to verify Willow Wilkins is, in fact, a real realtor.*
Beth: *And?*
Milo: *I can confirm that she is! Also, I may have stumbled down her Instagram wormhole.*
Beth: *<eye roll emoji> She has a lot of bikini pics.*
Milo: *Who posts that many bikini pics?*

Milo: *Damn, you type fast, lol*

Beth: *When you're good, you're good.*

Milo: *Not that I'm shaming her. She can share whatever she likes, it's just a lot.*

Beth: *She can. And she looks great, so why not flaunt it, right?*

Milo: *I guess.*

Beth: *What do you mean, you guess?*

Milo: *She's attractive, sure, but not really my type.*

Beth: *What is your type?*

Even re-reading this thread all this time later, I'll never forget the heart palpitations I had after sending that text.

I was on pins and needles, waiting for him to reply, watching those three bouncy dots appear then disappear about eight thousand times before his reply finally came through.

Milo: *My type is snarky bookworms who enjoy teasing me, make adorable little noises they might not even be aware they're making, and look great in black-and-white joggers, not unlike the ones you were wearing the day I inspected the house.*

I'll also never forget how I felt seeing that message, a heady combination of happy and excited and nervous and confused.

Even though it was only a text message, I could *feel* the sincerity of what he was saying.

It wasn't a line.

It wasn't something he doled out to countless girls in countless cities to get them to sleep with him.

He meant it.

Although I was slightly confused about the *little noises* reference. I never got around to asking him about it, but I don't make little noises...do I?

My eyes drift back to the screen.

Milo: *Just don't tell anyone I'm not into beautiful airheads. I have a reputation to maintain <winky face emoji>*

I scroll past a ton of photos of his children, more of my digs about his man bun, him sharing a link to an article about the history of the term *cul de sac*, me sending him a few strongly worded memes back.

Okay, so maybe they're not your average, *hey, would you mind if I borrowed your ladder?* neighborly texts.

They're veering into flirty territory. Yes, I see that. Despite being staunchly anti-love, I'm not completely oblivious.

But as it turns out, Milo might not be the big grump the world—and until recently, me—thinks he is. He's earned that reputation because he's quiet and reserved until he gets to know someone, along with his killer instinct on the hockey field. Rink? Arena? Whatever it's called.

Does he have an overinflated ego? He's a pro-athlete so the answer is, of course he does. He needs to. You don't rise to the top of any field by being humble and demure. You have to believe in yourself more than anything because the world is cutthroat, and if you don't have your own back, you won't get far.

But underneath that exterior, lies a gentle giant.

A gentle giant I enjoy exchanging occasional flirty texts with. That I can handle.

It's fun and friendly, but it's also safe because there's some distance there.

Just like there's literal physical distance between us now since Milo is currently in Tampa Bay to play against the... whatever the Tampa Bay hockey team is called tonight.

And as long as there's distance between us, I'll be fine.

8

Milo

We're leading *4-0*, when Alexis Trbojevic, the Tampa Bay Thunders' ruthless forward, intercepts a pass and makes a break toward me.

He skillfully glides past one of our defenders, then another.

I *thrive* on moments like this, when it's just me and a two-hundred pound goliath barreling toward me.

Adrenaline spikes in my veins, my eyes locked on him like a missile acquiring its target. I've kept the opposition scoreless all game, and I have no intention of letting anything get past me now.

I started playing hockey relatively late. I was in third grade. A PE teacher spotted my potential, and even though my home life was less than stable, I joined a junior team. That team became the only constant in my childhood.

On my darkest days, hockey pulled me through.

I could channel all my rage and fear and the gut-wrenching pain of being abandoned by an alcoholic mother and a drug-dealing father into a healthy outlet.

So I did.

And I still do.

Seven years in the major leagues later, I've got the highest save percentage of any goalkeeper in the past decade, and I'm in the top ten lowest goals against average goalies of all time.

That same rage, that fire, still burns inside me as Trbojevic approaches.

I grit my teeth, my heart racing, every cell in my body on high alert.

I live for this.

The only difference now is that it's not the only thing I live for anymore. I've got two small kids who depend on me to think about.

My eyes remain glued to Trbojevic as Josie and Jonah's sweet faces pop into my head.

I've finally got a purpose. A reason to do what I do that goes beyond making money, breaking records, and further inflating my already overinflated ego.

I want to give them the best start in life. The start I never had.

Trbojevic clutches the puck tightly to his stick.

The tension is palpable.

Whether he makes this shot or not won't affect the outcome of the game since there's less than a minute remaining.

Which makes this personal, a chance for him and his team to save face.

Not on my watch.

I square off against him, ready to defend the goal as if this were the Stanley Cup final, and not a Christmas week game.

He nears the crease, pulling his stick back in a smooth, practiced motion, and takes the shot.

The puck rockets across the ice.

My focus narrows to the small black disc gliding toward me. Years of discipline, dedication, and training merge with natural instinct as my glove meets the puck, the sharp snap of rubber against leather filling the air as I successfully block the shot.

With a sweep of my stick, I clear the puck from the danger zone.

We're in enemy territory tonight so the crowd boos loudly, but I don't care. I lift my stick in the air, goading them even more. The boos grow louder, and I can't help but smirk, enjoying every second.

After the up and down mess of last season, this year, the LA Swifts have come out swinging. It was a huge blow losing Culver so early, but those summer training sessions really paid off, and we're currently the top team in our division.

You can bet your bottom dollar I'm going to revel in it.

Why wouldn't I?

In hockey, you never know how long the good times will last, so you've got to make the most of them while you can.

After the game, Fraser jogs up to me as I'm leaving the arena, keen to get back to my hotel room. Even though the kids will be fast asleep, I still like to pop in and kiss them goodnight.

"Hey, man," he says when he reaches me. "I meant to speak to you earlier, but it slipped my mind."

"Winning does that."

"Heck, yeah, it does." We exchange exuberant high fives. "You were great."

"So were you, Mister Hat Trick."

He beams proudly. "This could be our year."

"Fingers crossed," I say, raising my crossed fingers. "Now, before we get sidetracked by our awesomeness again, what's on your mind?"

"It's about the wedding. Evie wanted me to pass on that we've saved you an additional two places."

"Two places?" I frown. "I'm not even bringing a plus-one."

Fraser bumps me with his elbow. "You have *two* little plus-ones."

"Oh, right. Thanks, but I already made plans for the kids. Their grandparents are coming to visit and will look after them," I explain. "I wasn't sure how you guys felt about having children at a wedding. Some people don't like it."

"Not us. We'd love for them to come. It's really no problem. Our wedding planner is fantastic and can adjust seating arrangements with no trouble."

"That's nice of you both, and I appreciate that. But I think the grandparents are looking forward to spending a few days with Josie and Jonah."

"Fair enough." He claps me on my back, then lets a beat or two pass before adding, "It's good to see you like this, man."

"Like what?"

He gives my shoulder a squeeze. "Happy."

Fraser is right. I am happy.

Having Josie and Jonah enter my life was unexpected, to say the least, but it's also been the best thing that's ever happened to me.

But becoming a father to two little ones has been a huge adjustment. I expected it to be tough, but juggling the intense demands of training, competing, and being on the road, all while trying to be the dad I want to be, is no easy task. There are times when I feel completely overwhelmed and wonder if I'm cut out for this. But then I remind myself, what choice have I got?

It's my job to give Josie and Jonah the best start in life. If that means working harder than I ever have and figuring everything out, then that's what I'll do. Because I cannot fail at this.

I'm also lucky. With an amazing nanny, Boden, supportive grandparents I can count on, and Josie and Jonah being wonderful kids, I'm managing to keep things together.

For the most part.

One thing I'm struggling with?

It starts with *bath* and ends in *time*.

It's the night before Christmas so I insisted Boden get home to his family in Milwaukee for the holidays. I assured him I could handle the kids on my own for one night. Turns out, I can't even manage a simple bath time on my own.

"Jonah, no," I say firmly. He halts for a second, his blue eyes sparkling with mischief as he stills in the tub. "No more splashing."

"Oh-tay, Daddy."

By now I've learned a valuable lesson—bathing a toddler means you're going to end up wet. There's no use trying to prevent it, but I can try to minimize it.

I wipe water off my brow as Jonah stops splashing and engages in his second favorite bath time activity—pushing his two floating boats around the tub. He's got a big grin on his face as he makes them race each other through the water. Occasionally, he collides the boats together, pretending they're in a crash, and giggles as they bounce off one another.

He's such a great kid. Playful, energetic, and unafraid of anything. The exact opposite of his sister. Josie is much more serious, calm, and cautious.

That actually works in my favor. Because while I'm busy chasing after Jonah, I can count on Josie to always be close by, keeping a watchful eye on things.

Like, right now. She's happily sitting in the corner of the bathroom reading a book about crayons that have come to life.

I turn over my shoulder to look at her...and her chair is empty.

"Josie," I call out.

Nothing.

"Josie!"

No response.

What the heck do I do now?

I can't leave Jonah alone in the tub, but I have to find out where Josie has wandered off to. Why hasn't anyone invented a way for parents to clone themselves so they can be in two places at once?

With no answer after shouting again, I quickly scoop up Jonah, wrap him in a blanket, and hurry off to look for Josie.

I find her in the kitchen drinking a glass of water.

She stops drinking and looks at me like I've lost my mind. She might not be too far off with that assessment.

"You all good, sweetie?"

"Yep." She lets out a satisfied *Ahhh*. "I was thirsty."

Think, Milo. Think. What's the best way to handle this situation? I don't want to scold her for simply getting a glass of water because she hasn't done anything wrong. But I do need to tell her that while Daddy may still be young, having constant panic attacks is a surefire way to an early heart attack —without scaring her.

"I have an idea," I say to buy myself some time since I currently have no freaking idea. "Let's play a game."

"What sort of game?"

"Uhhh...a game where we tell each other things."

"How do you play?"

"Well, for instance, when I'm giving Jonah a bath and you're reading a book and want to leave to get a glass of water, you let me know before you go."

"That doesn't sound like a very fun game."

"Oh, it is. It's so much fun. And hey, you can tell me things that I need to know. That way, we always know what's going on."

"I guess." She places her glass by the sink and walks over to me. "Can we play the game now?"

"Sure, sweetie. What do you want to tell me?"

"You're getting water all over the floor!"

"Huh?"

I look down, and she's right. I may have bundled Jonah up but I'm soaked and dripping water everywhere.

"I'll get it cleaned up," I say as I take her hand in mine so she doesn't slip..."Right after I finish giving Jonah a bath. Then it's time for bed so Santa can make his visit."

The living room is bathed in the soft glow of lights from the Christmas tree. I'm sitting on the couch, watching Josie and Jonah, both still dressed in their festive pajamas, tear open their presents.

Well, Jonah tears open his presents, his little fingers making fast work of the gifts I stayed up all night wrapping. I now realize there was no point spending all that time watching instructional YouTube videos on how to *level up my gift-wrapping game.*

The last thing he's paying attention to is the layering effect I painstakingly applied to his race car set or all the ribbons I ironed on low heat to make curling easier before attaching them to his swing set.

His delighted squeals fill the room and make all the effort worthwhile, even if he is too young to appreciate it.

But Josie's another story.

She's sitting on the carpeted floor, holding a wrapped gift —a collection of animal-themed books if I remember correctly —not saying or doing much.

"What is it, sweetie?" I ask, putting my mug down on the coffee table and joining her on the floor.

"I miss..." Her blue eyes start to water. "I miss Mommy."

"Oh, sweetie."

She falls into me, sobbing as I hold her in my arms,

frantically hoping my touch is comforting her because I sure as heck can't find any words. What could I even possibly say?

All three of our lives have changed in the most unexpected ways this year.

If you'd have told me last Christmas this is what I'd be doing a year later—spending the day with my kids in a small town where I bought a house next to a woman who seesaws between tolerating and hating me—I would have laughed in your face.

But that's life, isn't it? You've got to expect the unexpected.

And if all this change has been a lot for me, I can't even begin to imagine how hard it is for the kids.

In some ways it's good that Jonah's so young, he seems to be coping well. He asks about his mom from time to time, and I tell him she's always with him, looking out for him, that all he has to do is close his eyes, and remember her, and she'll never leave his heart.

But Josie is just that little bit older, and she feels her mother's absence more acutely. What words can you find to explain to a five-year-old that their mother is gone forever?

I hold her close to me and rub my hands up and down her small back.

Given all the changes they've experienced, they're both coping remarkably well. They've gone from losing their mother, to being shipped off to live with their grandparents for a few months, to traveling all over the country with me.

I may be their father, but until only a few short months ago, I was also a complete stranger.

And my lifestyle is anything but kid friendly, something that's become abundantly clear to me as we traipsed from city to city in the lead up to the holiday break.

But that's a problem I'll deal with another time.

Jonah drops his plush toy and toddles over to us, managing to slink his way between us to get in on the hug, too.

"Don't be sad," he says, giving his sister a reassuring pat on the back.

"That's right," I say softly. "Mommy loved you. Nana and PopPop love you. And I love you. Both of you."

Josie pulls away and sniffs, wiping her nose with the back of her hand. "You do?"

"I do. Very, very much. The three of us are a family, and I am always going to be here for you."

"Promise?"

Emotion catches in my throat. "I promise."

"I wuv you, Daddy," Jonah says, giving my bicep a press with his tiny fingers.

"I love you, too, Jonah. And I love you, Josie."

Josie looks between us, not saying anything.

Jonah started saying *I love you* to me after only a few weeks.

Josie hasn't said it yet.

And that's okay.

She needs time, so time is what I'm going to give her. I'll keep saying it to her, though, because I want her to always know that she is loved.

The kids go back to opening their presents, Josie still unwrapping hers way more cautiously than Jonah. Even at this young age, I can tell that he's going to be fearless, an *act first, think later* type, whereas Josie is a lot more measured and likes to take her time to assess things before jumping in.

I start scooping up all the wrapping paper and stashing it into a pile in the corner when my phone buzzes. I snatch it from the arm of the sofa and smile when I see who the message is from.

Beth: *Save me! Please! It's not even seven and my smile muscles are all maxed out. My family is way too chipper.*

I smile at the image of Beth surrounded by her family, who, from what she's told me, are the complete opposite of her. I believe her exact words were, 'They're so happy it depresses me.'

Milo: *At least YOUR smiling face doesn't scare away children.*
Beth: *Is that your way of telling me you've frightened your own kids and possibly ruined Christmas for them forever?*

I chuckle at that.

Some—*most?*—guys might take offense to the constant stream of insults and teasing that come my way, but I guess I'm not like most guys because I love it.

Milo: *Happy to report that the kids are having a great time...even with me and all my smiling.*
Beth: *It's a Christmas miracle!*
Beth: *Anyway, I won't keep you. Just wanted to wish you all a great day.*
Milo: *Thanks. Same to you and your family.*

I tap the side of my phone, wondering if I should ask how she's getting to Fraser and Evie's wedding. She's already up on the mountain since that's where her folks live, so I assume she'll spend the next two days with her family, and then drive straight to the venue from there.

I hold off from asking. She probably already thinks I'm a weirdo, why give her any more ammo?

The truth is, I'm dying to see her again. It feels like it's been an eternity since we've had a conversation that doesn't involve using our phones.

Don't get me wrong, I'm glad we're keeping in touch, but nothing beats seeing her in person.

Would I like for something more to happen with Beth?

No.

I'd *love* for something more to happen with Beth.

But I'm also a realist.

I'm a single dad with two children under five, a career that sees me crisscrossing the country eight months out of the year, and what am I forgetting?

Oh, yeah. She low-to-mid level hates me.

Teases me about my man bun.

Knocks my taste in music. Books. TV shows. You name it.

Has opinions she is not afraid to share about pretty much anything I say.

My phone buzzes in my hand.

Beth: *Merry Christmas, x*

I stare at that *x* for way longer than any grown man should stare at a single letter, my stomach suddenly feeling weightless.

What does the *x* mean?

Was she being festive? Did her finger slip? Or is that how she signs off on text?

I know the answer to that last question is no, because in all the months we've been texting, she's never once let an *x* slip through before.

Jonah shrieks excitedly at his pirate ship, so with a shaky thumb—*why is my thumb suddenly shaking?*—I click into the reply field, tap *Merry Christmas, x*, and hit *Send*.

I drop the phone as if it were a sizzling skillet then tuck it in between the sofa cushions so that I can't see it because that's a perfectly logical thing to do.

I can face off against a player charging at me on the ice, but sending someone a message that ends with *one letter* sends me into a tailspin?

I need help.

I also need to refocus.

So I wander over to Josie and Jonah and clap my hands together. "Who's ready for pancakes?"

9

Beth

"Oh, come on, start you stupid thing."

I turn the key in the ignition again.

Nothing.

No cough. No sputter. Not even a wheeze.

My car has officially conked out on me.

I first noticed it started making a funny noise driving down the mountain, so I did what any responsible car-owning adult would do in that situation—I ignored it, turned the music up louder, and prayed I made it back safely.

My prayer was answered, and I got home fine yesterday.

Sure, I could have stayed with my family since it would have been a shorter drive to the wedding venue, but that would have meant an extra thirty-six hours in their company, and I had to make a decision—spend time with them or remain sane.

I made the right choice for everyone involved.

As much as I love hanging out with Dad and Schapelle, I can't deal with Mom's constant nagging—*When are you going to get a real job? Why aren't you seeing anyone? You know, it's not too late for you to go to college like all your sisters have*—being forced to make polite chitchat with Tenley to gloss over the fact we have nothing in common, and fighting over the silliest things with Allie, which always happens whenever we spend more than a few hours together in close quarters.

Not to mention, they're all way too perky and optimistic for my liking. Like, all the time. Mom can switch from criticizing my life choices to chatting about a good news article she found on Reddit in an instant. Even Dad, with his ex-military background, has this whole life-is-good attitude going on. I'm the only Moore who inherited the snark gene.

I really shouldn't complain because I don't have some sad sob story about my childhood. So many people had it much tougher than me. Constantly relocating because of Dad's military career was the most difficult thing we went through, but it actually wasn't all that bad for me.

Being on the bigger side, I quickly came to see that wherever we went, the insults remained predictably the same. That helped in not letting the cruel things people said about my size get to me.

That, and retreating into books.

There's that famous quote about readers getting to live one thousand lives. That's so true.

Long before I was old enough to read romance, I used to love YA, fantasy, and adventure books. I'm talking old-timey classics like *Robinson Crusoe* and *Treasure Island*. Immersing myself in the lives of others, from far-off places and worlds so unlike my own, helped me cope with the constant moving and bullying.

When Dad left the military, we relocated here in my senior year of high school because Mom had always wanted to live in a picturesque small town. I knew right away that Comfort Bay was my soul home. It just felt right. I'd never had that feeling in any of the other places we lived.

When Mom and Dad moved up the mountain to Cedar Crest Hollow a few years later, I stayed behind. And I'm glad I did. I know my life isn't glamorous or exciting, but I get all the excitement my brain and heart can handle through books. I actually like the simple life I've carved out for myself.

Even if Mom thinks I should aim for more than working in a bookstore, I'm happy here. I have a close group of friends. I was able to buy a modest house thanks to Mom and Dad helping me out with a deposit. The early morning walks here are the best. And Comfort Bay is the first place where I feel like I belong. There's enough quirky folk in town that it makes my quirkiness not stand out all that much.

I let out a sigh and give the key another turn, hoping that whatever the issue is has miraculously fixed itself in the past sixty seconds, but nope, nothing.

I drop my head. Talk about bad timing.

Evie and Fraser's wedding starts in less than two hours. Since it's such a busy time of year, they've kept it simple—just a ceremony followed by a reception. That's it. No bachelor or bachelorette parties, and the wedding party only includes their siblings. It's a little disappointing since it would've been nice if the Fast-Talking-Five were more involved, but it's their wedding, and I totally respect that.

"Okay, okay what are my options here?" I say to myself.

I could call Dad. He'd drive down to have a look at what's wrong with my car. But there are two issues with that plan.

One, it would take him at least an hour to get here, assuming he could come over right away, and two, there's been some light snowfall up in the mountains these past few days, so I don't want him driving if he doesn't have to.

I take out my phone and scroll through my friend list.

I can't contact Evie since it's her wedding, and she's got enough on her plate.

Hannah and Culver had a huge, combined family Christmas in Starlight Cove and are driving up today, too, but they're taking Chester and Katie with them, so there'd be no room for me.

Summer and Amiel both left yesterday and are already up there.

So...great. I have no one to ask for a ride.

"Dadddyyyyyy!"

My ears prick.

I glance over at my next-door neighbor. Milo, his kids, and

two elderly people, who I'm assuming are the grandparents, are on the front porch.

Milo is crouched down, and I can see Jonah clinging to him. Even from this distance, it's evident the little guy doesn't want to see his Daddy go.

Maybe I could ask Milo for a ride?

No.

I couldn't...

Could I?

I watch as Milo gives Josie and Jonah one more hug, and it makes my heart clench. It's amazing how much his life has changed these past few months and how well he seems to be handling it. He's taking to fatherhood so naturally.

"Stay focused, Beth," I remind myself, noticing the time on the dashboard clock.

I chew on my nail, desperately trying to come up with a solution that ignores the most obvious one directly across the lawn from me.

I mean, Milo *is* driving to the same place I'm going. Asking him for a ride makes sense.

But no...I can't.

Sending friendly, slightly flirty texts back and forth for the past few months is fine.

Sending friendly, slightly flirty texts on Christmas morning to escape the Hallmarky sweetness of my family by reaching out to the grumpiest person I know in the hopes of basking in some of his grouchy glow, also fine.

But spending an hour, in a car, alone, with Milo?

Sooo not fine.

Nope. I need to keep my distance from him. I've already let him slip under my first round of armor, that's as far as he's going to get. I've reached the edge of my comfort zone, and I am not prepared to go any further.

There's a tap on my window, and I scream.

It's Milo.

With my hand on my pounding heart, I shove the car door open, step out, and glare up at his stupidly handsome face, stubbled jaw line, and man-bunned head. "You scared me half to death."

"Well, it's great to see you, too." His green eyes meet mine, a hint of a smile curling his lips. "What are you doing here?"

"I live here, remember?"

"I mean, what are you doing back home? I thought you were with your family."

"I was. Got back yesterday. Needed to escape."

"Got it. Um..." He scratches the back of his neck. I don't know if he's wearing a super tight Christmas sweater on purpose, or whether the sweater material has no choice but to cling to his massive muscles, but either way, I've got front row seats for the Milo Payne gun show.

Also, aren't Christmas sweaters meant to be cheesy and not at all sexy?

And also number two..."How come you're not wearing a suit?"

"I don't like driving in a suit," Milo explains. "If I leave now, I'll have time to get changed when I get there."

"Right."

"Um..."

"That's the second time you're *ummming* at me," I say. "Spit it out, already."

"Okay. Well...You were home all day yesterday?"

"I was."

"Had I known, I would have...uh...you...You could have come over, you know?"

"But I had books to read."

"Of course you did." He bites back a smile and taps the roof of my car. "Everything okay?"

"No. The stupid thing won't start. And don't say it." I point a finger at him, but I overreach and the tip of my index finger lands on his pec.

His granite-hard pec.

A crease forms on his forehead. "Don't say what?"

My finger remains superglued to his body. "Don't say something like, *'Want me to have a look at it...'*" I try to mimic his deep voice, but it's a poor imitation since his voice is *actually* deep. And masculine. Not that that's important right now.

I continue, because I'm just warming up. "...assuming I know nothing about fixing cars. To which I'll respond with a relieved, *'Oh, yes, thank you, Milo. Why, I don't know what I would have done without you.'*"

Not exactly sure why I put on a Southern belle accent when I do not speak like a Southern belle, but I'm too deep into my rant to pause and dissect that right now.

"And then you'd smile, all pleased with yourself, and say something like, *'Well, why don't you pop the hood?'* your voice laced with innuendo. And then you'd take your sweater off because you wouldn't want it to get dirty or something. And then before you know it, you've got grease stains all over yourself. And of course you can't be a normal guy with a normal body, *nooo*, you've got to be all rugged and muscular with an eight-pack because six-pack abs are so three years ago. And then, because I feel bad you got so dirty fixing my car, I'd offer to sponge the stains off your chiseled torso and before you know it..."

He steps in closer, his eyes twinkling with amusement. "Please continue. I want to hear how the rest of this scenario plays out."

"You know..." I tap my foot then glance at my trusty ol' Corolla hatchback. "We'd be having car-trouble-related sex."

He chuckles then quickly clears his throat. "We would be?"

"Yes. Duh. I'm a romance novel junkie, remember? I *know* how these things work."

"I'm clearly reading the wrong genre," he mutters under his breath, running his thick fingers over his stubble.

I go to move back, but the car traps me in place, so I awkwardly sidestep past Milo to create some space between us because...what...what... *What. Was. That?*

I have no idea what just came over me. How did it go from Milo asking if everything was okay to me creating—*and voicing*—a scenario where he and I are having sex in my car?

Oh. I know.

His granite pec.

The reason it's so hard is because it's not actually flesh, skin, and muscle, but rather a portal to my subconscious mind with the power to cause me to blurt out my most private—and inappropriate—thoughts.

Also, I just finished a blue-collar romance series about a group of hunky mechanic brothers that each find love with a curvy girl. That could have something to do with it.

An awkward silence fills the air.

"I actually wasn't going to offer to look at your car," Milo says eventually, kind of looking at me, but kind of not looking at me, as if sensing I'm embarrassed by...I still don't know what that was...and giving me some much-appreciated breathing room. "Mainly because I know nothing about cars apart from how to change a tire. But also because I distinctly remember a certain someone telling me that chivalry is dead."

Normal Beth would insert a quip here.

Mortified Beth has the good sense to stare at her feet and listen to what he's saying while wishing Milo's rock-hard pec wasn't a portal but a time machine so she could go back and redo the last five minutes.

"So." Milo takes a breath. "I'm going to say this, and I hope that you hear it in the way I intend it. I'm being practical here, nothing less, nothing more. You and I are going to the same destination. I have a car that works. It's cold and starting to rain. It'll take time for someone to come out here to look at your car, and the wedding starts soon. So, I'm offering you a lift. I am not being chivalrous. I'm prepared to offer you thirty percent control of music selection, and you can pay for half of the gas if that makes you feel better."

A long beat passes.

I feel...I don't know how I feel.

And I think that's the problem. I'm on shaky ground around Milo for some reason, and I don't like it.

But he's right.

We are going to the same place, and let's face it, I don't have any other options. Because for all my bluster about being faux-offended about a potential offer to look under the hood, I don't actually know anything about cars, either.

I glance upward at the gloomy, gray sky. It's started to rain and the wind has picked up, too. I wonder what the conditions are like on the mountain. Is it worse up there, snowing heavier than when I left?

Because that wasn't a fun drive.

And Milo *is* offering.

And he hasn't laughed directly in my face about my mini-brain explosion.

I take half a step toward him, keep my hands glued to the side of my body so I don't inadvertently poke any portals or time machines on his chest, lift my eyes to meet his, and say, "Music selection is fifty-fifty, and I'm paying for the gas. Deal?"

He smiles. "Deal."

10

Milo

"You're weird," Beth says, about five minutes into our drive.

The first thing she did when she got into my car was take full advantage of the fifty-fifty song selection. We've currently got Sabrina Carpenter playing, and as a twenty-seven-year-old dude, I've never come across her before. The track is cute and boppy and definitely not something I would have picked Beth as liking.

And that's the first thing she's said to me.

I don't mind though. I plan on using my allocated music selection on Mariah Carey's Christmas album because I'm a freak who can never get tired of listening to her belt out those holiday tracks. There may even be a rumor going around that I have every single word to every single song memorized, which I am not prepared to either confirm or deny. Don't want it messing up my whole grump image.

"*I'm* weird?" I say, increasing the speed on the wipers. "Do we want to explore your car-related sex story?"

"But that's just it. That story would scare most normal men away. But not you. Hence, I stand by what I said. *You're weird.*"

I glance over at her way too briefly but am quickly forced to return my attention back to the road. It's really starting to come down heavily now.

I checked the weather report this morning, and it's been snowing lightly up on the mountain these past few days, but the conditions are forecasted to get worse today.

That's just great.

We live in Monterey County, California, so my tires are not equipped for snow. I plan on taking it slow and steady. I'm going to need to keep my wits about me. As much for the weather, as well as due to my unexpected—but *very* welcome —travel companion.

"Firstly, I have never claimed to be normal, so that's on you for jumping to the wrong conclusion about me. And secondly, you don't scare me."

"I...don't?" I catch her head turning out of the corner of my eye, like she can't quite believe what I said. "Why? Why don't I scare you?"

I chuckle. "Because I'm weird, remember? And it's nice to interact with a woman who's smart and strong and funny. And you're all three things."

She adjusts how she's sitting. "Well, I can't fault your people-reading skills, I suppose."

To say Beth looks stunning would be a huge disservice to the word. I don't think there even is a word to describe how beautiful she looks in a burgundy long-sleeved, floor-length gown, a camel-colored, mid-length coat, and a pair of black heeled boots. Her hair is long enough that she can tie it in a short ponytail, whatever makeup she's wearing makes her skin glow, and her lips are a bright, striking red that drew my eye the moment I saw her.

"Does this mean you don't find my teasing insulting?" she asks.

"Correct. But I need to make sure you're not one of *those girls*? And just so you know, I'd use air quotes around *those girls* if it wasn't raining so much and I didn't have to keep both hands on the steering wheel. And also if a certain someone hadn't banned me from using air quotes."

"I'm glad you remember." I can *hear* the smile in her voice. "And what girls are you referring to?"

"Oh, you know, the type of girls that can dish it out but can't take it back. What's the word I'm looking for? Oh, yeah. Weak girls."

She huffs out a breath. "What's your middle name?"

"Excuse me?"

"Middle name, Milo."

"Garrett."

She clears her throat. "I can assure you, Milo Garrett Payne, I am definitely not one of *those girls*."

"You...you middle named me."

"I did."

"And I'm pretty sure I saw you lift your hands and use air quotes around those girls."

"It's an allowable exception. I had to make my point." She shuffles in her seat. "Did I make my point?"

I smile, my chest flaring with an unfamiliar but very pleasant warmth. "You sure did."

"Good. Now that that's settled, you need to drive a little faster or we'll be late."

"In case you haven't noticed, it's raining. I'm going as fast as I can."

"In case *you* haven't noticed, we just got overtaken by a group of nuns."

"Yeah, well, they've got God on their side," I mutter.

She harrumphs and folds her arms.

The rain is really coming down hard now. The wipers are on max, and it's barely helping. Visibility is shot.

Beth sits up and leans toward the windshield. "It's snowing."

Even though I'm seeing the flakes falling with my own eyes, and I heard about snow in the weather report, it still feels a little surreal. "How is this possible? We're in California."

"We're in the mountains in California," Beth explains. "It's a microclimate up here. It's been snowing lightly up here all week."

I squint and peer over the steering wheel. "This doesn't look light to me."

She turns the music off and switches over to the radio, just in time for us to catch the weather report. "*...a fast-moving, unprecedented weather situation developing affecting multiple areas on the mountain.*"

"That doesn't sound good," she says, and I can hear the worry in her voice.

I slow down even more, keep my eyes glued to the road, and say, "Can you turn the volume up please?"

She leans forward and rotates the dial. "Of course."

"*Meteorologists are predicting snowfall amounts of up to three feet in some areas of Cedar Crest Hollow...*"

Cedar Crest Hollow, that's where Fraser and Evie are getting married.

"*...The snowfall is expected to be heavy and wet, making road conditions extremely hazardous.*"

That *really* doesn't sound good, but I try not to let my concern show on my face.

I'm a good driver. Not that experienced in these sorts of conditions, granted, but we'll be fine.

We have to be.

I have to keep Beth safe, and I've got two kids who are counting on me to make it back in one piece.

"*All non-essential travel should be avoided until this weather event has passed and roads have been cleared.*"

"The wedding." Beth covers her mouth. "Poor Evie and Fraser."

I guess my cool and calm demeanor is working if she's more worried about the wedding than our current driving predicament.

"*Major highways and mountain roads will be closed due to the dangerous conditions. Local authorities are working to set up*

emergency shelters for those who cannot make it home. If you are
currently driving in or around Cedar Crest Hollow, you are strongly
advised to find a safe place to stop and seek shelter immediately."

"Oh my gosh." She clutches at her chest and starts taking rapid, shallow breaths as reality hits her. "We're in danger."

"It's okay," I say, keeping my voice calm. "Just keep breathing, nice and steady, and stay calm." She doesn't respond, but I can hear her breathing slowly return to normal. "We need to get off the road. You know these mountains better than I do. Is there anywhere we can pull off close by?"

"Actually, yeah. There's a left turn coming up ahead. Whispering Pines is a few miles away."

"Then that's where we're going."

I see the turn and take it.

"I'm pretty sure they have a motel," Beth says, pulling her phone out. "Shoot. No reception. I wanted to make a booking."

"It's fine. I'm sure we'll find something."

She sighs. "I hope so."

Worrying about accommodation is a future problem. Right now, my only concern is staying on the icy road.

I squint harder.

The headlights, though on full beam, only illuminate a dense wall of white, and the sound of the engine is muffled by the howling wind. It's crazy how quickly conditions changed from a drizzle to a full-blown snowstorm.

About ten minutes later, we approach a barely visible flickering motel sign. I let out a relieved breath as I ease into the parking lot, coming to a stop right in front of the building. I kill the engine but the windshield wipers stay on, fighting a losing battle against the snow pelting us.

"I'll go in and get us two rooms," Beth says, and I'm smart enough not to argue with her because heaven forbid she launches into another rant that ends up with us having sex for some inexplicable reason.

On second thought...maybe I *should* goad her just to see what wild tale she spins up this time.

Before I can say anything, she slams the door shut and is bolting inside. I unbuckle my seatbelt and lean back in my seat, left to wonder what might have been if this trip hadn't got hijacked by a freak blizzard.

Had the weather remained drivable, how much more could we have bantered? She didn't even get the chance to start on me about my man bun, my cheesy Christmas sweater, and whatever new insults she's been dying to dish out. Sure, she can rib me over text—and she does, believe me—but nothing beats a face-to-face teasing.

I'm bummed we'll never get that chance.

She's right.

I *am* weird...

Annnd I'm okay with that. Because I'm weird *for her*.

She's so unlike anyone I've ever met, and it's the coolest thing. I never know where conversations with her are going to go, I can't predict what she's about to say, and I'm not even fully sure whether she likes me or merely tolerates me.

Just being in her company gives me a bigger rush than stopping a crucial shot in overtime. So if that makes me weird, step aside ladies and gentlemen, and make some room for the king of weirdos.

A few moments later, Beth hops back into the car. I reach around to the back and grab a clean—well, clean-ish—towel and hand it to her.

"Thanks." She starts patting down her wet hair, face, shoulders, and arms before resting the towel in her lap. She looks straight ahead, not saying a word.

"So how'd it go with the room?" I ask, ignoring the strange vibe she's giving.

She continues looking straight ahead but raises her right hand. There's a room key twirled around her finger.

"You got us a room. Excellent. We can wait things out."

She shakes her head silently. A few beads of water drip from her jet-black strands, landing on her shoulders.

"Is something wrong?" I ask, because she's starting to freak me out a little—and not in the usual Beth-way I like so much.

"Is something wrong?" she mumbles quietly to herself. The head shaking intensifies before she stops and slowly turns to stare at me. "Yes, something is wrong. How many keys am I holding up?"

"One," I reply, then add, "You're also giving me the finger."

She gasps and quickly lowers her hand. "Sorry. That was unintentional."

"Oh, please. You totally did it on purpose."

"Believe me, you'll know if I do it on purpose."

She's got a point there. It's not like she holds back on expressing her true feelings around me.

But that doesn't explain why she's acting so strange.

"One key means one room," she says.

"Okay. So why didn't you get two rooms then?"

"Oh my gosh. You're so clever. Why didn't I get two rooms?" She thwacks me across the chest. It's adorable if she thinks that hurts me. I barely feel it. "You don't think I asked for two rooms? I *begged* for two rooms, Milo. I said I'd pay literally anything they wanted to charge for two rooms. But they only have one room left because people are annoying and like to travel for the holidays."

She exhales then looks at me expectantly, waiting for me to respond.

So I give her a response.

Just maybe not the one she was expecting.

"Now, when you say you *begged*, did you just say the words, or did you literally fall to your knees and beg? Because in my mind, that's a true beg. If you're not on your knees, it's more pleading than begging."

She makes a sound I can't even begin to decipher. "*That's* your takeaway from what I just told you?"

I shrug. "I'm a visual person, and I want to make sure I'm taking in the full picture of what you're saying."

Her eyes meet mine.

I *could* be a jerk and mention a recent story of hers that I will be picturing for a very long time to come, but she seemed genuinely embarrassed by her car-trouble related sexcapades tale. There's a clear distinction between teasing and having fun and being plain mean. I never want to cross that line with her.

She's still glaring at me.

"So we have to share a room. Big deal. At least we're out of this." I gesture to the snowstorm engulfing us. "We'll be safe."

"*I'll* be safe," Beth shoots back. "You better sleep with one eye open, mister, because not only am I smart and strong and funny, but I also have a black belt in Brazilian Jiu-Jitsu."

"You do?"

She falters for the tiniest fraction of a second before saying, "Whether I do or not isn't as important as you thinking I do."

"Got it."

I smile—hopefully my smile game has improved over these past few months, and it's no longer at scare-the-kids level scary—in the hopes of reassuring her that she can and should feel safe with me.

I'm a total gentleman. She has nothing to worry about on

that front. Besides, I like her too much to take advantage of the situation.

That said, even though I do feel bad for the havoc this freak blizzard is causing for Fraser and Evie's wedding, I'm not entirely mad about it. Because it means I get to spend a lot more time alone with Beth.

And suddenly, this road trip got a whole lot more interesting.

The next few hours pass by with the two of us holed up in a pretty decent motel room. Soft, warm lighting gives the space a cozy ambiance, the walls are painted a shade of light beige, and nature-inspired paintings by local artists line the walls.

I called Mike and Robyn to let them know that we're both safe, and that we may be delayed in getting back. They said it's no problem, and that the kids are fine.

Beth has been texting with Evie and her girlfriends in their WhatsApp group. Evie is obviously distraught at the disruption this freak blizzard is causing, but everyone is safe where they are, so that's something at least.

I've been listening to the radio, and unfortunately, the forecast isn't looking good. With at least half the guests stranded in various places throughout these mountains and the wedding venue currently flooded and without power, the chances of Fraser and Evie getting married today, or even possibly rescheduling to tomorrow, don't look very promising.

I glance over at Beth, perched on the sofa by the large window, which I assume normally has a nice view. Now, you can't see anything. Total whiteout conditions. I've never seen weather change so quickly. I guess there's a reason why they're calling it a *one in a hundred years* weather event.

She's changed out of her gown into black leggings, an oversized beige knit sweater, and fuzzy-patterned socks. Her feet are tucked under her body, and her attention shifts between the book she's reading—a romance, by the looks of the bright pink cover and the illustration of a guy and a girl— and her phone which keeps buzzing every few minutes.

She made her displeasure with the whole only-one-bed situation abundantly clear when we first got into the room, but I think she's starting to feel better about it. Her periodic five-minute grumbles are now spaced out to much more measured twenty-minute intervals.

"Whatcha readin'?" I ask as I join her, sitting down in the spare seat by the window. I extend my legs, resting my feet on the small, round table between us.

She raises an eyebrow.

I drop my feet to the floor.

Okay. Not a fan of feet on the coffee table. Noted.

Resting her book in her lap, she looks at me and sighs. "I'm reading an enemies-to-lovers romance."

"Enemies to lovers," I repeat, trying to understand how that would work. How can you fall in love with your enemy? That doesn't make any sense. "I don't get it."

She stares out the window and lets out a long sigh. "You and me both."

Now I'm even more confused.

"Hey. I'm meant to be the weirdo in this rel—er...in this—" I stop talking and let me waving my hand between us fill in the blank. "Why are *you* acting weird? Is it about the wedding?"

"Uh, yeah. The wedding. Let's talk about that. Or anything else that isn't an enemies-to-lovers romance where the two main characters get trapped in a snowstorm and are forced to share—I'll stop talking. I think I've done enough ranting for one day. What would you like to talk about?"

Right on cue, my stomach grumbles. "Food?" I suggest.

She grins.

Then catches herself and immediately stops.

She mutters something under her breath that sounds a lot like, "Do not start seeing him in a new light," but I can't be sure with the wind howling outside.

When we checked in, the receptionist explained that due to the weather, they'll be offering room service rather than have people leave their rooms and make their way to the on-site restaurant. It's a safety thing.

"I can order us some food to the room, if you like?" I suggest.

"Sure."

"What would you like?"

"Um, a salad would be great. Dressing on the side please."

"Any particular type of salad?"

"Surprise me."

I get up out of my seat. "One Oreo and Twinkie salad coming right up."

I walk over to the phone, and when I check back on her, I see her grinning face in the window reflection.

She's not going to make this easy for me...and I like that.

A lot.

See? Weirdo.

The food arrives half an hour later—a California cobb salad for her with the red wine vinaigrette on the side, and a chicken fried steak, fish tacos, some pasta, and club sandwich for me because I have a few days off and can indulge in whatever food I want.

There's not enough room on the small table by the window for all the plates, so we eat at the breakfast bar by the kitchenette.

"Did you have a nice Christmas with your family?" I ask, taking a bite of my fish taco.

She nudges her food with her fork and shrugs. "Yeah. I guess."

I don't really know what the deal with her family is, but from the little snippets she's shared with me, I get the sense that they're not necessarily bad people, she simply feels different to them, like an outsider.

But I gleaned that information from her via text. I'm not sure if we're at the place where I can press her for more details in real life.

I take a calculated risk.

"How are things with your family?" I study her face for any reaction. She inhales deeply through her nose and says nothing. "We don't have to talk about it if you don't want to," I tack on, giving her an out.

"No. It's fine." She rests her fork against the side of the bowl. "I'm the black sheep in my family. Literally, I'm the only one with jet-black hair."

I slow my chewing. "Okay."

"They're all very accomplished in their fields. Dad's ex-military, Mom runs a national nonprofit, Schapelle is a best-selling author, Tenley holds a top position in management within a luxury resort chain, and Allie founded and runs a super successful 'elite training center to the stars' in Hollywood."

Hearing the heaviness in her voice, I try to brighten her up a little. "I'll make an exception and allow the use of air quotes this one time."

She cracks a tiny grin. "Thanks."

"But you're accomplished, too, though."

"No. I'm not. I work in a bookstore. *Retail*, as Mom likes to call it when she really wants to drive the point home of how beneath me she thinks it is."

"People need books, Beth," I say. "Reading is one of life's greatest pleasures. You help people find stories that will make them laugh and cry, feel all sorts of things, and see the world and themselves in brand new ways. That's not nothing."

"I guess." Her eyes travel to the window, and there's a sadness in her that I can't quite place. "I'm just so different from my family. They're all optimistic, energetic, outdoorsy people. I hate the outdoors, except for my morning walks. I'm not a pessimist by any means, but I'm not as cheery and hopeful as they are. My idea of a perfect afternoon is enjoying homemade banana bread, a cup of tea, and nonstop reading. And..."

I steeple my fingers and fix my gaze on her. "And what?"

She turns back to look at me, and I can tell she's nervous, weighing up whether to tell me this next thing or not.

I keep my eyes focused on her, sensing now is not the time to back down and praying my instincts are right. We're on the verge of something here. I can feel it.

"I used to be fat," she says bluntly, pushing her plate away. "So, not only am I the complete opposite of my family career-wise and personality-wise, but I've always had to deal with being the only big one, too." She tucks a loose strand of hair behind her ear. "Sorry, I shouldn't be dumping all this on you."

"Don't be sorry. I asked."

I see her fingers tapping the countertop, and I have this sudden urge to reach across it and take her hand in mine.

But my brain kicks in—my survival instinct, too—and I have the good sense to keep my hands to myself.

Beth opening up to me is one thing.

Me touching her—even if it is purely innocent and solely

motivated by wanting to comfort her and nothing else—is another thing entirely.

We are definitely not there yet.

"Has your family ever made you feel bad about yourself?"

"Oh, gosh. No. It's never been an issue. Not even for Mom, who literally criticizes every decision I make. My size has been the sole thing I had a pass on."

That's something. I would have hated for her to be dealing with added pressure or criticism from the people who are meant to love you unconditionally.

There is something else I'm wondering about, but I have to phrase it carefully. "Do you mind if I ask how you..."

"Lost the weight?"

I nod and take a bite of my sandwich, feeling awkward for wanting to know. It's not that it matters to me. It doesn't. I'm sure Beth was just as beautiful then as she is now. I'm just curious.

"It's nothing too exciting. I didn't do any crash diets or anything drastic. I made small incremental changes to my diet, I walk every day, and I limit the sweets I eat. It took about three years for me to get to this size, and yeah, that's how I did it."

She makes another one of her noises, and I wish there was some way to catalog them so that I can access them whenever the need to feel close to her arises.

Because yes, I'm the weirdo who's so infatuated by a girl that he wants to create a library of the noises she makes because he can't get enough of them.

Can't get enough *of her*.

"Anyway, enough about me." Beth picks up her fork and pierces it through a leaf of lettuce. "Let's talk about something else."

"Sure." I polish off the last of my sandwich. "Like what?"

"I have a *looong* list of things to tease you about."

I finish chewing and let out an exaggerated sigh of relief. "Finally. I've been waiting all day. I thought you'd never grill me for details about myself then proceed to judge and critique all of my responses in your typical acerbic fashion."

She giggles, then quickly brings her hand to cover her mouth. "Is it wrong that I like you using the word *acerbic*?"

"Not at all. I only hope it doesn't shatter your image of me as a total dumb-dumb."

Her eyes flash to mine. "I...I don't think you're a dumb-dumb." She makes a light clearing noise. "Let's start with that." She points at my chest.

"My Christmas sweater?"

"Uh-huh. You're a father now. What's with all the muscles? Where's the dad bod?"

"I believe there's a twelve-month grace period before the dad bod era officially kicks in."

She smiles at my joke. I like seeing her smile, but what I like even more is that she's checking me out. I bought the sweater online and despite being the correct size, it sits a little tight on me.

She noticed.

And it seems she approves.

I sit up taller, and hey, it's not my fault if I subtly puff my chest and flex my arms a little. If she likes what she's looking at, who am I to deprive her?

"How are you adjusting to everything?" she asks. "With the kids, I mean. I imagine it's a lot."

"It is. But I'm focused entirely on Josie and Jonah. They're my entire world. All I care about is that they're okay."

She smiles. "They're lucky to have you."

"I'm lucky to have them," I counter. "I mean, how else am I going to practice smiling so I no longer scare kids away?"

"Good point." She giggles. "It sounds like family is important to you."

"Uh, yeah."

Family *is* important to me, especially since I've never had a proper one. Which is why I'm determined to do everything I can to make sure that Josie and Jonah do.

"What's your family like then? Tell me, are they as bad as mine?"

Oh.

No.

She was probably thinking this would continue being a light and fun conversation, but my family situation is anything but light or fun.

Reading my face, she winces. "Uh-oh. Did I just step into a minefield?"

"Kinda, yeah."

"It's okay. Like you said to me before, we can talk about something else."

I should take her up on it.

I *never* open up to anyone about my family, but...I don't know. For some reason, I feel comfortable talking to her about it.

I need to give her fair warning, though. Let her know just how minefieldy the minefield we're about to step into is. My childhood was bleak, and there's no way to sugarcoat it.

"I'm okay to talk about it, but I have to give you a heads-up, it was pretty intense. Are you okay with that?"

She straightens, aiming those gorgeous hazel eyes at me. "I can handle it."

"Okay. Good." I bob my head a few times, working up the strength I need to get the words out. "I was an orphan. My mother was an alcoholic and my father was a drug dealer. He died when I was four, which sent my mom spiraling even more. Child services got involved, and I was taken out of her care when I was seven."

"Oh, Milo." Her eyes go glassy. "I'm so sorry."

The painful memories I've buried deep inside bubble to the surface, proving that while time may heal all wounds, they never disappear completely.

My chest tightens, but I force myself to keep going. "I bounced around from foster home to foster home. At the time, it felt horrible. I felt so unloved. But now, having heard some real horror stories, I see that maybe I didn't have it so bad."

"What do you mean?"

"Well, I was never abused. Never experienced any violence. That sort of thing."

"That's a basic requirement for raising children, Milo."

"I know. And don't get me wrong, I was one angry, hurt, and confused little kid who thought he'd gotten a rotten deal and that the world sucked because why did everyone else get to have a family and I didn't?"

I push through the pressure in my chest. "Luckily, I found hockey, and it saved me. Gave me a purpose. A healthy outlet for me to channel my emotions into. Much better than dealing drugs or getting into trouble with the law, which happens all the time to kids in a similar situation. I had talent, and thanks to a great PE teacher, Mr. Lawson, I made it into the juniors. Hockey was my ticket, my shot at a better life, so I was determined to work my butt off and take it all the way."

"And you have."

I shrug, feeling a little lighter. "I guess."

"Don't be modest." Her breath hitches, and I shift my gaze to her. She grins. "It scares me."

I grin back. "Sorry. Give me a minute, and I'll be back to my egotistical self."

"Good." She nods firmly. "And I know you've made it all the way. Your defense rebound and SPG stats are incredible."

Defense rebounds is definitely not a hockey term, and *SPG*?

"What's SPG?" I ask.

"You know, stop-puck-goal. I've been speaking to Evie, and while she may have used the proper official terms with lots of numbers that made no sense to me, my takeaway was that you're very good at stopping that puck thingy..."

"It's just called a puck, no need to add thingy."

She smiles. "Right. You're very good at stopping that puck from going into the goal...thingy."

I smile right back. "Yeah, I guess I am."

We fall silent, and I can see her processing the stuff I told her about my family because as the smile fades from her face, it's replaced by a pained look of empathy.

She reaches across the table and curls her soft, delicate fingers around mine. This is the only second time she's touched me—the first being at the fence when she placed her hand on mine after I shared the news about my sudden fatherhood—and it fills me with warmth.

"I'm so sorry you went through that, Milo. I really am."

11

Beth

It's not often that I find myself unsure what to say.

Or feel so powerless in the face of someone sharing something real and honest and painful with me.

And I'm shocked that of all people, it's Milo who's opening up to me like this, and that it's the story of his childhood that's affecting me so deeply.

The way he's choosing his words carefully and taking his time makes me think this isn't something he shares with many people. So for him to be opening up like this makes me feel... Well, in all honesty, it makes me feel like an idiot.

And there I was, droning on and on about how I feel like an outsider with my family and how awful that was. It's not perfect, sure, but at least I have a family who loves me. I didn't lose one parent and get abandoned by the other. I wasn't shipped around from foster home to foster home.

Yeah, we moved a lot because Dad was in the military, but we did it as a family. We had each other to rely on. My parents rarely drank, have never touched drugs in their lives—as far as I know—and I have three sisters who, despite our differences, I adore and who I know love me.

And what family does Milo have?

None.

Well, except for his two children now.

As I reflect on what he just revealed, a few more pieces of the Milo puzzle slot into place.

"Is that why you settled in Comfort Bay?" I ask. "To give your kids the type of childhood you never had?"

He smiles softly. "It is."

"And is that why you chose a small house in a nice neighborhood over a mansion on the hill?"

"Bingo."

I force a smile.

Great. I'm not just an idiot. I'm the reigning queen of Idiotland. I've completely misjudged him.

I had Milo pegged as a one-dimensional, grumpy and arrogant guy with a questionable hairstyle when he's actually a very down-to-earth, smart, strong person who's overcome a traumatic childhood many people wouldn't even survive, much less come out of as a successful athlete, and now, a loving father.

He's handled this whole instant fatherhood situation in the most awesome way possible. He didn't shirk from his responsibilities when he easily could have, because, let's face it, he didn't exactly have any good parental role models growing up.

But that's not what he did.

He stepped up and didn't just take ownership of the situation, he's gone above and beyond.

Moving to Comfort Bay so that his kids can have a nice childhood.

Choosing a small family home filled with character over a soulless mansion.

Adopting Jonah, who isn't even biologically his child, so that he and Josie could stay together.

I'm...I'm blown away.

He gets up, comes over to my side of the table, and taps me on my shoulder.

"Hand it over," he says.

I lift my gaze to him, confused. "What are you talking about?"

"Your pity."

"Excuse me?"

"I don't want you looking at me like that." He takes hold of my wrist and transfers my imaginary pity into his hand. He clenches his fist, holds it up in the air as he walks over to the entry. He opens the door. A gust of wind roars into the room as he throws the imaginary pity out and closes the door.

He strides across the room in that Christmas sweater that looks like it's practically glued to his sculpted chest and arms. Then my eyes slide down his body to those thighs encased in denim right now, and my mind fills with the vision of him in those deliciously tight white tights at Fraser's party, and holy heck, what is wrong with me?

I should *not* be checking him out right now.

But for the first time in a really long time, I'm genuinely attracted to a guy.

Yes, he's hot, and yes, that's part of it. But it's more than just physical attraction. I'm really liking Milo as a person.

He uses his outward demeanor the way I use my snark—for protection. Being prickly and unapproachable is a defense mechanism, a way to not get hurt again.

But underneath the image he projects, I'm seeing more and more of the man he is.

He's a lot smarter than I initially gave him credit for, and I like a man who knows words. I wonder if he's a reader, and if he is, what his favorite genre is.

He's a devoted Dad. If the major life changes he's made and the stream of pictures he sends me weren't proof enough, the way he ran back to kiss and hug Josie and Jonah one last time before we left was nothing short of adorable.

He's not afraid to make fun of himself...or for me to make fun of him as is more likely to be the case.

And he's a survivor.

By the sounds of things, he's all alone in this world, and yet, he's never let that stop him from achieving his full potential, working hard, and creating a good life for himself.

And nope, nope, nope...What am I doing? I cannot allow myself to see Milo this way.

I can't.

It's too scary, and I am one hundred percent not ready for the feelings he's stirring up in me.

Milo resumes his seat on the stool, picks up his fork, and points it at me. "I'm not sure where you want to start, but you promised me a grilling, so you need to deliver. My man bun and love of Mariah Carey's Christmas album are easy targets, so you can start there until you gain some momentum. Now go!"

It takes me a moment to adjust my head—and my heart—back to our usual back and forth ribbing.

But this is good.

This is what I need.

Teasing him about what artisanal shampoo he uses to wash his hair and asking if he's strapped for cash since the Christmas sweater he's wearing is so ridiculously tight he must've bought it from the children's department dials back the...whatever it is...simmering between us and creates some much-needed distance.

Well, as much distance as there can be between two people stuck in a blizzard, sharing a motel room.

Humor as a deflection tactic is my superpower, and I need to summon it now more than ever. Because after reading many, *many* romance novels where this exact scenario plays out, I need to have my wits about me and be on my A game.

I cannot—*I will not*—let this forced-proximity situation be the catalyst for anything starting between Milo and me.

I. Will. Not. Let. That. Happen.

After we finished dinner, we were able to diffuse the situation even more. Mainly by giving each other a wide berth.

I plonked myself down by the window and continued

reading a new book since I packed several and I was *not* in the mood to read a sweet hockey romcom about a grumpy goalie and a snarky librarian who get trapped in a cabin in the mountains. I may work in a bookstore and not a library, and Milo and I are stuck in a motel and not a cabin, but it was still hitting way too close to home. A nice post-apocalyptic, dystopian, sci-fi romance is just what I need at the moment.

Milo took the couch. I half expected him to ask if he minded if he watched some sports game match thingy on TV. But instead he pulled out a book and started reading. When I asked him what it was, he lifted the cover for me to see it was Bill Reynolds' latest psychological thriller.

I smiled. So he likes to read. I had a feeling he did.

He then asked if it was okay if he put his feet on the coffee table, to which I replied I had no problem with that and to stop acting like such a weirdo.

He smiled the way he always does whenever I sass him. Why does he like my teasing so much?

I place my book on my lap and look over at him on the couch. He's untied his man bun and his hair flows down past his massive shoulders. It's really nice hair, too. Light brown with a few streaks of a golden, dark-blond. It's thick and silky. Maybe he really does use an expensive artisanal shampoo, and if he does, I need to get the name of it.

His long legs are stretched out in front of him, and boy, his socked feet are huuuge. I'd guess a size thirteen at least.

And it's all proportional, right?

He's a tall guy with big hands, big feet, big shoulders, big arms...My next thought takes a detour...*southward.*

I suck in a breath.

Loudly.

So loudly Milo hears it.

He swivels on the couch and glances over at me. "Everything okay back there?"

"Yep. Fine."

"Okay." He saves his place in the book and puts it on the coffee table. "I was thinking about taking a shower. Unless you want to use the bathroom first?"

"Nope. You're fine. Just leave the toilet seat down and no towels on the floor, please and thank you."

"Yes, ma'am," he says, giving me a mock-salute as he heads toward the bathroom and closes the door behind him.

My eyes slide over to the queen-size bed.

The *one* queen size bed in the room.

Ugh, I've been putting off dealing with that all day.

I'm pretty sure the sofa he was sitting on is one of those pullout ones, so I guess he'll just take that. I should probably chill out because there's a good chance that in real life, these situations aren't as awkward as romance novels make them out to be. Maybe in real life, the guy offers to take the couch and that's the end of it. Matter resolved.

After Milo is done in the bathroom, I walk in to find it... immaculate. Like, you wouldn't even know someone had just been in here. There's not a drop of water in the sink, the mirror is fog free—did he actually wipe it down?—the toilet seat is in its correct position, and there are no towels or clothes in sight.

"Well done, Milo," I say to myself.

I take a nice long shower, letting my thoughts stray from Milo to the other thing that's been plaguing me all day—Evie's wedding.

It's officially been canceled. They can't even reschedule for tomorrow. The wedding lodge is in no state for a wedding.

She messaged about an hour ago.

I'm devastated for her and Fraser. This wedding was

exactly what they—not their mothers—wanted. Yes, it was a little last minute and on a whim, but they found a way to make it work. The stars aligned and they secured a great venue, found an incredible wedding planner, and then nature had to come along and ruin everything.

I step out of the shower, dry off, then take a long hard look at my night clothes. Obviously, I wasn't expecting to get stranded with Milo nor have any other company, so I packed my favorite Hello Kitty pajama set.

"Just pretend it's a normal evening," I mumble to myself as I put on the long-sleeved top and matching pants, dreading the teasing I'm sure I'll cop from Milo the second he sees me.

I fix my hair in the mirror and put on some lip gloss, which is absolutely something I do every night when I'm alone at home and definitely not an attempt to make myself look better for my new and unexpected roommate.

I place my hand on the door handle, close my eyes, and take a deep breath.

This will be fine.

I'm ninety-nine percent sure Milo will have used the time I've been in the bathroom to get the pull-out sofa made up for himself.

I'll make a beeline straight for the bed.

If he happens to notice my pajamas, cue his jokes, to which I'll smile and say he got me, then dive under the covers.

We'll say goodnight.

Lights will go out.

And that will be that.

Everything will be nice and normal, despite the unusual circumstances.

I open the door, step out into the room, and everything is not nice and normal.

The couch remains, well...a couch. Milo hasn't set it up as a sleeping space.

And where is the man of the hour himself?

Why, he's made himself quite comfortable *in. the. bed.*

"What do you think you're doing?" I demand, taking a few steps closer to him, stunned by what I'm witnessing. Any concern I had about what I have on has vanished.

"What does it look like I'm doing?" Milo, who is not only in the bed, but he's also lying *under the sheets*, hooks his hands behind his head, grinning from ear to ear. He casts a glance up and down my body. "I like your pajamas."

He sounds sincere. Where's the teasing? The mocking?

"Uh, thanks."

Still grinning, he tips his chin toward the sofa. "I'm sure you'll be fine on the couch. Yell out if you need a hand setting it up."

What?

What???

He can't be serious.

Step aside Cool Beth, and let Raging Beth take things from here.

I stomp over to the bed, get right up in his face, and grit out, "Leave this bed right now."

He watches me with that grin still on his face, his normally intense eyes brimming with playful mischief. It'd be nice seeing him like this if it didn't come at my expense.

"You said chivalry is dead, so here we are, living in a post-chivalrous world. Enjoy the sofa."

He moves to switch the bedside lamp off, so I lunge forward and catch hold of his wrist. "Are you for real?"

"I am." He pauses, our faces separated by barely a few inches. I can smell the motel body wash wafting off him.

Or is it coming off me?

We're so close I can't tell whose smell I'm smelling.

He lifts a brow. "Or..."

I let go of his wrist. "Or, what?"

"Well, I suppose I could share my bed with you. But no funny business. I don't want you taking advantage of me just because I'm a pro athlete with a soft spot for snarky bookworms."

Ooh, no fair. He's playing dirty. Any shot I had at making a rational comeback flies out the door the second I hear those words.

He...he has a soft spot for me?

Me?

No way.

I shake my head.

As nice as that sentiment may be, I'm no pushover. And if he wants snark, then here's a big ol' helping of the good stuff coming right up.

"Fine." I circle the bed and climb in on the other side. "But make a move and touch me, and you won't be able to have any children, mister."

Wow. I'm so off my game after that *soft spot* comment, I don't even realize my mistake until Milo kindly—and with that annoying grin plastered on his face—points it out to me. "You might want to update your reference, Beth. I already have kids, remember?"

I cannot give him the satisfaction of seeing my grimace, so I school my features and calmly reply with, "Any *more* children."

"Right." He folds his pillow in half and angles his body so he's facing me.

"What?" I say after a few moments of him staring at me in silence.

"Can I say something?"

"As long as it's not stupid."

"It's not stupid."

"Are you really the best judge of that?"

"Fair."

"How about you just say what you want to say, and I'll determine where it lands on the stupid-o-meter."

"Deal." He grins again. Or it's the same grin continuing from before. I can't be sure. He's doing a lot of grinning. "I had a really good time with you today."

He swings his gaze to me, like he's waiting for a score on his statement.

Ha. Joke's on him. I can barely talk, much less run numbers after *that*.

I suck in a breath.

That's a totally stupid thing to say...but I had a good time with you, too.

Oh, boy.

Did I say aloud or was I able to keep it to myself?

Milo's still looking at me expectantly, so, okay...maybe I haven't said anything at all?

His stupid *soft spot* comment coupled with the whole *I had a really good time with you today* has totally scrambled my brain.

And then, just when I think my thoughts can't get any more jumbled, Milo utters four words that send me into a complete tailspin.

"Can I kiss you?"

12

Milo

I'm a dead man.

A dead, stupid man who ruined what was, up until that point, the best day I've ever spent with a woman—freak blizzard aside—by asking one stupidly stupid question.

What was I thinking?

I guess I wasn't. I guess by opening up to her the way I did earlier and then seeing her not freak out completely when I told her I'd had a good time with her—yes, I'm taking her silence as a win—gave me the courage to ask a question that will likely destroy any of the goodwill I'd built.

I hold my breath, waiting for her to respond with a mixture of anticipation and fear for my life as Beth probably weighs up the best way to dispose of my body after she kills me.

Even if my life does come to a sudden, tragic end, I meant what I said. I've had a really good time today.

Despite our conversation about our families taking a darker turn—my fault entirely—I'm glad I opened up to her, and I enjoyed learning more about her family dynamics as well.

Then after eating, we both just read, and it was nice. I've heard people talk about sharing a 'comfortable silence' with someone, and I never really understood what they meant. I do now. Beth was engrossed in her world of romance, I was invested in my psychological thriller, two completely separate worlds, and yet, we were still together.

And of course, no time spent with her would be complete without me being on the receiving end of her taunts and jaunts, and I like serving them back to her, too. And since she's not one of *those weak girls*, I enjoy seeing how she handles a challenge once in a while.

That's why I claimed the bed.

For the record, if she really didn't want to share it with me, *of course* I would have taken the sofa. I just wanted to see how far I could push it.

And when she emerged from the bathroom in that black Hello Kitty pajama set that complemented her hair and made her natural beauty shine through even more, I almost lost it. How is she able to look so stunning in pajamas I'll never know, but man, does she ever.

Everything was going great, and then I had to open my big, stupid mouth and ask to kiss her.

When we're in bed.

Together.

In the middle of a snowstorm.

Talk about a bad move.

Bad timing.

Bad everything.

I'm so screwed.

After the silence stretches way too long, I accept my fate, peel the comforter off me, and swing my legs out of bed. I can admit when I've lost, and I've definitely gone too far here.

I'm *such* an idiot.

As I make a move to get up, a soft hand lands on my shoulder. "One."

I slowly turn my head back to her. "One?"

Our eyes meet.

She pins me with a heated stare, giving a subtle nod. "One kiss. That's it. That's all I'm giving you. And then we never speak of it again. Deal?"

"Deal," I reply without a second's hesitation.

"And not in bed," she says, pulling the comforter off her as well. "Because that would be..."

"Weird?" I offer.

"Yeah." She locks eyes with me. "And..."

"I'm weird enough for the both of us."

She climbs out of the bed. "Hey! Stop stealing all my lines."

"Sorry, sorry." I grin. "Okay. So where would you like to do this totally *non-weird* kiss? And for the record, I refrained from using air quotes for you."

"I'm honored."

She strides over to the kitchenette and flicks on the overhead light. It's one of those super-white, fluorescent lights, and we both blink a few times to adjust to the brightness.

"What are you doing?" I ask when she turns the tap on.

"I hate wasting water," she replies.

"So why did you turn the tap on if you're not using it?"

"I need to arm myself. This kiss cannot turn into anything more, and it can't go on for too long, either. Now hurry up and get over here."

"If this is your idea of foreplay..." I reach her and smooth my hands over her soft upper arms. "Then I am all in."

"You are *so* weird."

"That's already been established. Now, if you're trying to *un-romantic-ify* the moment as I suspect you are..."

"Not a real word but continue."

"...Should I turn the TV on? Maybe find one of those annoying infomercials so that as we kiss, we'll hear the announcer say something like, 'If you act now, you'll receive this special bonus!' to break the moment?"

"Yes, yes. That's perfect."

I chuckle to myself as I scoop up the remote from the coffee table, find an infomercial channel, and increase the volume.

I wonder if she realizes she could have ordered me to do *anything*—skydive out of an airplane, climb an erupting volcano, scuba dive with sharks—and I would have done it in a heartbeat for the chance to kiss her.

I return to the brightly illuminated kitchenette and get in nice and close.

I have no idea why she feels the need to 'arm herself,'—I may have stopped using air quotes around her, but I'm still allowing them in my private thoughts—but if I only get one kiss with her, I'm going to make it the kind of kiss she reads about in her romance novels.

The kind of kiss that will ignite her entire body, from the top of her head all the way down to the tips of her toes.

The kind of kiss that she'll have no choice but to remember every time she looks at me.

"You ready?" I check, aiming for a casual tone and definitely not sounding like a man about to embark on the most important kiss mission of his life.

"I am." She nods. "And make it quick, the water's running."

"Stop turning me on."

"Call now and we'll double your order. That's right, folks, you won't just get one amazing..."

We look at each other and smile. "Come on, Payne. What are you waiting for? An embossed invitation?"

The lighting is all wrong, the water is pooling in the sink and making a gluggy noise as it goes down the drain, and the announcer yaps away loudly in the background, but as I slide my hand around her neck and bring my lips to her, everything that isn't her fades away.

A tiny whimper escapes from the corner of her mouth as I secure my other hand around her waist, bringing our bodies close.

Not touching, but close.

Close enough I can feel the warmth radiating from her skin.

Close enough it makes me wonder if she can feel my heart racing in my chest.

Her whimper turns into a moan as my tongue sweeps inside her mouth.

I rein in the primal impulses raging through my body and tell myself to go slow, determined to remember every single thing about a moment I never thought I'd be lucky enough to have.

After a few seconds, Beth returns the kiss, pushing her body against mine and forcing my back against the wall.

I figured she'd be a woman who took charge, and she does not disappoint. The only thing better than kissing Beth is getting kissed *by* Beth.

"There," I whisper, using every ounce of willpower I have to pull back from her ever so slightly. I run the pad of my thumb over her lips. "One kiss."

"One kiss," she repeats with a soft murmur, lifting her eyes to meet mine.

An intense, euphoric joy—a sensation I've never had before—envelops me, and as I stare into her hazel eyes. This wasn't just a simple 'one kiss' for me. It was so much more than that. It was—

"This deal won't last, so get in quick, folks. And remember, satisfaction guaranteed or your money back!"

We turn our heads to the television at the same time.

The moment may have been broken, but whatever spell she's cast over me is alive and well. It's not just the kiss, it's the months leading up to it. From the moment I saw her giving me the stink eye at karaoke all those months ago, I was smitten.

Her teasing turns me on because I'm weird like that.

Her presence makes me feel safe to be vulnerable.

And one kiss with her confirms what I've known all along —I'm crazy about her. Certifiable, even.

I've never met anyone like her, and I've never felt this intensely about anyone before, either. She's enchanting and playful and smart and beautiful and whatever reasons she has for building a wall around her heart, I'm determined to find them and dismantle that wall, one brick at a time.

I don't care how long it takes or how many man bun jibes she throws at me, I am determined to make Beth mine.

I stare intently at her and drag a hand through my hair before I'm finally able to find my voice. "I'll turn the TV off, you get the water."

It takes her a few seconds to respond. "Deal," she whispers with a breathy tone.

As I trundle across the room, it hits me just how much of a lunkhead I am for agreeing to Beth's condition.

How on earth did I ever think that one kiss would be enough?

13

Beth

My eyes snap open.

Something is wrong.

But what?

I blink a few times.

I know what day it is—the day after what was supposed to be Evie's wedding until nature decided to be a pain in the you-know-what.

I know where I am—a motel room we were forced to spend the night in because nature decided to be a pain in the you-know-what.

And I know whose big arms I'm wrapped up in.

Milo.

I inhale sharply.

I'm wrapped up in Milo's strong, heavy, protective arms.

That's what's wrong.

Actually, wait.

No.

That's not it.

I exhale just as sharply.

I'm wrapped up in Milo's strong, heavy, protective arms... and I don't hate it.

That's what's wrong.

Why don't I hate it?

Yes the man gave me the best kiss of my life last night—a considerable feat given the intentionally unromantic setting—and yes, he's breaking my no-touching-in-bed rule, but I...I don't care. There's something so nice about starting a new day wrapped in someone's arms that sure as heck beats waking up alone.

Milo stirs behind me.

A few seconds pass, and then he sucks in a deep, whooshing breath. Is he having a moment of post-kiss clarity? Remorse? Regret?

He breaks away from me. "Oh, man. Beth, I'm so sorry. I don't know how we ended up—how my arms were around—why I held—Okay. I'm clearly having trouble finishing a sentence, but in my defense, the threat of imminent death will do that to a man."

I bite back my grin and roll over to face him.

My breath catches in my throat at the sight of him, and I let out a sputter.

What is it with us this morning?

He can't complete a sentence, and I'm having trouble remembering the basic in-and-out pattern required to breathe and, you know, stay alive.

Milo's long, shoulder-length hair is tousled from sleep, falling gently around his face, which is lit up by the soft glow of morning light filtering through the curtains, and his light-gray T-shirt clings to his muscular frame. If waking up in his strong arms is an excellent way to start the day, being greeted by this spectacular view runs a close second.

"It's okay," I say, partly to reassure him I'm not mad, and partly so I have an excuse to run my hand up and down his massive bicep.

"So I'll still be able to have kids?"

I stop rubbing his arm. "It's too early for your so-called comedy."

"Six seconds in and you're already insulting me. That's a new record."

"Yeah, well. I think you like it."

"Another thing that's already been established." He reaches

over and tucks a strand of hair behind my ear. "So. Do we do the awkward post-kiss thing where we pretend like it never happened, or is it okay if I'm upfront with you and say that was the single most spectacular kiss of my life?"

My heart starts beating way too fast, but I make an effort to not let it show. "Option B sounds good."

He smiles, and a beam of light catches on his green eyes, making them glitter. "Well, it was. Just wanted to put that out there before you go back to mid-level hating me."

"You've been downgraded to low-level hate," I say. Then, not liking the way the word *hate* makes me feel, amend, "And *hate* is too strong a word. You've been downgraded to low-level annoyance."

He beams like I've just declared my undying love for him. "Even though I'm bummed for our friends that this trip didn't turn out as planned, at least I got that."

That reminds me. "The wedding." I sit upright and look out the window. "It's sunny."

"It is."

I race over to my phone I left charging in the kitchenette. "I'm going to message Evie," I say loudly over my shoulder. "Maybe the wedding is back on somehow? You know, post-Christmas miracle, and all that."

"Fingers crossed." He gets up as well. "Mind if I use the bathroom?"

"Not at all." I'm tempted to throw in some quip about wanting him to leave it clean, but after the pristine condition he left it in yesterday, I don't see any reason to.

I pick up my phone and tap into the Vinaigrettes WhatsApp group chat.

Beth: *Hey, it's sunny here in Whispering Pines. Any chance the wedding can get un-canceled and you can have the ceremony today?*

Evie: *I wish. There's been a landslide, and the road in and out of Cedar Crest Hollow is cut off. Plus, the lodge has sustained damage.*

Summer: *Oh, Evie. I'm so sorry this has happened.*

Beth: *Me, too.*

Hannah: *Me, three.*

Amiel: *Me, four. How are you holding up?*

Evie: *We're trying to focus on the good. No one got hurt, and we will still get married. It just won't be this time.*

Beth: *And how are you really feeling?*

Evie: *Disappointed. Frustrated. Sad. Angry. And guilty that I can't focus on the good things like I should be.*

Summer: *Don't feel guilty. You're allowed to feel the way you feel.*

Evie: *I guess. I know it doesn't change anything between Fraser and me. He loves me, and I love him. I just want to be his wife so we can...you know, be together as husband and wife. <raised eyebrows emoji> It's been HARD waiting.*

Beth: *I bet it has <eggplant emoji>*

Hannah: *lol*

Summer: *lol*

Amiel: *Why am I always the last one?...lol*

Beth: *Sorry, sorry, sorry. Now is not the time for my world-famous humor.*

Amiel: *And how was YOUR night, Beth?*

Beth: *Fine.*

Amiel: *<raised eyebrow emoji>*

Summer: *<gimme hands emoji>*

Hannah: *<ears emoji> <ears emoji> <ears emoji>*

Evie: *<eggplant emoji> (For revenge)*

Beth: *You guys! Stop it!*

Hannah: *Give us the goss, and we will.*

Beth: *There is no goss.*

Amiel: *Did you and Milo kiss?*

Wow. They are not messing around this morning.

Beth: *We did.*
Hannah: *That means there's goss.*
Beth: *There's no more goss apart from that. We kissed once, and it was nice.*
Amiel: *Nice???*
Beth: *Okay. It was slightly better than nice.*
Summer: *Slightly???*

I sigh and do the smart thing—cave.

They're relentless when they get like this, and I'd know since I'm usually the one leading the probe for romantic details.

I'm not used to being on the receiving end of it, though.

Beth: *Okay, fine. It was the best, most mind blowing kiss I've ever had in my life. Even though the lights were on, the tap was running, and an obnoxious infomercial was blaring in the background.*
Amiel: *Why were any of those things happening?*
Beth: *It was my attempt to un-romantic-ify the situation.*
Amiel: *That's not a real word.*

I want to disagree with her, but she's right. It isn't.

Summer: *I think I get what you mean, though. That's so you.*
Evie: *It really is.*
Beth: *Is that a bad thing?*
Hannah: *Absolutely not. We should never be anything but ourselves.*
Evie: *Milo's a smart dude. He knows what he's doing.*
Beth: *You think so?*

Evie: *I know so. Okay, this is strictly confidential and doesn't leave the group...but Fraser told me Milo's been asking about you. A lot. Like, alllllll the time.*

Amiel: *I'm squealing over here.*

Summer: *As someone in the room next to Amiel, I can verify that squealing is happening.*

Evie: *Apparently it started over the summer, after the karaoke night.*

Hannah: *That was such a good night! <smiley heart eyes emoji>*

I smile because that was a big night for Hannah and Culver.

And *not* a big night for me and Milo.

I basically ignored him all night, barely said two words to him—and I'm pretty sure whatever I did say to him came with a side order of sass—and even after all that, he liked me enough to ask about me.

Multiple times.

An uneasy combination of guilt and pining swirls inside me. Guilt for not treating Milo as well as I should have and pining for—well, let's not go there.

A new message pops up.

Hannah: *Are you happy, Beth?*

Beth: *Remind me again what happy feels like?*

Summer: *Generally characterized by not hating everything and everyone.*

Amiel: *Accompanied by a light feeling in your chest and a bounce in your step.*

Evie: *Other physical signs—symptoms?—include: smiling, laughing, relaxed posture, and calm breathing.*

Beth: *I...don't know.*

Evie: *Don't know or not ready to deal?*
Beth: *The last part.*
Evie: *Fair enough. There's no pressure.*
Hannah: *There really isn't. Look at me and Culver.*
Evie: *Or me and Fraser...Or Summer and Bear?*
Summer: *<eye roll emoji> Not this again. Let's keep moving.*
Amiel: *I'll keep it moving. Beth, what was it like when he came to your room this morning? Or, wait, did you go to his? Was it awkward?*

Oh, yeah. I *maaay* have possibly kinda accidentally overlooked telling my friends Milo and I were forced to share a room.

Oops.

Beth: *So about that. Funny story, actually. When we got to the motel, they only had one room left so we were forced to share.*

Amiel would like to switch to video chat

I hit decline because even though Milo is in the bathroom, that is still way too close. The last thing I need is him walking in on an avalanche of excited screaming from my girlfriends.

Beth: *Sorry, Amiel. I can't talk. He's showering.*
Amiel: *Fair enough. I only have one question to ask anyway, and the answer to this question will tell me everything I need to know.*

I groan.

As a fellow romance reading junkie, I have a hunch I know what she's going to ask.

Beth: *Go ahead.*

Amiel: *I'll make it real simple.*
Amiel: *You like multiple choice, right?*

I groan loader.

Beth: *Sure.*
Amiel: *Okay...*
Amiel: *In that case...*
Amiel: *How many beds are in the room you shared with Milo. Option A: 1. Option B: 2.*
Beth: *Option A.*

Before I'm on the receiving end of a lightning-round inquisition, I quickly tap out a lie.

Beth: *Guys, Milo is coming out of the bathroom. I have to go.*
Amiel: *Ooh, go, go! Can't wait to get the FULL details.*
Summer: *Same. And also, Evie, if we can do anything for you, let us know.*
Beth: *Yes. Anything at all.*
Evie: *Thanks, guys. There's nothing anyone can do. Just stay safe and keep in touch. Okay?*
Hannah: *Will do!*
Summer: *I will.*
Beth: *Same.*
Amiel: *<sigh emoji> Always the last one...Me, too.*

I get off the phone and turn on the TV to a local news station, needing a distraction from all the Milo-related thoughts whirling in my brain.

How *do* I feel?

Happy?

I...guess. It's fifty-fifty.

The first fifty is yeah, I am happy. I like Milo. He's a great guy. I feel safe with him. I had a great time yesterday talking and hanging out together.

The other fifty is taken up by a not-so-happy feeling—the lingering remnants from relationships past.

Letting my guard down with Milo seems to have triggered some muscle memory. I've let two other guys in before, and they both ended up treating me badly and really hurting me.

Logically, I know Milo isn't them and that this situation is different. But try telling that to my only recently mended heart.

The weather report comes on, and I force myself to pay attention. It looks like parts of the mountain are still cut off, but where we are isn't, which means we'll be able to return to Comfort Bay today.

A few moments later, Milo steps out of the bathroom, and it's like I'm seeing him for the first time.

His hair is loose and a bit damp, falling down to his muscular shoulders. He's dressed in a flannel top, unbuttoned, over a white T-shirt emblazoned with the LA Swifts logo, and a pair of straight fit dark-blue jeans that show off his muscular thighs nicely.

It's a normal outfit, something I've seen him wear a few times. Nothing out of this world, and yet for some reason, it feels out of this world.

Milo looks different somehow. I...I can't explain it.

Guess that's why I'm not the author in my family.

I turn the television off. "I have good news and bad news. Which do you want to hear first?"

He walks over and sits down on the couch next to me. Not too close, but not too far, either.

"The bad."

"Okay. The bad news is the wedding is still off."

He runs a hand through his damp hair. "Oh, man, that's rough. I feel awful for Fraser. How's Evie?"

"Devastated but putting on a brave face."

"Understandable." His eyes drop to my lips. "And what's the good news?"

Suddenly, the thought of going back home doesn't feel like such good news. Which is silly. It's not like we can stay holed up here in this motel room forever.

Can we?

And we definitely can't kiss again since I'm the one who instigated the one-kiss rule. I can't break it less than twenty-four hours later.

Can I?

No, Beth, you cannot. Now stop wasting time and answer Milo's question before you cross over and join him as co-mayor of Weirdsville.

"The good news is we're fine to travel back to Comfort Bay. The roads on this side of the mountain have reopened."

"That's great." His eyes stay on my lips for a few more seconds before he lifts his gaze and offers a slight nod. "What would you like to do?"

Is it just me or is there a raspy edge to his voice?

Stay here and keep kissing you, is what I want to say. "Go home, I guess," is what I actually say.

"All right. Let's go home then."

"Before we do." I hesitate, unsure whether I want to bring this up, because if I do, there'll be an unspoken implication for him to join me.

And I don't know how I feel about that.

I'd like to do it with him, but then again, I've never done it with a guy before.

I shake my head. "Forget it."

He shuffles closer and hooks his fingers under my chin,

gently tilting my head up until my eyes meet his. "You can tell me anything, Beth. *Please.*"

There's something about the warmth in his voice, the sincerity shining in his eyes, that gives me the courage to break through a piece of that old resistance and say to him, "I'd like to go for a walk."

"Oh. Okay." *Come on, girl. Don't stop now. He's clearly waiting for you to invite him.* "Want to come with me?"

"I'd love to." A radiant smile spreads across his face. "I thought you'd never ask."

I smile back.

I almost didn't.

～

Thirty minutes later, we're hiking along a trail behind the motel.

Milo's been quiet.

We both have been.

I'm doing it. I'm actually going on an early morning walk with a guy I like. I know it's not the biggest achievement in the world, but it feels like a breakthrough for me. Apart from my girlfriends, and my mom when I was younger, morning walks have always been a solo activity.

Neither of the guys I dated expressed any interest in joining me. Not that Milo and I are dating, but it's nice he was so enthusiastic about coming along.

My head is still spinning.

I'm walking with Milo, and he told me our kiss last night was the most spectacular kiss of his life.

Guess I can add emotional intelligence to the list of traits I assumed he didn't possess, because what type of man says something like that?

The sincerity in his voice and the conviction in his eyes as he said it, made me believe him. And when you've been lied to by guys in the past, you develop a sixth sense for these things. He wasn't feeding me some throwaway line, he meant what he said.

I pick up the pace a little. "Can I ask you something?"

"Sure," he replies, matching me stride for stride.

"What was Josie and Jonah's mom like?"

"Ah."

"If it makes you uncomfortable, we don't have to talk about it."

"No. It's fine. The thing is, I wish I knew more about her, because the truth is, I don't. Her name was Isla, and I met her on a post-victory night out six years ago. She was really pretty and seemed different from the normal ditzy girls who hung around hockey players. She was in college. Read sci-fi. Loved manga. Spoke three languages."

"She sounds cool."

"She was. In a nerdy way, which made her even cooler to me because I'm weird like that."

I smile as I take in his self-deprecating joke. I've never met a guy who's so comfortable making fun of himself.

He continues. "We had an immediate attraction, which only increased when she told me she wasn't interested in hockey players."

"Wait. You *liked* that?" He nods. "You really are a weirdo."

He grins. "I really am."

The trail breaks off in two separate directions. The left loop is two miles, the right is five. I flick my fingers between them. "Are you up for a longer walk?"

"Sure. You?"

"Let's do it. So what happened with you and Isla?" I ask as we set off on the right trail.

"Well, after we slept together, I found out that she'd also been with one of my teammates and at least two other players I knew. I'm not judging her for that, but I was hurt by her dishonesty. She *was* into hockey players. Big time. She also told me she was interested in more than just a one-night stand, only for me to discover that that was another lie."

"You never heard from her again?"

"Nope. After our night together she ghosted me completely. Didn't answer my texts or phone calls. I spoke to my teammate, and we put two and two together pretty quickly. She was yet another puck bunny."

"I'm sorry that happened to you."

"Thanks. I'll be honest, it did affect me for a while. I'm not a quick-to-trust person at the best of times, so after that experience, I closed up even more."

"That makes sense."

"For a long time, I regretted sleeping with her. But then..."

A smile stretches across his lips, and I *know* who he's thinking about. "How did you learn you were a father?"

"My manager got an email from Isla's mother saying that Isla had been killed in a car crash and that she had two children—a five-year-old girl named Josie, and a two-year-old boy named Jonah—and that there was a chance I was the father of Josie."

"Holy moly. What did you do?"

"We looked into it. Part of me suspected it might have been someone's idea of a sick joke, but I didn't want to dismiss it outright, either. We hired an investigator, and the story checked out. I took a DNA test, and yeah, it turns out I'm Josie's father."

"What about Jonah?"

"That was the snag that made the whole custody slash adoption process take so long. I'm obviously not his father since I never saw Isla after our night together. Despite a comprehensive search, his biological father hasn't been tracked down. I obviously wanted custody of Josie, but at the same time, I didn't want her to lose her brother. They'd already experienced too much loss, so I...I adopted Jonah, and he *is* my son."

He declares it proudly and with such conviction, leaving no room for doubt that he is Jonah's father.

I have to blink faster to keep the tears welling in my eyes at bay. I'm speechless. What a beautiful, selfless, kind thing to do.

"What about you?" Milo asks, ducking out in front to remove a fallen branch from the path. "You want kids?"

As I pass him closely, I catch the subtle scent of the motel body wash from him. "Uh, sure. I guess."

"You hesitated."

"No, I do. I want kids. But in some abstract, future tense way, you know? I don't even have a boyfriend so it's a little too soon to be thinking about kids."

He opens his mouth, closes it, then opens it again. "And how come you don't have a boyfriend?"

I sigh and slow down a little to take a swig from my water bottle. "Remember how I said I used to be heavy?"

His jaw tightens. "I do."

"There's your answer. Guys aren't into big girls, or if they are..." I lock my focus on the forest straight ahead, my chest filling with a sense of shame I haven't been able to shake even though, rationally, I know what happened wasn't my fault. Both times.

We spot a bench up ahead, and without saying anything, we approach it and sit down.

"Did someone hurt you?" Milo guesses.

I smile sadly. "Try someones. Plural."

"I'm sorry." His arm twitches, and for a moment I think he's going to touch me, but he doesn't. Instead, he rests his hands in his lap, clasping them firmly. "You don't have to tell me anything. I'm curious, and I'd like to know what happened. You can tell me to stick my nose anywhere you like."

His words are like a release valve to the pressure that had been building in my chest, and despite his offer, I'm ready to tell him.

"I've had two boyfriends," I begin, staring straight ahead. "Liam after I graduated high school and Dylan about a year after Liam and I broke up. Two very different guys, but one very common theme in why I ended things."

I take a breath and carry on. "With Liam, I overheard a conversation between him and his best friend. They were talking about me."

"What were they saying?" Milo asks in a gentle tone.

"It wasn't very nice." I drop my head. "Basically, his friend was making fun of my size, and Liam was laughing along. He said something along the lines of, the only reason he's dating me is because he can treat me any way he likes and he knows I'll take it because I'm so..." I close my eyes to prevent the tears from escaping. "Desperate."

"Oh, Beth."

I shake my head, trying to loosen the stranglehold of emotions clawing at me. "I ended things right after that, but it still hurts. And I hate that. I hate that after all this time, it can still affect me."

"I don't know what to say."

I glance at Milo.

He's tense, gripping his hands so tightly his knuckles have turned white, jaw ticking, and brow furrowed.

But his voice?

His voice this whole time has been soft and gentle and filled with nothing but concern.

"It gets worse," I say with a heavy heart. "If I thought Liam was a grade-A jerk, Dylan was the supreme overlord of the jerkdom. We were only dating for a little while when I found out that he and his friends had a competition..." I halt, the repugnant words lodged in my mind, too awful to voice.

"A competition?"

"Yeah." I whisper the next part. "A competition to see who could sleep with the most plus-size girls."

Milo bolts to his feet and furiously punches the air. His whole body is heaving with rage. He leans over, resting his hands on his knees, his massive back and shoulders swaying with every breath he takes.

Then he straightens and returns to me. "May I?" he says, dropping his gaze to my hands.

"Yeah."

He crouches down and takes my hands, brings them to his mouth, and peppers my knuckles with delicate kisses. Then he looks me straight in the eye. "There's nothing I can say. That's absolutely disgusting behavior that makes me sick to my stomach."

"It's okay," I tell him, not used to seeing a guy get so enraged on my behalf like that. My girlfriends, yes, but a guy?

It's oddly comforting.

"It's not okay," he mutters to himself then swings his eyes to meet mine. "I'm sorry about my reaction. Off the ice, I'm not a violent person at all, but that was just..." He blows out a breath. "That was a lot."

"You're fine," I assure him. "Really. It was...kinda nice actually."

He releases my fingers and lifts his hand up, hovering near the side of my face. "May I?"

I'm not quite sure what he's asking permission for this time, but I nod anyway.

He smiles tenderly as he grazes my cheek with his fingers. My heart melts at the tenderness of the gesture.

He stops suddenly and pulls back, staring at my hands. "Oh no. I just broke the one-kiss rule."

"Technically, you did." But him kissing my knuckles before was such a sweet thing to do, I'm willing to let it slide. "But if we're getting all technical about things, I meant kisses on the lips."

"Right." His voice has turned husky. "Okay..."

I can tell he's itching to say something more. "Yes?" I prompt.

"Well, you weren't exactly clear about something else either."

"And what might that be?"

Our eyes meet. "Whether your one kiss rule meant one kiss *ever*, or one kiss *per day*."

"Hmm. I guess I didn't spell that out."

"No. You didn't. That was incredibly confusing of you."

"Shut up."

"You know, I could probably sue you for emotional ambiguity."

I giggle. "Shut *up*."

He grins. "Make me."

Oh, I'll make him all right.

I scooch over to get closer to him, grab the sides of his face, and launch into a frenzied kiss.

Some guys might get funny when the girl takes the lead, but I'm confident Milo doesn't mind the way my hands are messing up his hair, the way my tongue is probing his mouth like a search team on a mission, or the way my hands slide across his chest, tracing the hard muscles under his T-shirt.

My only note about last night's kiss was that it was too short, so I make sure not to repeat the same mistake today.

"One kiss a day," I clarify, murmuring hungrily into his mouth.

He responds by tightening his grip around my waist, signaling his approval of our arrangement, and I can't help but moan at the heated touch.

It's only the sound of approaching footsteps that eventually makes me let go of him.

"So," I say, straightening my shirt and fixing my hair.

"Right," Milo says, doing the same.

By the time the middle-aged couple walk by us, exchanging friendly hellos, we manage to erase all signs of this kiss.

Which doesn't feel good because I didn't want to erase all signs of the kiss.

But maybe it's for the best?

Even though I'd rather not, I have to face reality. This weekend took one giant unexpected turn, but that doesn't change the fact Milo and I lead two very different, very incompatible lives. There's no point in even daydreaming about this leading to anything more.

Maybe he can join me for an occasional early morning walk when he's in town, and we can enjoy a kiss now and then.

"What are your plans for when we get back?" I ask, as we resume the walk.

"I'll spend today getting ready to leave. We're back out on the road tomorrow." He hesitates. "You know..."

"Yeah?"

"I'm playing in LA in a few weeks if you feel like joining Evie and coming down to watch."

"I hate hockey," I remind him on the off chance he's forgotten.

"I'm well aware."

"I also may or may not still find you low-level annoying."

"Another fact I know all too well."

"Did I already say I hate hockey?"

He licks his lips, smiling. "You did."

"Can I think about it?"

"Of course. You know where I live, and you have my number."

"Yeah." A grin tugs at my lips. "I do."

14

Milo

Rage fuels my hockey.

It's not the only thing, obviously. I train hard, work hard, and possess a degree of natural skill and athleticism.

But underneath it all, rage has always been my secret weapon.

When I first started, it was my outlet to deal with the pain and anger of dealing with the crappy hand I'd been dealt.

In my teen years, I started realizing I wasn't the only one who got a raw deal. I saw how the world worked, and I didn't like it.

How poorly some people get treated because of things they can't control, like the color of their skin. How those with money have so many more doors opened to them while those of us who don't have cushy bank balances have to fight for everything we have. How, despite decades of progress, there are still men out there who think it's acceptable to talk about and treat a woman the way Beth's exes talked about and treated her.

I've been playing some of the best hockey of my career these past few weeks, in no small part based on the fury Beth telling me about her experiences with men unleashed in me.

And I'm really on fire tonight knowing she's in the stands, watching me.

The Bullets star forward Matt Padalecki advances, closing in on me with a fierce determination. I stand steadfast at the net, my eyes locked on the puck, every muscle in my body coiled and ready to react.

Padalecki fakes left, then right, attempting to throw me off balance.

I don't even flinch, my eyes solely focused on the puck.

He winds up for the shot.

The puck rockets off his stick like a bullet.

The crowd holds its breath as the puck hurtles toward the net.

I drop to my knees in the butterfly position, pads spread wide to cover as much of the goal as possible. My gloved hand extends out for the intercept. There's a deafening thud as the puck makes contact with the glove, but it's not over yet.

The rebound bounces off my glove, and another opposing player swoops in, attempting to capitalize on the loose puck.

I spring to my feet and lunge forward, stick outstretched, to poke the puck away only to be met with a fierce slapshot from yet another opponent.

I dive sideways, stacking my pads to form a wall of protection. The puck deflects off my leg pads, flying high into the air.

I push myself back to my feet.

As the puck descends, it becomes a mad scramble in front of the net with players from both teams battling for control.

I manage to locate the puck amidst the chaos and pounce on it, smothering it under my glove.

The whistle blows, signaling a stoppage in play, and the arena erupts in a deafening roar.

Breathing heavily, I rise to my feet as my teammates converge, burying me in a wall of hugs and backslaps. The euphoria of the successful save washes over me, but my eyes seek out one person and one person only.

Scanning through the sea of jubilant faces, my eyes dart past a blur of banners and waving hands, searching, searching.

And then I spot her.

Well, first I spot Evie, who's hard to miss, leaping up and down with the exuberant energy of the Energizer bunny.

But Beth is right there beside her, dressed in all black with an LA Swift scarf wrapped around her neck, which I'm sure she'll roll her eyes as she tells me later that she only wore it ironically.

She may not be bouncing around like Evie, but she's smiling and she looks happy. And when she sees me staring at her, she does the cutest thing ever.

She waves.

Then she looks around and raises one fist in the air, in what I'm guessing is her attempt at a sports-fan gesture.

It's so awkward.

And so freaking adorable.

She's completely clueless about how to cheer, and something about that releases another wave of adrenaline in my body.

There's still a few minutes left in the game, so I wave back and take my position.

She doesn't leave my mind, though.

I could tell Beth was a strong woman from the moment I met her, but after hearing about her awful experiences with men, my respect for her has only grown.

And I guess understanding her past helps explain some of her initial harshness toward me. After the way she's been treated, I don't blame her for being suspicious of men and quick to think the worst.

I've been on the road with the kids ever since we returned from Fraser and Evie's wedding that wasn't, so my only communication with Beth has been through messaging each other every day.

She's teased me about the photos in my *Hockey Illustrated* story—admittedly, the hipster outfit chosen by the stylist wasn't my preferred choice for the shoot, but I went along with it to not be difficult—she's texted a thumbs-up emoji after every one of our victories, and she's been sharing stories from the bookstore, recounting all the amusing and funny things customers say and do.

But one of my favorite text exchanges with her?

That would be the one from two nights ago.

Beth: *Against all my better judgment and knowing I am going to hate every minute of it, I've decided to tag along with Evie to LA to watch the game.*
Milo: *You mean, to watch me play. <eyebrow raise emoji>*
Beth: *You have a talent for exuding arrogance, even via text, you know that?*
Milo: *Arrogant and weird is an unbeatable combination.*
Beth: *You talk a good game.*
Milo: *I can back it up, too.*
Beth: *Can you now?*
Milo: *<sunglass wearing smiling emoji>*
Beth: *You better win, is all I'm going to say to that.*
Milo: *We will.*
Beth: *Time will tell. See you Saturday, x.*
Milo: *x*

It's the second time she's ended a message thread with an x, and this time, I'm proud to report it didn't send me spiraling.

I hit that *x* key and pressed *Send* without a second thought.

With our forwards dominating in the dying seconds of the game, I'm left alone to think in the goal crease. Like always, Beth occupies my every thought. Between her and the kids, it feels like that's all I ever think about.

After a couple of unexpectedly heavy conversations during our trip up the mountain, Beth's returned to her usual intoxicating mix of insults, jabs, and expressing her low-level annoyance at me any chance she gets.

That's clearly her comfort zone, so I'm going to respect that. And honestly, I like the to-and-fro banter between us.

But there is something I'm struggling with.

As much as I'd like to continue down our semi-friendly, semi-flirty path, in light of what she revealed about her past treatment, I'm not sure how to navigate things.

If I compliment her appearance, am I inadvertently reinforcing that she looks good only because she lost weight? Because I don't mean it like that. I think she'd look great at any size, but this is the only size I've seen her.

And I don't know how to proceed on the, uh, physical intimacy side of things, either.

Based on her dating history, there's a high probability she hasn't been with anyone yet. My experience on that front has only been with women who are very forward and clear on what they want.

I don't want to treat Beth differently simply based on an unconfirmed assumption I have, but if I am right, I want to tread carefully and make sure she always feels safe with me.

Because she is.

I will always give her the respect and care she rightfully deserves.

Another thing I'm not sure about?

That would be our kiss arrangement.

Sure, she clarified that she meant one kiss a day, but did she mean it hypothetically or for real that we could actually kiss every day. And if she meant the latter, does that apply only to days when we're together, or is there a running tally, in which case, we are woefully in arrears and will need to do a lot of kissing to square the kiss ledger.

The final buzzer sounds, and we end up winning the game.

We've won a lot of games this season, our turnaround from this same time last year truly remarkable.

It's January and midway through the season. Our record stands at 28-12-3. Twenty-eight wins. Twelve losses. Three overtime or shootout losses.

We're leading our division by a comfortable margin, but neither me nor my teammates are resting on our laurels. A lot can happen between now and the finals, and we are staying focused and determined.

I race through my post-game stretches and bypass the ice bath for two reasons.

One, my kids are here because Boden had to fly home to Wisconsin yesterday after his mother took a nasty fall and broke her hip. I've hired an interim nanny from the agency. Patricia seems great, and maybe I'm overthinking this, but I didn't feel comfortable leaving the kids alone in the hotel with her, so I dragged them all along to the stadium.

And two, Beth is here as well.

She'll meet my kids for the first time tonight.

I keep telling myself that it's no big deal. That if I were a normal person living a normal life, they would have already met by now. But we haven't been back to Comfort Bay since Christmas.

Besides, it's not like I'm introducing them to my girlfriend. We're just neighbors. One of us may be infatuated with the other, while said other tolerates mildly annoying me.

I pull my head through my shirt and let out a weary sigh.

If my lifestyle isn't kid-friendly, it sure as heck isn't girlfriend-friendly, either. It's funny, neither one of those two things even crossed my mind before. Now it's all I can think about. Even though Beth and I aren't even dating.

"You ready?" Fraser asks as he approaches my locker.

"Yeah." I throw the rest of my gear into my duffel bag. "Let's go."

We take off for the family lounge.

He and Evie have rescheduled their wedding for Valentine's Day. They were able to book the same venue since it'll be repaired by then. I'm hoping they'll have better luck with the weather this time.

As if reading my thoughts, he says, "I got your RSVP to the wedding."

"Great."

"Beth RSVP'd too."

I stop walking and turn to him. "Yes, and?"

"Well, one of the only bright spots of the wedding debacle was, you know..." He rocks on his feet, wagging his brows, and I recognize that goofy look on his face from when he and I were ribbing Culver over his situation with Hannah. Teasing someone about their love life is always more fun when you're not the target.

"I have no idea what you're talking about," I say, despite having a ninety-nine percent idea I know what he's talking about.

"Oh, come on, man." He flicks my arm. "You and Beth. Holed up in a motel room with a blizzard raging outside. It's like a scene ripped from one of the romance novels she's always got her nose buried in."

"It was nothing like a scene from a romance novel," I argue, hating that my cheeks always get warm when I lie.

"Then why are you blushing?"

"I'm not blushing. I did, however, limit the Bullets to only score once, so forgive me if the price of our victory tonight is a little more color in my cheeks."

"Uh-huh. Uh-huh." We start walking again. "That's not what Evie said. About your stay in the motel, I mean."

Don't bite. Don't bite. Don't bite.

"Why? What's Evie told you?"

Damn. I bit.

"Oh, nothing." He smiles annoyingly. "Besides, I don't really like to gossip."

I snort. "I may be Comfort Bay's newest resident, but I'm yet to meet anyone who lives there and can say that truthfully."

"Look, without betraying anyone's confidence, I'll say this —she doesn't hate you."

"Super helpful." I say it with a smile because I can read between the lines of what he's telling me.

With Beth, not hating someone is a *very* good sign.

We enter the family lounge. "Daddyyyyy!" Jonah runs up to me. "You stopped da puckeys."

I crouch down, and he launches himself into me. "I sure did, buddy," I say, ruffling his hair. Josie walks up to us. "Did you enjoy the game?" I ask her.

"I liked the nachos. The game was boring."

I'm still adjusting to the unfiltered honesty only an almost-six-year-old can pull off.

I smile. "Yeah. The food here is pretty great."

There hasn't been any progress on the *I love you* front, either, but I can wait it out until she's ready and comfortable enough to say it to me. I need to earn her trust, and I will.

Hmm. That seems to be a recurring theme in my life with females at the moment.

I exchange a few words with Patricia, the fill-in nanny, who comments how well-behaved the kids are. When she moves on to general chitchat, I survey the lounge, seeking out—ah, there she is, talking with Evie and Fraser.

Heat surges in my chest.

Beth cuts a striking figure, decked out in a black sweater and black jeans with the scarf now hanging over one shoulder.

As if sensing I'm looking at her, she turns her head, and

our eyes meet. I hold her gaze for a solid few seconds, curious what she's thinking about and wondering if missing her way more than expected is a silly one-way thing.

She gives a small wave, and I tip my chin and greet her with what could possibly be one of my scare-children-away smiles. I've been making progress on the smile front, but I'm suddenly nervous so maybe I'm reverting to my old ways.

Tapping Evie on the arm, she excuses herself, and of course, Fraser and Evie make no effort to be discreet as they watch her making her way over to me.

Nerves churn in my stomach even more than they did before the game tonight. Why do I care so much if she gets on with my kids, and why am I hoping they both like Beth?

She reaches us, and before I can get introductions underway, she drops down and greets Josie and Jonah with a friendly smile. "Hey, you guys. My name is Beth, and I'm your next-door neighbor in Comfort Bay."

Josie gets a little timid and mumbles a quiet hello, while Jonah bulldozes past Josie and lifts his tiny hand to exchange a high five with Beth. "I wike your hair," he says, and her smile widens.

"Why, thank you."

"It's b'ack."

"Yes it is black," she says, and I'm impressed she didn't miss a beat understanding what Jonah was saying.

I scoop him up in my arms before he can lunge at her and touch it—he's going through a touchy-grabby phase at the moment—and introduce Beth to Patricia, hurrying to explain why Boden isn't with me when her eyes widen in surprise.

After they've said hello, it's my turn, and I don't know the best way to greet her.

A hug? Maybe.

A kiss? Definitely not.

Since I'm hesitating, Beth makes the first move by...sticking her hand out.

"A handshake?" I sputter.

Jeez.

My heart sinks.

I expected her to play it cool—if for no other reason than to not give our friends, who are currently gawking at us from across the room, any ideas—but a freaking handshake? Even the locker-room attendant high fived me after the game.

"Take it," Beth whispers out of the corner of her mouth.

"Take what?"

I have no idea what she's talking about until I drop my gaze and spot the edge of a bright blue piece of paper wedged in her palm. "And be discreet, dude."

I smile as we shake hands, *discreetly* taking the piece of paper from her.

Unfortunately, the next thing I do?

Not so discreet.

She slaps the side of her face and scoffs in disbelief as I unfold the paper out in the open.

"What?" I ask.

She tips her head toward Evie and Fraser who are staring at us, grinning. "Smooth," Beth mutters, rolling her eyes.

I shrug, figuring the damage is already done and read her note.

Except it's not really a note.

It's more of a coupon, actually.

A coupon that entitles me to the one thing I've been missing and thinking about every day I haven't been with her these past few weeks.

One free kiss.

"I'd like to cash in my coupon, please," I say as soon as I shut the door to the kids' room behind me and make my way to Beth, who's sitting on the couch in my hotel suite.

"I still can't believe you read the note in front of everyone," she says, closing the book she's been reading while I tucked Josie and Jonah in. Because as she told me when I asked her about it, she never leaves her house without one. "I was trying not to raise suspicions."

I drop down next to her. "Are you really that embarrassed to be associated with me?"

"Of course I am," she says with a smile. "I also love how you have literally zero chill and are claiming your kiss the second the kids are asleep."

She has no idea how much I've been missing her, craving her, dreaming about kissing her again. But seeing as I'm already a weirdo who has zero chill, I don't want to add *comes on too strong* on top of that.

"Me having zero chill is only part of it. Jonah's developed a habit of getting up a few minutes after I put him down and bringing me random things he collects."

"Why"

"Not sure. I think he thinks he's being helpful."

"That's so sweet." Beth smiles. "They're both great kids."

My chest warms at the compliment. "Take after their old man, I guess."

"Whatever."

She may have rolled her eyes, but that doesn't stop her from leaning over and sliding her hands over my shoulders then just as quickly sliding them off and retreating to her side of the couch when she catches Jonah bounding into the room with a remote control in one hand and a notepad in the other.

He extends his arms and proudly displays his latest haul. "For you, Daddy."

"Sorry," I mutter to a giggling Beth, before glancing at Jonah.

"Thanks, buddy," I say, taking the items from him. "Want me to tuck you in again?"

He nods and lets out a yawn. "Yes, pwease."

"I'll be back soon," I say to Beth.

She waves her book at me. "Take your time."

I don't.

I can't help feeling a little guilty as I rush through tucking Jonah back into bed. But come on, I haven't seen Beth in *weeks*. I'm sure when I tell him this story one day when he's found his person, he'll understand my hurry.

I freeze.

"What iz it, Daddy?"

"Nothing, buddy." I kiss him on his forehead. "Sweet dreams. I love you."

"Wuv you, too."

He rolls over, and I sit on the edge of his bed for a moment, fixated on the thought that casually slipped into my head even though there's nothing casual about it.

Is Beth *my person*?

I realize it's way too early to make that call. We've only started getting to know each other. I'm probably still on her list of mildly annoying people she tolerates, like Doyle, the grocery store owner everyone has a problem with back home.

Plus, she's got every good reason not to trust men.

But I can't deny that there is something between us. An attraction, sure. A desire to kiss, yeah. But it runs deeper than that. I'm at a loss for how to describe it. One thing is certain, though.

My feelings for Beth are unlike anything I've ever felt in my life.

So I turn the bedside lamp off, quietly slip out of the room, and return to her, ready to redeem my kiss coupon.

15

Beth

"So what's going on with you and the grumpy goalie?" Courtland asks as we're standing behind the counter at the bookstore in a rare moment of quiet.

"Ooh, yes, I'd like to know, too," Amiel says, sneaking in from the side.

"What are you doing here?" I ask surprised, having missed her coming into the store and possibly also hoping the deflection gets me out of answering Courtlands's question.

"It's Valentine's Day Eve, so I'm stocking up." She lifts a pile of three books and grins. "Apart from going to Evie and Fraser's wedding tomorrow, my only other plans involve spending time with several high-quality book boyfriends."

"Same." Courtland sighs, then his eyes widen when he realizes what he said. "Except, book girlfriends, in my case. Oh, and hanging out with my cats, of course."

Amiel grins. "You're the first guy I've met who reads romance."

He thumbs his glasses up his nose, getting all serious like he does from time to time. "It's hard to pinpoint exact numbers, but industry figures suggest men make up about ten percent of the romance reading market. So for every thousand romance readers, about a hundred are men. That's not a huge amount, by any means, but it's also not insignificant."

"That's really cool," I say.

Please keep talking about romance industry readership figures and not me. Anything but me.

"So while the two of us have our Valentine's Day plans with fictional characters sorted..." Amiel smirks my way. "One person amongst us might have a real life romantic prospect in the works."

There goes that wish.

I become the target of two stares.

"I have no idea why you're both looking at me," I say, glancing around the store, desperate to find a customer in need of my help.

But nope, everyone seems fine browsing.

Great.

"Oh, stop denying it, Beth, and tell us already." Amiel leans over the counter. "Where exactly are you and Milo in your enemies-to-lovers journey?"

"I'm guessing second base," Courtland answers for me.

"No. I'm guessing first," she counters, using her close friend advantage and knowledge of my dating history to more accurately predict where things stand with Milo and me.

"I don't know sports, so I have no idea what bases mean," I say with a hand flourish.

It's an obvious lie, and neither one of them buys it. All romance readers—even if they've never watched a second of baseball in their lives—know what the bases mean.

First base is kissing.

Second is touching above the waist.

Third is touching below the waist.

And fourth is...a home run.

Milo and I are firmly in first base territory, even if the kiss after last month's game *almost* veered into second.

Well, actually, it did a little. From my end, not his.

After tucking Jonah in for the second time, he practically sprinted back into the living room to cash in his coupon. We started kissing, and I couldn't resist the urge to run my hands all over his strong, muscular arms.

And shoulders.

And chest.

Milo was definitely into the kiss, but he was a little more

restrained than I was. Probably because his kids were asleep in the next room, and if one of them came in at any moment, he wouldn't want them catching their dad in a compromising position.

But I get the feeling that maybe he was holding back for another reason, too. He's a smart guy, and now that he's aware of my dating history, he's probably put two and two together and come to the conclusion that I'm sexually inexperienced.

That could explain why he never oversteps with physical closeness.

And I have to say, I like that.

I like that a lot.

It makes me feel respected. Like he cares about me as a person and doesn't see me as some target or joke or *object* the way my exes did. And if some jerk made some joke or off-color remark about me, Milo's the kind of guy who'd stand up for me.

I *really* like that.

"You did go to his hockey game last month," Courtland points out.

I pick up some papers and start shuffling through them. "So?"

"You hate hockey."

"I love hockey romances," I rebut.

"Not the same thing, and all three of us know it."

"What happened *after* the hockey game is what I'm interested in," Amiel says, her eyes dancing with a playful glimmer. "You've been unusually tight-lipped about what went down when you went back to Milo's hotel."

Courtland's mouth flies open, and I hold up my hand. "It's not what it sounds like." I lower my hand. "Okay. It's a little what it sounds like. Fine. Yes." I let out a defeated breath. "I went back to his hotel room and we made out a little. But I'm being sensible about this and have imposed a strict *one kiss per day* limit."

Courtland grins. "Right. Because nothing screams *I have no interest in a guy* than coming up with a kiss rule."

Amiel joins in, because sure, let's all pile in on me, shall we? "Please don't tell me you made Milo sign an agreement to that effect."

"No. Of course not," I reply, jamming the papers into the top drawer and closing it a little too forcefully. "I'm not crazy, you guys...I made him a coupon."

Uh-oh.

My eyes dart between them. Hearing it back, and seeing their faces, I wish I hadn't said that.

"That is *sooo* sweet," Amiel says, placing her books near the register. Courtland starts ringing them up. "I'll bet you fifty bucks they're together by the end of spring," she says to him.

Courtland shakes his head. "You're underestimating how stubborn she can be. My money is on by the end of summer."

"Deal."

"Deal."

They shake hands on it like I'm not literally standing less than six feet away from them.

"Ooh, speaking of the end of summer, the season after that is fall, which just so happens to be when someone's sister has a new book coming out." Courtland is positively beaming as he turns to me, in full fanboy mode. "Your sister's agent confirmed we've secured a spot on her book tour."

"That's awesome," I say. "Congratulations on nabbing her."

"That's so cool," Amiel squeals excitedly, and while she and Courtland gush over my incredible author sister, my mind wanders to Milo.

He gets in late tonight, and we're going to drive up to Evie and Fraser's wedding together tomorrow.

I'm excited to see him but also a little nervous. I don't know where things stand with us, or if there even is an *us* in the first place.

Yes, we've been messaging each other, but nearly a month has gone by since we were in the same room.

Will it be awkward being confined to a car with him? Will things feel uncomfortable? Will we have anything to talk about?

I sigh.

I guess there's only one way to find out.

~

"Hey, Beth. You look great," Milo greets me at his front door, a wide smile on his face.

"Uh, thanks. You look great, too."

Understatement.

He looks incredibly dapper in his charcoal gray, tailored suit. It fits him perfectly, highlighting his broad shoulders and trim waist. He's tied his hair into a low bun, and his neatly trimmed stubble adds a rugged edge to his polished appearance.

I stand there for a moment, unsure what to do next when Milo steps out onto the porch, slides his hands around my waist and asks in a hushed tone. "May I cash in one of my kiss coupons please?"

I smile. "Anyone ever told you that you have zero chill?"

He smiles back, his green eyes shimmering. "None at all when it comes to you."

My tummy flutters, and I nod. He brings his lips to mine, and it's just what I need to settle my nerves. I'd been worrying all morning that things would be weird between us.

But as he kisses me with a perfect blend of strength and

delicacy, I realize the past few weeks apart haven't dampened the energy between us.

"Da-ddy!"

Milo pulls back slightly. "You ready for the kids?"

"Of course."

I crouch, and Jonah bounds into me, giving me a big hug. Josie is hanging back, and as I straighten, I notice the children's grandparents approaching.

Milo introduces Mike and Robyn to me, and we chitchat for a few minutes. Milo told me they were really nice, and it checks out. They seem lovely, and I'm glad Milo is developing a good relationship with them so that they can be in their grandkid's lives.

"We should get going," he says after a short while.

"I agree. And I'll drive this time since we'd like to get there sometime this year."

Josie giggles. "Daddy drives slowly."

"I drive to the speed limit," Milo says a touch defensively but with a smile.

He gives Josie and Jonah a big hug, answers Mike's question about the TV system, reminds them he'll have his phone on him at all times even though reception may be spotty, and then turns to me.

"Right. I think I'm ready."

I smile. "Let's go." I give Jonah a high five and say goodbye to Josie, who's inched forward a little.

"Hope you like the red heart," she says, looking up at me with a small grin.

"Red heart?" I look at Milo, confused.

"Uh, we should get going," he deflects, then grabs my arm and leads me over to my car.

With a wave, we set off for Evie and Fraser's second attempt at a wedding. Due to the time constraints of the hockey season, there's no rehearsal lunch or dinner, just a quick, intimate ceremony today before Fraser, Milo, and the rest of the Swifts jump on a red-eye for their game tomorrow night in Chicago.

Evie is possibly the only girl in the world who isn't bothered by spending her honeymoon watching her new husband play hockey.

"Well, the weather couldn't be any better," Milo observes from the passenger seat, leaning toward the windshield, his handsome face tipped up to the brilliant blue sky.

"First thing I did when I woke up this morning was race to the window to check," I say.

"First thing I did when I woke up this morning was step on Jonah's fire truck that has way too many sharp and painful edges for a children's toy."

I smile. "Mike and Robyn seem nice."

"Yeah. They're great. They're always going to be in the kids' lives, so I'm glad they're cool people."

"How are the kids doing?" I ask.

"They're fine."

I'm driving, so I can't peel my eyes off the road for too long, but Milo's tone doesn't match his words. "What's the matter?" I ask.

He huffs out a breath. "Nothing. Josie and Jonah are both doing great. It's just...a life on the road isn't a life meant for kids."

"Are they struggling?"

"No. They love it. Room service is their favorite thing ever. I'm the one wracked with guilt."

"About what?"

"About them not having a normal dad who has a normal life and lives in a normal house. I want them to grow up in one place, feel safe, have roots, you know?"

"I get that." I drum my fingers against the steering wheel. "Well, the season ends in April, June if you make it into the playoffs, right?"

"That's right. How do you know that?"

"I may have only ever watched one hockey game in real life, but I've read *alllll* the hockey romance books. I've picked up one or two hockey-related things. The point I'm making is that the season is coming to an end. You can figure stuff out then."

"True."

"And maybe my hardly-ever-there neighbor might actually be, you know, there."

"We will definitely be home all summer."

I contain my smile. "That's...cool."

"How's the bookstore going? Did you manage to get that issue sorted out with the supplier?"

I shuffle in my seat. I'd forgotten I mentioned that in one of our texts. But that was, like, two weeks ago. "I'm surprised you remember that."

He snorts. "In addition to being able to read, I also have great comprehension and memory skills."

I grin. "I didn't mean it like that. It's just that it was a minor detail I texted about weeks ago."

I quickly turn and see him shrug. "I remember everything you text."

"You...you do?"

"Of course."

"Really?'

"Yep."

"Everything?"

"Uh-huh."

"Prove it."

"Okay."

And then he does.

He literally starts reciting our exact message thread where I told him about the supply chain issues one of our smaller suppliers was having and how it meant we were woefully low on a number of children's titles. And he isn't paraphrasing, he's saying it back to me word for freaking word.

As he's talking, I flick my head several times to make sure he hasn't somehow taken out his cell phone and is secretly reading the texts. But nope. I can see both his hands, and he is recalling the messages verbatim.

When he finishes, I remark, "Why didn't you tell me you have a photographic memory?"

"What? And ruin the illusion that I'm a numbskulled hockey player? No, thanks."

My chest tightens uncomfortably.

He's not calling me out, but he very well could.

I completely underestimated his intelligence when I first met him. I prejudged him through the lens of a tired stereotype—the dumb jock athlete. And for months now, Milo has been revealing himself to be far more than I ever expected.

"Some music?" I suggest to quell the uneasy feeling gurgling in my chest.

"Sure." He answers slowly. "Are you okay? Did I say or do something wrong?"

"No. I'm the one who did. I...I'm sorry, Milo."

"Normally those three words are in the top five things I like hearing from you, right up there with 'You're the best, Milo' and 'You're always right, Milo,' but I don't like unwarranted apologies."

"Oh. It's warranted, all right. I jumped to all sorts of conclusions about you when we first met. It was wrong of me, and I'm sorry for that."

He pauses. "I accept your apology. Thank you." Another pause. "But you still hate my man bun?"

"Well..."

"Please tell me you hate it, otherwise I'll start to think I've been sucked into some alternate reality."

I laugh. "Okay. I hate your man bun," I say without meaning it. I'm not going to go out and buy an *I Love Man Buns* T-shirt anytime soon, but I don't hate it anymore, either. Truth be told, it kinda suits him.

"Can I say one more thing, and then we can drop it?" he asks.

"Okay."

"I get why you may have formed a low opinion of me, Beth. I've been hurt by people in the past, too, so I know what it's like to feel like you have to protect yourself."

I remember what he told me about his tough childhood and growing up, so I guess in a way he can relate to my horror dating history. Totally different circumstances but hurt and pain and betrayal are universal.

"I'm sure you do. You're not mad at me for the way I acted when we first met and I totally ignored you? Be honest. Because if you are, it's totally justified."

"No, I'm not mad," he says warmly.

"Really?"

"I'd tell you if I was. If anything, I'm constantly blown away by you."

"Why?" I turn my head and find both his eyebrows arched. "I'm not fishing for compliments," I clarify. "I'm genuinely curious."

"Okay. I'll tell you. But remember, there's only room for one giant-sized ego in this car." I giggle as he goes on. "I think you're amazing, Beth. You're strong and confident. You're who you are and you don't apologize for it at all because you know you don't need to. I love your passion for books. How much you enjoy your career. How important your friends are to you. And I..." He falters for a second. "I like how you make me feel."

I grip the steering wheel a little tighter and force myself to swallow. "And how do I make you feel?"

He lets out a long breath and stays silent for a while.

A long while.

Just as I start to think he's not going to answer the question, he replies with one softly spoken word.

"*Seen.*"

Capital *W*.

Capital *O*.

Capital *WWWW*.

I honestly don't know what to say to that. Neither does Milo it seems, as we get enveloped in another stretch of silence.

He flicks the dial, and we spend the rest of the drive listening to a local radio station, my mind so consumed by what Milo just said I don't even mind the static hisses and crackles that increase as we climb higher up the mountain and out of range.

I make him feel seen.

It's hands down the best compliment I've ever received. It'll definitely take me some time to wrap my brain around the enormity of that.

As we pull up to Cedar Crest Haven, the wedding lodge where Evie and Fraser will be married, my body thrums with an energy I can't quite pinpoint.

It's a gorgeous spot, nestled among towering pine trees and overlooking a breathtaking valley. Elegant wooden structures and delicate fairy lights blend harmoniously with the natural beauty, creating a romantic atmosphere. An idyllic place for a wedding.

"We're here," I say, pointing out the obvious as I turn the engine off.

"And a few minutes early," Milo says with a grin, like he's in on the joke about him being a slow driver.

"Yeah." I release a deep breath. Some fresh air might clear my head and help get my thoughts in order. "Should we go in?"

"Uh, before we do. I just want to check if you're okay? We've both been quiet since I said...the thing."

He looks worried, and I hate that he's maybe thinking I'm freaking out about *the thing*. I mean, yes, I'm freaking out about *the thing*, but not in a bad way.

"The thing you said was..."

"Too much?" he guesses.

"No. Not at all. It was the most beautiful thing anyone has said to me. I just need some time to process it."

He lowers his head, his eyes finding mine. "Are you sure that's all it is?"

I nod. "I am." A few people walk past our car, reminding me we're here for one of my best friend's wedding. "We should probably—"

"One more thing. Last thing, I swear. No words will be spoken this time, I promise."

"Okay, weirdo."

I have no idea what he's doing. Even as he grins and slides his paw of a hand into the inside pocket of his jacket and produces a cream envelope, it doesn't hit me.

"I didn't know if you had a Valentine, so I thought..."

Now it hits me.

"Oh, Milo."

Seriously. What is going on here?

This feels like a scene straight out of a romance novel, and I'm swooning so hard I can barely breathe. It's terrifying and unfamiliar and also the sweetest gesture ever all at the same time.

With trembling fingers, I open the envelope and pull out a card with an illustrated red heart on the front.

"Josie drew that," he says proudly.

"Oh, right." I trace my fingers over it. "That explains her red heart comment before we left."

"It does. She's great at drawing, not so good at keeping secrets."

I smile and open the card. The handwritten note inside reads, *I enjoy facing off with you. Milo, x*

There's also a coupon entitling *me* to one free kiss per day every day from today. The **every day from today** is in bold and underlined.

"I wanted things to be perfectly clear."

"What do you mean, clear? What's not clear?"

"Your one-kiss policy. I have questions. Many of them."

I giggle. "Like what?"

"So, we've established it's one-kiss per day. But what happens on days when we don't see each other? Do those kisses get saved up so I'm essentially banking kisses? If so, how do I claim them? If not, is there a manager I can speak to about reviewing this?" His grin has grown into a full-watt smile. "As you know, I'm a weirdo so I could keep going."

"I'm sure you could."

"That's why I said *every day from today* in my policy. So that includes days when we're not together, too."

I try to match his smile but I'm not sure if I succeed. He just keeps blowing me away, more and more and more.

"Turn the coupon over," he says.

I flip it over and..."Oh my goodness."

I have to bring the paper right up to my face to read the

tiny fine print that covers the entire back section of the coupon.

This coupon is issued by Milo Garrett Payne and entitles the holder, Beth <middle name currently unknown> Moore, and ONLY Beth <middle name currently unknown> Moore, to one additional free kiss per day on top of the already established one kiss policy that exists between the two parties. The coupon is valid from whenever you can no longer deny your attraction to me to whenever you get sick of me and never want to see me again. This coupon cannot be used in conjunction with any other offer, discount, or promotion.

"Oh, Milo." I blink back a few tears and lean closer to him. "This is so sweet and wonderful and...Thank you."

He rests his arm on the center console. "So I take it you don't have a Valentine?"

"I didn't." I chew on my lower lip. "But I do now."

The smile that blooms on his face is pure radiance. "You sure do."

"Oh, and it's Anne," I say.

"Excuse me?"

"My middle name. It's Anne."

"Ah, okay. Good to know. I'm committing that to my photographic memory."

I giggle again, then I grab him by the shirt and tug him in to me. When I'm less than an inch away from his lips, he pulls away abruptly. "Just checking, is this kiss part of our pre-existing kiss policy, or are you cashing in your coupon?"

I shake my head and giggle some more. "Just shut up and kiss me already."

His green eyes sparkle. "Yes, ma'am."

∼

Evie radiates elegance and grace as she's escorted down the aisle by her beaming dad. Her golden hair cascades in soft waves, perfectly framing her face, and her makeup is beautiful yet understated.

She looks like a woman ready to marry the man she loves.

Oh, and the wedding dress?

Di-vine.

The gown features a classic bateau neckline that highlights her collarbone, and the fitted bodice seamlessly flows into a gentle A-line skirt that sways gracefully with each step. A delicate, sheer veil cascades from a simple tiara, gently trailing behind her as she moves.

The only splash of color comes from the vibrant bouquet of yellow roses she's holding, the flowers holding special significance for her and Fraser.

We sit down when she joins Fraser, who I've never seen look more elated.

I'm so relieved their first wedding attempt was just a minor blip on what I'm sure will be a beautiful, lifelong marriage, and that it wasn't a sign or omen. Because these two *belong* together.

The ceremony gets underway, and as beautiful as this old church is, it's also very small. Combined with a large guestlist, everyone is crammed into rows of wooden seats.

I'm sitting next to Milo—AKA *my Valentine!*—and his leg is barely a few inches away from mine. He's tucked his hands on his lap, like he's trying to take up less space.

Ha. Good luck with that. The span of his shoulders is at least double mine, and despite his efforts, he can't make himself small. But it's nice of him to try.

Without thinking, I place my hand over his and rest our joined hands on his firm thigh. He smiles and rubs his thumb over the top of my hand.

He's such an amazing guy, and the more time I spend with him, the more I realize just how wonderful he is.

He's kind. A devoted dad. Rocks a pair of tights. Smart—photographic memory, hello. Thoughtful to get me a Valentine's Day card. Adorable with the whole kiss policy thing. And emotionally intelligent to be able to say what he said to me in the car on the drive up here.

And just in case all of that wasn't enough, he's humble and good looking and funny and likes to read, too.

Talk about a dream guy.

He gently presses the side of his leg against mine, and a shudder rolls through me.

A big shudder.

Actually, it's more like a tremor.

And I'm not the only one feeling it.

The minister pauses, and a low murmur breaks out amongst the assembled guests.

And then we hear it.

The unmistakable sound that can only mean one thing.

"Earthquake!" someone yells out.

Horrified shrieks fill the air as people rush to their feet, clamoring toward the nearest exit.

Despite knowing I have to move, I'm temporarily frozen, in shock that mother nature is ruining Evie's wedding—*again.*

Thankfully, Milo's got his wits about him. He grabs me by the wrist and guides me in front of him. "We need to get out of here."

With his hand pressed firmly in the small of my back, he leads me toward the nearest double doors.

People are panicking all around us, but not Milo. As if his touch wasn't reassuring enough, he keeps saying, "Keep going, we're going to be all right," into my ear as we move swiftly along with the crowd of fleeing people.

And then it happens.

A thunderous crack that makes everyone turn their heads toward the front of the church right as a massive chunk of the ceiling caves in.

"Evie!" I scream, because that's where Evie and Fraser and the minister were standing not less than a minute ago.

We've reached the double doors, and Milo nudges me through them. "Go!" he shouts to be heard over the screams. "Find shelter!"

And then he then turns, racing back inside the crumbling building.

"No!" I yell after him, but I'm being pushed away, caught up in the stream of people frantically pouring out of the church. "Nooo!" I cry again even though it's futile, before spinning around and running to...I don't know where to go.

Staff from the venue are directing people to several temporary shelters scattered throughout the grounds.

I get shoved...right next to Summer.

"Oh my goodness, Summer!" We embrace. "What about Evie?"

"Shhhh." She pats my back as I sob into her shoulder. "She'll be okay. They all will be."

I pull back, tears streaming down my face. "Milo went back in."

"He what?"

"He went back in. He made sure I got out safely, and then he turned around and ran back inside."

Summer's eyes widen. "He'll be okay, too."

I know she has no way of knowing that, but I cling to her words anyway.

She peels open her purse and yanks out her phone. "Shoot," she grumbles. "No reception."

I lift onto my toes, hoping to spot Amiel or Hannah or

Culver or anyone I know, but it appears there are multiple safe zones, so just because they're not in this one doesn't mean they're not safe in another one.

But Evie? And Fraser? And the minister? Where are they? They were standing right where the ceiling collapsed.

I can't even think about it.

A stab of anger shoots through me at the memory of Milo charging back into the crumbling building, but that's quickly replaced by guilt for having such a selfish thought, which then morphs into an overwhelming sense of pride that he's the sort of man who would risk his own life to pull his friends out of danger.

It feels like an eternity, when in reality probably only about ten minutes pass, before we're allowed to leave.

Apart from the collapsed side of the church roof, all the other buildings on the sprawling property seem unaffected. From the outside, at least.

"Beth! Summer!"

We both spin around as Hannah and Culver race over to us.

"You're safe," I say, hugging her.

"We are. Are you both okay?"

"We're fine," Summer answers. "Did you guys happen to see Amiel?"

She shakes her head.

"You guys stay here. I'll go look for her," Culver says.

He kisses Hannah on her forehead and takes off.

"We're going to remain positive," Summer says, her voice dipping into what I assume is her lawyer-sounding voice. "Until we get any information, we're going to choose hope over fear. Okay?" When neither Hannah nor I say anything, she repeats. "Okay?"

"Yeah, okay," Hannah says, craning her neck in every direction.

"Uh-huh." I'm not paying attention, either, desperately searching through the crowd of people to see a familiar face.

Nothing, nothing, and then...two intense green eyes flash into view.

Milo.

Someone gets in the way, and I lose him.

"I just saw Milo," I tell the girls. "I have to go."

"Stay safe," Summer says as I take off.

"I will." Moving in the direction I spotted him, I catch fleeting glimpses of him through the gaps in the crowd.

I squint to make sure I'm seeing right.

His face is covered in dirt, and he's limping. I think. I can't make him out for long enough to be sure.

My heart pounds furiously, but as I get closer, I see it's not Milo who's limping, but an elderly man who he's assisting. His hair, face, and shoulders are covered in a heavy coat of dirt and dust.

I finally get to him. "Hey," I pant. "Are you okay?"

"I am." A paramedic appears at the same time I do, and Milo explains to them, "This is Mr. Walsh. I pulled him out from under the rubble. His right leg hurts badly, and he has a cut on his face."

That's when I see the giant gash on the side of Mr. Walsh's face and the blood dripping from it.

The paramedics take over, and as soon as they do, I launch myself into Milo's arms. "Are you hurt? Anything broken? Concussed?"

"I'm fine."

I cling to him for a few more moments, feeling his chest beating against mine, his strong arms wrapped around me.

"Really?" I check.

He pulls back and braces my arms. "*Really*."

I stare into his piercing green eyes. "I should be mad at you for doing that."

"Don't be mad. I had to."

"You didn't have to." I hug him again. "But I'm so proud that you did."

"Would I be pushing my luck if I used this as an opportunity to negotiate a doubling of my daily kiss allowance?" he asks, squeezing me right back.

I laugh.

Then sob.

Then hold onto him extra tight for a few moments, before regaining my composure and moving back slightly. "No more coupons. I say we move to unlimited daily kisses. We can kiss whenever we like, how many times we like."

"That's the best news I've had all day." He smiles, and his teeth look extra white against his dirty face. "I want to show you something. May I?"

He brings his hands to the sides of my body, and I have no idea what I'm agreeing to, but when I nod, Milo picks me up and lifts me above the crowd like I weigh nothing.

"Look to your left," he instructs from below. "Fraser, Evie, and the minister got out through a door by the back." I spot the three of them, huddled together, surrounded by their families. He lowers me down. "They're fine, too. Safe and uninjured."

I let out a relieved breath. "That only leaves Amiel."

"I'm here," she says, and I spin around. She throws her arms around me. "I'm here."

I hug her back hard. "Oh, thank goodness."

Culver, Hannah, and Summer also join us, which means everyone I know and love is accounted for. Now I only hope no one else was seriously hurt.

As everyone starts talking, Amiel leans in closer to me and

whispers, "I've been here for a while, but it looked like you two were having a moment, so I didn't want to interrupt."

"We've just survived an earthquake, and you're using it as an opportunity to make a not-so-subtle point about me and Milo?" I whisper back.

"Exactly. We *survived* an earthquake. If that's not a reminder that life is short and to not waste time, then I don't know what is."

When she puts it like that...

I turn to Milo, who's half-listening to the conversation between Hannah and Summer. When his eyes land on me and he tips his head up, a current of heat fizzles through my entire body.

I don't know if it's because I'm running on an adrenaline high having survived an earthquake, or whether I'm finally ready to accept my true feelings for the first and only guy who's ever given me a Valentine's Day card, but I march right up to Milo and lift onto my toes.

The conversation comes to an immediate halt as I cup the sides of his face. Not even the slight taste of dirt on his lips can stop me from kissing the man I'm falling for.

16

Milo

"Can I get you anything else?" Beth offers for about the gazillionth time.

"I'm fine," I reply, for about the gazillionth time.

She's been fussing over me ever since we got checked into this room. The wedding is well and truly off, and no one is staying, but venue staff instructed all guests to wait a few hours in their rooms to make sure there are no aftershocks before heading back. Beth and I have ended up in a room together. Seems to be a thing.

I don't mind her attention one bit, I just wish it came under different circumstances and that she didn't look so worried. I really am fine.

After racing back into the church, I quickly found Culver and a couple of our other teammates. Through the dusty haze, someone yelled out that Fraser, Evie, and the pastor had escaped through a side door. That left us free to help the remaining people still inside.

I came across a dazed-looking elderly man. He told me his name was Andrew Walsh and that he suspected his leg was broken. He didn't say anything about the gash on his face, and I didn't, either. If he didn't know about it, what good would it have done for me to point out he was bleeding?

I helped Mr. Walsh to his feet and got him out of there as quickly as I could. Thankfully, we were met by a paramedic right as Beth came over.

"Come 'ere," I say, patting the sofa. "Relax. Everything's fine. No one died or was seriously hurt."

Turns out it was a relatively minor earthquake. Well, as minor as an earthquake can be. Not being from the west coast, any earthquake is pretty major in my book. I suppose I'll need to get used to that. A few people sustained minor injuries, including Mr. Walsh, but he should be fine.

Beth drops down next to me. "You realize what this means?"

"No. What?"

She huffs adorably. "You're now my hero, and I have to respect you."

"You don't strike me as the type of woman that does anything she doesn't want to."

She bites back a grin. "Stop it. It's bad enough you're brave. Don't add charming to the list."

"I'm slightly offended you're overlooking my incredible handsomeness."

She releases a soft giggle. "Stop it."

I raise an eyebrow and stretch my arms out across the back of the couch. "Make me."

I'm expecting to be met by one of her usual quick-witted retorts.

I am not expecting her to jump into my lap.

But I'll take it.

This is *way* better.

She runs her hand through my hair, which I've left untied after taking a shower and cleaning up.

"I'm starting to like...this," she says, twirling a strand around her fingers.

"My hair?"

"No." She caresses my cheek. "This. *Us*."

My heart breaks out into a gallop in my chest, but I do my best to stay composed. Because there's an us. She just said there is.

Which means that my feelings aren't one-sided. My obsession about my daily kiss allowance? Totally a 'me' thing because, as has been well established, I'm weird. But the feelings I'd sensed, hoped, prayed, she was feeling, too, are real.

I gaze into her captivating hazel eyes. "And what would you like *us* to be?"

She rests her forearms on top of my shoulders. "I...I don't know."

"I don't believe you."

Beth is strong. She's the type of woman who knows what she wants and isn't afraid to say it.

Most of the time, anyway.

She lets out a shaky breath. "You make me feel things I'm not used to feeling."

"Right back at ya."

She bites her lower lip. "I have baggage."

"I have more."

"I also trust issues, Milo. Big ones."

"So do I. But..."

She squints. "But what?"

"I trust *you*. I always have, right from the start, Beth. Even when I was pretty certain you hated me—"

"Just your man bun," she interrupts, smiling.

"Right." I run my hand up and down her back. "I've opened up to you more than I ever have to anyone else in my life, and I don't fully know why."

Her fingers skim over my stubble. "Because I make you feel seen?" Her voice is barely more than a whisper.

I swallow hard. "Yeah. You do. It feels like...like you're the only one who ever has."

"Does that scare you?"

I think about it.

It should scare the freaking life out of me. I've never opened up like this, been so raw and vulnerable with somebody. I'm accessing parts of myself I didn't even know I had. I should be petrified.

So why am I so calm?

Why does this feel so right?

What is it about her that makes me feel so seen?

I curl my hands around her waist. "No. It doesn't scare me. It should. But it doesn't. I generally have good instincts about people."

"And what do your instincts tell you about me?"

"That you're special. And funny. And smart. And beautiful...no matter your size." My gaze meets hers, searching for a reaction.

I went there.

Was it too far?

I stop breathing.

She smiles shyly. "Thank you for saying that."

I exhale then curl my fingers around her waist. "I mean it."

"So, to answer your question about what I'd like us to be..."

"Yeah?"

"I'm ready to take the next step. I'm ready to go from friends...*ish* to friends." Her smile widens. "And leave the door open for anything else that might happen in time. How does that sound?"

"Sounds like the best thing I've ever heard you say."

"Better than my suggestion of unlimited kisses?"

I tap my chin, thinking about it. "Okay. Equal best thing. Sorry. I have the most beautiful girl sitting on my lap, so you'll have to forgive me if my cognitive function is slightly impaired."

Her cheeks get dusted by the cutest blush I've ever seen.

She leans down, and we kiss.

Being called beautiful might be a new thing for her, and

I'm going to have to walk a fine line between telling her how I feel without making her self-conscious or uncomfortable.

"There's something I should tell you," she says, her tone shifting as she climbs off my lap and perches herself next to me on the sofa.

"Go on."

"I'm a virgin."

"Okay." I run my hand through my hair. I suspected she was, so it's not exactly a shock. "I'm...not."

"Having children was kind of a giveaway." She bites her lip. "But is that a problem for you?"

"Why would it be a problem?"

She shrugs and looks away. "I don't know. Some guys—"

"*Ahem.*"

Her eyes meet mine, and her grin returns. "You're not *some guys*, I know."

I nod decisively. "I've worked extremely hard to establish my weirdo status with you, thank you very much. Please don't take it away from me."

"Stop. It."

I angle myself so that I'm facing her and take her hands in mine. "Beth, it's honestly not an issue for me."

"It doesn't change how you see me?"

"Of course not. Why would it?" She opens her mouth, and I bring my finger to her lips. "If whatever you're about to say includes the term *some guys*, I'm afraid there will be a punishment."

Her eyes shine with amusement. "Oh, will there now?"

"There will. I may just be forced to kiss you."

"You're saying your kisses are so bad that they're a punishment?"

"Er, wait." I chuckle. "Maybe I didn't think that one through."

"You're allowed a pass after what you did today."

I shrug it off, not wanting to make it a bigger deal than it is. Culver and my teammates did the same thing. I think most people in the same situation would.

I glance at her. I'm glad she's opening up to me, and I hope it's a sign she feels safe and trusts me. And I like that we can have a serious conversation in a lighthearted way. But there is something I need to know.

I gently lift her chin, guiding her eyes until they meet mine. "What do you need from me?"

The ball's in her court.

It has to be. She's in control here. I want her to know that.

She takes a moment to think about it before replying, "Time, I guess?"

"You got it," I say straight away.

"Are you sure?"

"I am. You can't get rid of me that easily." I look her in the eye. "What about the kids?"

"What about them?"

"Well, I'm kind of a package deal. Three for the price of one. That's a lot. Some women might—"

For a moment, I think we're having an aftershock only to discover it's actually Beth clearing her throat. "Some women?"

I laugh. "My bad. You're not *some women*."

"Thank you."

"I just wanted to raise this because we haven't spoken about it yet. I'm a father, and I take that responsibility very seriously. Josie and Jonah are a huge part of my life, and they always will be. I hope that's not a dealbreaker for you."

"It isn't."

"Really? Because I remember you saying you weren't thinking about kids since they weren't in your immediate future, which is totally fine—"

"Milo." She curls her soft fingers around mine. "I think Josie and Jonah are great."

"Yeah. They are."

"So let's just take it one step at a time, okay?"

I nod. "I'm sorry. I don't know how to navigate this or what to tell them."

"Neither do I. But we'll figure it out. For now, tell them we're neighbors."

I grin. "Neighbors who give each other cards with hearts on them."

Her eyes twinkle. "Exactly."

Having kids totally takes over your life. It changes everything—including dating. But Beth is giving me all the right signals that she's cool with it. It's not like we're getting married or anything, so I should probably just chill a bit.

"I love how you are with them," she says, looking me right in the eye. "Seeing you in dad mode is heartwarming and..."

"And?"

"And a little sexy."

I grin. "You realize my dad bod era is getting closer and closer by the day."

She giggles. "Stop it."

"So we're cool? About this? About everything?"

Her head bobs. "We are. And if things change, we'll talk. Right? I hate miscommunication."

"We'll talk." I switch hand positions and give her fingers a protective squeeze. "No miscommunication."

"Okay. Good." Her gaze meets mine, her eyes clouded with introspection. Something is still playing on her mind, I can tell. "I do want to have sex," she says softly after a beat. "I'm not waiting for any other reason other than...Well, I haven't met the right guy yet."

Could I be that guy?

Can't help it. It's the first thought that pops into my head.

A surge of hope courses through me, but I do my best to tamp it down. She's being vulnerable and alluding to the horrible way guys have treated her in the past, something that fills my vision with red rage whenever I think about it. My only job right now is to be here for her.

"I've been burned by guys before, so I need to feel safe. And I do feel safe with you, Milo. I do. But *that's* a whole other level of safe. *Annnd* I'm going to stop using the word *safe* now."

I swipe my thumb across her cheek. "You can say *safe* as many times as you like. I completely understand where you're coming from."

"You do?"

"You got treated badly. It's only natural you feel the way you do. I'll never pressure you, Beth. I swear."

She looks me straight in the eye, and it's almost like I can see her inner struggle, how she's torn between wanting to trust me and the doubts that linger because of her past experiences with guys.

I'm determined to do everything in my power to be a man worthy of earning her trust.

"I want you to know that you're the one calling the shots here," I assure her. "Anything that happens between us—or doesn't happen, and that's fine, too—takes place on *your* timeframe. Okay?"

She nods, but I can tell I haven't convinced her entirely, so I add, "Good things come to those who wait, Beth. And I need you to know I can be a very, *very* patient man."

Her whole body relaxes and she lets out a massive breath. "Thank you."

I extend my hand, hoping she'll take it, but she does something even better. She scooches down the couch to get in nice and close, slides her smooth palm across my cheek, and brings her lips to mine.

The kiss is soft and tender and...different somehow. I've never felt this close, this connected to anyone.

It's been a whirlwind of a day with the earthquake and the wedding falling through again. I feel terrible for Evie and Fraser, they really have the worst luck. But on the positive side, every time they try to get married, it ends up bringing Beth and I closer.

And today marked a huge turning point for Beth and me.

We're officially an *us*.

Even if I have no idea what our future holds or how to solidify an *us* into a real relationship.

Turns out, becoming an *us* with Beth isn't that much different from how we were before.

And it's all on me.

Well, on my insane schedule.

I've often wondered how players manage to have any semblance of a romantic relationship when the demands of the season are so grueling.

The travel. The training. The games. The media attention...

In the four months since Fraser and Evie's second wedding attempt—no word yet on whether there'll be a third—Josie, Jonah, and I have been in Comfort Bay three times for a grand total of less than eight days.

Subjecting the kids to a three-hour drive isn't fun, so most of the time off I've had after playing in LA, we've stayed in the city out of convenience. It's just easier that way.

Doesn't mean I'm happy about it.

The nagging sense that this can't continue has been intensifying and becoming harder to ignore.

Josie starts school in the fall. Jonah should be in preschool. And I want to be closer to Beth.

I need to make a decision.

Correction, I've already made a decision. What I need to do now is put it into action.

But first things first, I've got to deal with the seriously angry-looking forward barreling toward me.

It's the Stanley Cup final, LA Swifts versus the Boston Bullets.

The atmosphere in the arena is electric as the clock ticks down. We're leading by one with less than sixty seconds to go.

Padalecki charges down the ice, intent on closing the one-point gap and forcing a sudden death overtime.

I'm not going to let that happen.

With my gaze locked on him, I bend my knees slightly, ready to spring in any direction. My gloved hand hovers just above the ice in case he decides to shoot low.

Padalecki fakes left, then right, but I'm able to read him well. I've kept him scoreless against me all season, and I know how much he hates that. He's been trash talking me every chance he gets. Not gonna lie, the competitive, egotistical part of me loves that.

He takes the shot.

The puck sails into the air.

It only takes a split second for me to miscalculate.

The puck sails just out of reach, above my outstretched glove, finding the back of the net with a resounding clang.

The deafening roar of the Boston home crowd conceals my outburst of expletives. I hate letting the team down, and because of me, we're going into a sudden death overtime.

That's where the first team to score a goal wins the game and the entire championship.

"Don't blame yourself," Fraser says to me as we return to the locker room to wait out the fifteen-minute intermission. "You were great tonight."

"Thanks, man," I reply glumly.

"I'm serious. Don't beat yourself up. I missed a shot in the second period."

I clap his back, and he smiles tightly. I know how much he wants to win. Evie's dad is an LA Swifts legend, so winning the Stanley Cup would be extra special for him. "We'll refocus, and we'll kill it out there."

He slaps my back in return. "Yeah, we will. Go, Swifts!"

The team gathers around the coaching staff to discuss strategies and adjustments. I throw back a Gatorade, determined to refocus. What's done is done. I can't do anything about that. I can only control my future—both on and *off* the ice.

I want to win as much as Fraser does. All the guys do. The ultimate dream of every pro hockey player is to lift the Stanley Cup.

And if we win, it'll be extra special for me, too, because this will be the last game I ever play.

Yep, I'm retiring.

It's the right thing to do, and it's what I want to do. I've never been more certain of anything in my life.

We head back out onto the ice.

The tension in the arena is palpable, the roar of the crowd a constant hum in my ears, but I block it out, focusing solely on the ice in front of me. It's sudden death overtime—everything is on the line.

As the puck drops at center ice, I crouch low, every muscle in my body coiled and ready. The Bullets take control, their players moving fast, weaving down the ice with precision. My defense struggles to keep up, and before I know it, Padalecki is winding up for a shot.

Time slows as the puck rockets toward me. I drop into a butterfly, pads out wide, and feel the thud as the puck slams into my pad. No time to think, just react—I sweep the puck away with my stick, sending it to the corner.

The crowd's roar intensifies, but I'm already back on my feet, eyes scanning for the next threat. My teammates regain control, pushing the play up the ice, but I stay sharp, ready for anything.

Suddenly, there's a breakaway—Fraser slips past the Bullets' defense, racing down the ice. The noise from the crowd swells to a deafening level, but all I hear is the pounding of my heartbeat and the rush of blood in my ears. Fraser approaches their goalie, the puck dancing on his stick, and then—he shoots.

For a moment, time stands still.

I hold my breath, my entire being focused on that one instant. Then, the red light flashes behind their net, and the horn blares through the arena.

My teammates leap over the boards, rushing toward Fraser, who is already being swarmed at the other end. Relief floods through me, followed by a wave of pure, unadulterated joy. I push off the ice and join the celebration.

We did it! We won the Stanley Cup!

The victory feels extra special because it was Fraser who secured the winning goal.

I'm cheering next to him on the ice when he pulls away from the team and finds Evie in the stands. She is jumping up and down like a pogo stick on caffeine, losing her freaking mind.

My eyes only notice the black-haired beauty standing next to her.

Beth is smiling, beaming with pride. She gives me one of her cute awkward waves, and as I wave back, my heart melts into a pool of gushing gushiness.

My feelings for her have never made sense.

She ignores me when we first meet, and what happens? I can't stop thinking about her.

She makes fun of everything about me, and my infatuation for her only grows.

She acts immune to my charms, and my feelings only intensify.

And as we slowly open up to each other over the past year and progress from a tightly regulated kiss regime to an uncertain future that hangs on the thread of a possibility of there being an *us*...I'm already gone.

Done for.

We're not even officially dating, but as I stare at Beth through the plexiglass panels, I know with all my heart and soul—I'm completely in love with her.

17

Beth

I pick up the pace on my early morning walk.

"Don't expect me to take it easy on you, mister," I say, accelerating my stride. "You've had two days to recover from basking in the glory of winning the Stanley Cup."

"I wouldn't dream of it," Milo mutters, catching up to me.

With his long hair tied up in a neat man bun, he looks great in a light blue athletic shirt and black shorts. The material is light and breathable and clings to his muscular frame. I am definitely not checking him out any chance I get.

We hike up the trail to Cuddle Cove Cliff briskly.

And quietly.

I've got a lot on my mind.

Actually, no, that's not true.

I've got one thing and one thing only on my mind—Milo, and specifically, what his plans for the future are.

Because I'll be honest, I don't know how Evie does it with Fraser being away for so long. I have even more respect for her now because I've experienced how hard and lonely it can be. These past few months since the earthquake at Evie and Fraser's second wedding have *draaagged*.

Milo and the kids have only been to Comfort Bay three times, and even though we hung out, it was never long enough. Last time they were back, Jonah proudly showed me he could count to ten, and Josie talked about the "Berenstain Bears" series I recommended Milo buy her. Then, they were off again way too quickly.

I've become attached to Josie and Jonah faster than I thought I would, and I miss them so much when they're gone. I've managed to catch a few games in LA, but the time we spend together is never enough. And if it's this difficult when Milo and I aren't even officially together, what will it be like if —*when?*—we are?

I like him a lot.

I trust him a lot.

But his career is...a lot, too.

And as strong as my feelings for him are, I'm not sure if that's something I can handle. I know hockey players have relationships, but I don't know if *I'm* cut out for the long-distance thing.

It's different with Evie and Fraser, and even Hannah and Culver because they all had a history before they started dating. Yes, Milo and I have only known each other for almost a year, but most of that time was spent apart, and the time we had together I was busy trying to keep distance between us because I was scared to let anyone in.

But Milo isn't just *some guy*.

Discovering he's a fantastic person, full of wit, intellect, and a refreshingly humble attitude. Observing his heartfelt devotion and unwavering commitment to his children. Witnessing his bravery as he risked his life and ran into a crumbling building to help save others.

Milo is the *best guy* I've ever met.

But do I have it in me to be a hockey player's girlfriend?

Maybe I do. Maybe we could find a way to make it work.

But do I have it in me to be a hockey player's girlfriend when said hockey player also has two kids?

I've been giving it a lot of thought. Josie and Jonah are always going to be a huge part of Milo's life, and if things between us develop, they'll also be a huge part of my life, too.

And I'm good with that. I really am.

So maybe we can try?

What's the worst thing that can happen? Oh, I know. I strike out in love again, making it three for three.

These thoughts have been whirring in my brain nonstop for weeks now. It's exhausting, and it's clear that Milo and I need to do the thing we'd said we'd do and communicate.

We reach the summit right on schedule—five minutes before the sun is set to rise.

The sounds of birds chirping and Milo glugging down some water from his bottle fill my ears.

I settle on the bench, my eyes sweeping over the charming town of Comfort Bay.

"This is my favorite part of the day," I tell Milo as he takes a seat beside me.

"Why do you like it?"

"Because it's so peaceful and quiet. People are friendly. All the craziness of the day hasn't started yet. It'd be nice if this was how life was all the time."

"Friendly people and less crazy does sound good."

"Makes it worth getting outside the house for."

He smiles, setting off a wave of flutters in my tummy.

"This okay?" he asks, clasping his fingers around mine.

"Yeah." Our eyes meet. "It's okay."

We watch the sun come up in silence, holding hands, my mind still racing and my stomach tied in knots. I hate that I'm overthinking this.

We need to talk.

Lay it all out there.

Figure out what we're doing so that we can make a plan, and I can stop imagining a million different scenarios that mostly all end in a fireball of hurt and devastation.

And they say romance readers have a tendency to be overly dramatic.

I open my mouth to say something, but Milo beats me to it. "So, I have some news."

"Oh. Is it a man bun update?"

"Yes." His speedy reply catches me off guard, and he laughs. "No. It's not. It's actually something important. Something I haven't told anyone yet. So please, keep this to yourself, okay?"

"Stops scrolling through her contact list looking for *NHL Digest Weekly,* which is totally the name of a real sports magazine and not something I just made up."

He chuckles. "You really are something else, you know that?" He takes a breath. "I'll make the official announcement in the next few days, but...I'm retiring."

My mouth falls open in shock. "You are?"

He nods. "Yep."

"But you're only twenty-seven. The Swifts just won the Stanley Cup, and you've had the best season of your career with a .920 save percentage and six shutouts."

His forehead wrinkles. "How do you know that?"

"Evie."

"Right. Of course." He lets go of my hand, strolls to the edge of the lookout, and then swiftly steps back.

I get up and join him. "Why are you retiring?"

He smiles, staring off in the distance. "A lot has changed this past year, and I realized that my old life isn't compatible with my new life."

"Are you referring to becoming a dad?"

"I am." He turns to face me. "Amongst other things."

A warm shiver races through me as I stare up into his green eyes. "Other things?"

"Yeah." His thick fingers slide softly down my cheek. "One thing in particular. She's five-six. As snarky as she is gorgeous. Obsessed with books. Someone I'm lucky to call my *friend* and am currently in an *us*-ship with."

I move in a little closer to him. "She sounds amazing."

He wraps his arm around me, tucking me into his side. "She is. There's only one problem."

"Oh."

"I can't get her out of my head. I think about her all the time. And when I'm away from her, I miss her like crazy."

A long beat passes.

"Really?"

"*Really*. I don't want to be away from you anymore, Beth. What's the point of buying a house in Comfort Bay if I'm never here? With Josie starting school soon, I want to make sure she and Jonah are settled and having a normal childhood. I want to do dad things like school drop offs and pickups."

"For gossiping with other parents?"

"Of course. Why else?" He grins. "I want to watch a million YouTube videos and learn how to build Jonah a treehouse. I want to have dinner at the same place at the same time every day, not room service from a different hotel in whatever city we're staying at."

"That's amazing of you."

"Actually, it's not," he replies. "Women give up their careers all the time. It's expected of them. My kids don't have a mom, so I want, no, I *need* to do this for them."

I'm at a loss for words as I so often am around him.

He goes on. "I'm lucky. I got to achieve my dreams. I made a successful career doing something that I love. And I went out on a winning high. I'm also in the very privileged financial position where I can take a few years off paid work to do, well, only the most important job in the world."

I smile and resist the urge to argue with him that he is amazing, despite what he says. He's right. Women make these sorts of sacrifices all the time, but it's still rare for men to do the same.

He braces my shoulders. "And I'd like a chance to see where things with us go. I'm not putting any pressure on you. But I would like to take you out on a first date, and who knows, see if you can tolerate being around me more often."

I brush my fingers over his stubbled jaw. "That doesn't sound like the worst thing in the world."

I cut off his chuckle with a kiss.

That evening, I'm messaging with my girlfriends, telling them about what Milo said on our morning walk.

I've been floating on air all day. Courtland kept checking in on me at work, convinced I've come down with something.

And I have.

It's called Milo-itis, and there's no known cure for it.

Beth: *And then he said how women give up their careers all the time and tried to downplay what he was doing.*
Summer: *Way to come through, Milo.*
Evie: *It's always the quiet ones who surprise you.*
Hannah: *Or the loud ones.*
Evie: *True. So...men in general.*
Summer: *<laughing emoji>*
Beth: *<laughing emoji>*
Hannah: *<laughing emoji>*
Amiel: *Why am I always the last one? <laughing emoji>*
Amiel: *And no one else knows?*
Beth: *Nope. He's only told me.*

My heart swells, thinking back to him telling me about the situation with Josie and Jonah before he shared that with anyone else, too. He does trust me, and he has right from the very start.

Which reminds me...

Beth: *I cleared it with him to tell you guys, but obviously, this doesn't go anywhere.*

I'm hit with four *Of courses* and smile when poor Amiel responds last as usual.

Hannah: *So...*
Beth: *Yes?*
Hannah: *Just curious about a little something.*

I grin to myself.

It's equally wonderful and alarming when one of your closest friends can be thousands of miles away, typing out a vague message, and yet you know exactly what she's getting at.

I save her the hassle of having to spell it out.

Beth: *No. We haven't had sex.*
Beth: *Yet.*
Summer: *But you want to?*
Beth: *I do. I feel safe with him and that's super important for me. But we're not rushing things. He's been amazing and is letting me control how fast things go.*
Amiel: *<furiously searches for advances in cloning technology> I wish all guys were like that.*
Beth: *Milo has definitely salvaged my faith in men. He's a good guy.*
Evie: *I can vouch for that. He and Fraser have gotten close lately. He's 100% trustworthy.*
Hannah: *Speaking of your fiancé, any update on the wedding front?*

Evie: *Yes! Apparently it is possible to have wedding-related PTSD. Fraser and I are currently taking part in a world-first study group.*
Beth: *Using humor to deflect is MY thing, thank you very much.*
Evie: *<laughing face emoji> x 3*
Evie: *We're taking a break from wedding plans which is annoying the life out of both our mothers. Eloping is looking VERY attractive right about now.*
Summer: *If it's what you guys want to do, go for it!*
Hannah: *Exactly. But please record it since we would like to see the ceremony.*
Evie: *I'm, like, 60% kidding. But I'll keep you all updated.*
Amiel: *What about you, Hannah? Any news from Italy?*
Hannah: *Actually, yes, I do have an announcement to make.*
Beth: *Good or bad? I need to prepare myself.*
Hannah: *Good. Very good.*
Hannah: *Culver and I are returning to Comfort Bay at the end of the summer!*
Evie: *Woohoooooooooo!!!!*
Summer: *<cartoon character jumping up and down with excitement GIF>*
Beth: *It's going to be so good to have you back!!*

I've missed Hannah so much, I'm glad she's coming home.

Summer: *Circling back to Beth, what's next for you and Milo and your us-ship (which I love, btw)?*
Beth: *He's taking me on our first official date this Friday.*
Evie: *Ooh, exciting! Where?*
Beth: *I have no idea. He won't tell me.*
Amiel: *Isn't the Comfort Bay Fair happening this weekend?*
Evie: *It is!*
Amiel: *He might take you there. That'd be cute.*
Beth: *It would be.*

Beth: *I'm looking forward to it.*
Hannah: *I'm happy for you. Also happy that you have FINALLY settled on whether you like him or hate him. I think you've made the right choice.*

I frown at her message, not liking the guilt that bubbles up inside me.

Did I ever really *hate* Milo?

That's a very strong word.

I made assumptions about who he was, pre-judged him, which is an unfair thing to do to anyone, and treated him more harshly than he deserved, but I never outright hated him.

Beth: *I'm not putting any expectations on it. It is only a first date, ladies.*
Summer: *True. But you've been in each other's orbits for around a year now, so it's not like an actual first date where you know nothing about the person.*
Amiel: *That's a good point. It's been a very long slow burn enemies-to-lovers situation with you guys.*
Beth: *Yeah. I guess it has.*
Evie: *Are you nervous?*
Beth: *Oddly, no.*
Summer: *That might have something to do with the fact that you know him.*
Beth: *I think you may be right about that.*
Amiel: *OMG, you guys! I just had a wild thought.*
Hannah: *What?*
Amiel: *What if Beth does something that's never been done in all of human history?*
Evie: *Which is?...*
Amiel: *What if she's able to enjoy her first date with a guy? No pre-date nerves, no trying on every article of clothing to see what looks*

best, no spiraling into anxiety. What if she's able to just chill and relax and actually have a really good time.
Hannah: *That would be AMAZING!*

I smile to myself.

Beth: *Yeah. It would be.*

18

Milo

"Why am I so nervous?" I ask myself, staring into the full-length mirror.

"Was that a rhetorical question?" I spin around to see Boden chasing after Jonah, who's traipsed into my room. He scoops my son up in his arms. "Sorry. Didn't mean to startle you."

"It's fine."

If having two kids under six and a nanny has taught me anything, it's that the only truly alone time I get is when I lock the bathroom door. Other than that, it's fair game.

"You look fine, by the way," Boden says, bouncing Jonah on his hip. "That's a nice shirt. Really brings out your eyes or something. Sorry. I don't really know how to compliment another guy on his appearance."

"Thanks." I manage a small smile and turn back to the mirror. I've gone with a red-and-black plaid button down, a pair of my favorite jeans, and dark-brown Chukka boots. Stylish, comfortable, and hopefully doesn't look like I'm trying too hard or spent way too much time overthinking my choice of outfit. I'm still undecided whether to take a summer jacket or not.

Why am I so on edge?

Oh, that's right. Because I'm in love with Beth, and the next few hours are a vital litmus test to see whether or not I have a chance at turning our us-ship into an actual relationship with the first and only woman who's ever set my soul on fire the way she does. No biggie.

"It's stupid to be this nervous," I mutter.

"Not if you like her, and it's pretty obvious you do."

"It is?"

Boden nods in the mirror. "I received an email from the International Space Station earlier today. They can see your attraction to Beth from up there."

"Right."

"For what it's worth, she's into you, too."

"Has that been confirmed by the ISS?"

He grins. "Yep. And by me, too. I've seen the way she looks at you. Just relax and have a good time. Don't get all first-datey about it. You've got nothing to worry about."

Oh, but I do.

Even though Beth and I have known each for almost a year, a first date feels different.

It *is* different.

I want it to be special and memorable. Plus, she's read more than her fair share of romance novels, so I have *a lot* to live up to. "You don't think going to the fair is pathetic?"

"Not at all. It's...cutesy."

"Hmm."

I finish tying my hair into a bun.

Cutesy.

Is *that* what I'm going for?

Well, I don't have any other ideas, and it's too late to change my mind now, so I cross my fingers and pray that Beth likes it.

"This is so..." Beth glances around the fair.

String lights are draped between trees and along stalls, sounds of laughter and cheerful music from a live band playing near the main stage mingle in the air, and game booths buzz with activity.

"Cutesy?" I offer.

"Yeah. Cutesy. Perfect word, Mr. Payne."

"Not as perfect as how you look tonight," I say, because man, Beth is even more stunning than usual.

And it's not just because of the stylish outfit she's wearing —a white linen blouse tucked into high-waisted, dark denim jeans, paired with black ankle boots, a simple silver necklace and delicate stud earrings.

Or the little extra makeup she's got on—like the bright red lipstick that makes her soft lips look even more inviting.

Or the spicy scent of her perfume wafting in the air—a captivating mix of cinnamon, cloves, and vanilla.

No.

It's more than that.

There's something about her—a confidence she's exuding —that is *really* doing it for me.

Meanwhile, I'm hoping I've put on enough deodorant to mask my underarm sweat so she can't see how much I'm freaking out.

I want tonight to go well, and I really want her to enjoy herself and have a good time.

And who knows? Maybe it could be the start of something more.

She knows I'm retiring and staying in Comfort Bay.

She knows I like her.

We've taken the first very tentative step toward a relationship.

Everything seems to be falling into place...I just wish the stars would hurry up and align already. All this waiting and anticipation is making my stomach churn. If all love is this stressful, I have no idea why Beth enjoys reading romance novels so much.

We walk past a ring toss. "Want me to win you something?"

She smiles. "Sure. Just don't get overly competitive about it."

I scoff. "As if." We walk over to the ring toss, and I tip my head toward the wall lined with prizes. "What would you like?"

She scans the options. "The stuffed pink bear holding a book," she says, pointing her finger toward the bear.

"Coming right up." I hand the attendant a twenty and smirk cockily at Beth. "This is going to be a piece of cake."

Ten minutes—and one hundred forty dollars—later, Beth's the one smirking.

"You don't have to keep going," she says softly so that no one can hear.

"No. I think I've figured it out. The perfect wrist flick to directional precision ratio. I'm so close I can feel it."

"If you say so."

Sweat is pouring down my back as I focus all my concentration on tossing the five rings over the targets.

I will win her that bear if it's the last thing I do.

Trying not to let my frustration show, I line up for my gazillionth attempt.

With a flick of my wrist, I toss the first ring. It lands securely around the neck of the first bottle with a satisfying clink.

I repeat it again and get the second bottle.

Then the third.

I'm not getting too excited just yet. I've been here several times before.

I take a breath and toss the ring again. It sails through the air and...makes it.

Yes!

I'm on a roll. Just one more to go.

I glance over at Beth and am treated to one of her beautiful smiles. It fires me up, and I know—I just know—I'm going to land this one for her.

I throw the ring.

It glides smoothly, hovering momentarily before dropping down and encircling the bottle in a perfect fit.

"Yay!" She claps then throws her arms around me.

The attendant, a spotty-faced teenager, hands me the stuffed pink bear with a look that clearly screams *weirdo*— can't argue with that—but I don't care.

The look of happiness on Beth's face is worth it.

We finally shuffle off, Beth cradling her new pink reading bear into her chest, me three pounds lighter from sweating so much. I swear that thing was rigged.

"I love it. Thank you," she says, lifting on her toes to kiss me on the cheek as we walk away from the ring toss from hell.

"You loved seeing me suffer," I say, tugging her into my side.

"I did not." She giggles, and the sweet sound infiltrates into my bones. "That was just an added bonus."

"Are you hungry?" I ask.

"Sure. I could eat."

We make our way over to the food stands.

But something's amiss.

"This doesn't seem right," I say, on the lookout for corn dogs, funnel cake, and cotton candy but only seeing a variety of international cuisines. Don't get me wrong, they all smell delicious, but I've got a hankering for some good old-fashioned fair treats. "Where are the corn dogs?"

"Blame Doyle," Beth says.

"The guy who runs the grocery store?"

"That's him. He's also town selectman, so he oversees all this stuff. And just so you know, he can be a massive pain in the you-know-what, so either stay on his good side or try to slip under his radar."

"And what does Doyle have to do with me not seeing any corn dogs?"

"He went to an inclusivity workshop recently and decided to incorporate international cuisine only."

"So, what? No American cuisine, then?"

Beth grins. "I think that may be the first time corn dogs have ever been referred to as cuisine, but yeah, sorry, you're out of luck."

"I'm boycotting that man's store," I grumble. "Come on. Let's see what they do have."

Ten minutes later, we're sitting at a table with an assortment of dishes laid out in front of us—gyros from Greece, a sliced-up Banh Mi sandwich from Vietnam, Spanish Paella, and some Japanese octopus balls.

"So, how am I doing?" I ask around a mouthful of seasoned lamb and pita bread.

She finishes chewing her Paella. "Doing?"

"Yeah. First-date wise."

"You want me to rate your first-date performance?"

"I do."

"Why?"

"You're basically the queen of romance, so I want to see if I need to up my game."

She snorts. "Queen of romance, hardly." Her eyes widen. "*Annnd* I just snorted."

"You snorted adorably. Romantically."

"That's not a thing. And there's no need for you to up your game, mister. You're doing great." She lifts her one hundred sixty dollar pink bear as evidence. "Just...just keep being you. And let's steer clear of all the hokey first-date topics."

"Like, *So tell me, what do you like to do in your spare time*?"

"Exactly." She smiles. "Or asking about birthdays and star signs."

"Or going through favorite movies, or shows, or music."

"Yes! And not being honest with any of your answers for fear of being judged, so you only say things you think the other person will think are cool."

I clear my throat. "You speaking from experience, by any chance?"

"Actually, yeah." She blushes a little. "Younger Beth was a lot more worried about what other people thought of her."

"I like this Beth better."

"You do?"

"For sure." I hesitate. "Tell me something embarrassing."

"Excuse me?"

"Well, if I scored highly due to not asking typical first-date questions, I'm curious to see what score I get for asking untypical first-date questions."

"You mean atypical."

"I'm pretty sure I'm rig—you know what, nevermind. I'll let you have the win."

"Nuh-uh. I'm *taking* the win because I'm right."

"Are we ever going to stop teasing each other?"

She grins. "I hope not."

"I hope not, too."

"Okay. Let's see. You want an embarrassing story, huh?"

"I do."

She takes a moment to think of something. "Okay. I have something. It happened recently."

"Go for it."

"Okay, so Mr. Forrester comes into the book shop. Do you know him?"

"No. I don't think I do."

"He's so lovely. When you think of a sweet grandpa, he's the guy who pops into your head."

I smile. "Got it."

"Anyway, he asked for a mystery book recommendation. That's not my genre, but I remembered Courtland raving about a mystery he'd just read, so I suggested that to him. Anyway, Mr. Forrester returns the next day, laughing, and tells me the book I'd recommended was actually a steamy romance novel. I'd gotten the two titles, *The Lieutenant's Secret* and *The Lieutenant's Promise* mixed up."

I chuckle. "Bet he didn't see that plot twist coming."

Beth giggles. "I realize it's not the worst thing in the world, but I *died*. I only hoped he stopped reading by page five because that's when the Lieutenant's, uh, secret, makes its first appearance."

My chuckle turns into a laugh. "That's too funny."

"Okay. It's my turn to ask you a non-first-date question. Hmm." She taps her chin. "Ooh, I know. Is Milo Payne, the gruffest and grumpiest goalie in the NHL afraid of anything?"

I study her for a moment. It's an interesting question to ask. Is she asking because she really wants to know, or is it a test to see if I'm able to admit to my fears?

"I'm good with a lot of things. Snakes, spiders, toddler poop." She giggles. "The only thing I'm afraid of is heights."

"Oh. Okay. Where does that come from?"

"It doesn't affect my day-to-day life, so I haven't given it that much thought. Most people have something they don't like, and height is my thing."

"Are you okay with flying?"

"I am. I even prefer the window seat. It's only when I'm outside, like if I were on a rooftop."

"Ohhh."

"What?"

"So that's why you took a giant step back at the lookout."

That was such a tiny detail, and yet she noticed, she remembers. I nod. "It is."

"I meant to ask you about it, but we were talking about your retirement plans, so I got sidetracked."

I shrug. "Like I said, it's not a big deal. I stepped back from the edge, and I was fine."

"So no Ferris wheel then?"

I wince. "I mean, if you really wanted to I suppose I cou—"

"Milo, I'm kidding. I've watched way too many amusement park disaster videos to ever go on one myself."

I huff out a relieved sigh. "Good. Okay. My turn. So this *is* a first-date question, but given you are who you are, I need to know."

"Should I be worried?"

I smile. "Not at all. What's your favorite book?"

"Perfectly Imperfect," she replies without hesitation. "And I'm not just saying that because it's my sister's debut novel. It's a legitimate bestseller, having sold millions of copies worldwide. She's in talks with a few streamers who want to acquire the rights for it, and it's just really good."

I love seeing her get so passionate. "What's it about?"

"It's a romance, naturally. A second chance which usually I'm not a fan of, but the way she was able to make me fall in love with both characters, I was drawn in from the first sentence."

"Is one of those characters a hunky hockey player by any chance?" I tease.

She laughs. "Funnily enough, no. They're both 'normal people'—"

"Am I ignoring your use of quotation marks?"

"You are if you know what's good for you," she quips with a grin.

"Fair enough. Continue."

"It's just so relatable. Two people who aren't perfect. In fact, they've both made a huge mess of their lives, but when they come together, they bring out the best in one another. It's nothing revelatory, but it was done really well. Oh, and Maverick Pendleton."

"Who's that?"

"He's the hero, and in my humble opinion, the ultimate book boyfriend."

"What on earth is a book boyfriend?"

She giggles before explaining, "It's the male character in a romance who is so wonderful that readers fall in love with him and imagine him as their book version boyfriend."

"I see." My eyebrows pinch together, and my voice gets a little gruffer. "And what makes Maverick Pickleton so great?"

"It's Pendleton, and I don't know..." She smiles bashfully, like maybe this isn't something she's comfortable talking about. I'm about to drop it and move on to another topic when she says, "It's how he made the heroine, Violet, feel. She'd been treated badly by guys before and had put up so many walls. He had the patience of a saint and treated her with nothing but kindness and respect, even when she pushed him away. It was beautiful."

Hmm. Why does the situation she's describing feel oddly familiar?

She clutches her chest and sighs wistfully. "And then the grand gesture."

"What's a grand gesture?"

"Wow. You really don't know the romance genre at all, do you?"

"I know *Romeo and Juliet*. Does that count?"

She emits a little huff and shakes her head. "That definitely does not count. A grand gesture is the pivotal moment in the story when a character expresses their deep love, regret, or desire to get back together in some big way."

"Okay, so what did this Plonkinton dude do that was so special?"

"You sure you want me to tell you? I don't want to spoil it for you."

"I'll survive."

"It's hard to explain without having read the book because it's not just what he did, but how he did it. He risked everything to give her something really special she'd lost as a little girl."

"It sounds like a good read."

She nods. "It's the best. Really. I know you don't read romance, but if you ever get the urge to try one, start there."

I smile. "Noted."

We must have spent longer than I realized talking, because by the time we finish our meal, the fireworks are about to start.

"Want to find a nice spot to watch?" I ask.

"Sure." She slips her hand into mine, and a rush of warmth fills my chest. I lead us away from the midway and the stands, hoping to find a less crowded area.

"This okay?" I ask as we approach a couple of empty lawn chairs in the picnic area. A few other people have had the same idea I have, but it's way less busy and the vibe is super chill.

"It's great," she says, plonking herself down.

Before sitting down, I shrug off my coat, grateful I decided to bring it, and drape it over her shoulders.

She looks up at me and smiles. "Thank you. You get bonus first-date points for that."

"I wasn't doing it to score points...but I'll take them."

I smile, she giggles, and as the fireworks begin and we look up to watch them, I've never felt this happy, this comfortable, this *right* with a woman before.

I'm convinced Beth is the one for me, but does she feel the same way, too?

I think so.

I hope so.

But I don't *know* so.

And it wouldn't be just me she's getting. The Milo Payne boyfriend collectible comes as a package with two bite-sized munchkins.

She knows that. She said she's fine with that.

But what if she's fine with it now, but her feelings change down the road? What then? I don't want to put any unrealistic expectations on us, but at the same time, I have to protect my kids. She's a natural with Josie and Jonah, and they're always asking when we're coming back to Comfort Bay to see Beth. I don't want them to get too attached only to lose her if things between us don't work out. They've both been through enough in their young lives.

Dude, chill. Get out of your own head and enjoy the moment.

I pretend to yawn, using it as an excuse to place my arm around her shoulder.

"Smooth," she says, not taking her eyes off the fireworks. She scoots in a little closer and leans against me.

The fireworks in the sky? Yeah, they've got nothing on what's happening inside my chest.

Once the display is over, we head back home, strolling through the streets hand in hand.

"When do I get my end-of-date score?" I ask as we turn onto our street.

"When I get my end-of-date kiss," she replies.

"That a challenge, is it?"

One of her eyebrows shoots up. "Maybe."

I chuckle. "In that case, challenge accepted."

We reach her house, and she turns to me. "Before we

restart our usual tit for tat, I just want to say something. Something serious."

"Will I need protective gear?"

A small grin. "No. I..." She looks away, then up at the sky, before returning her eyes to meet mine. "I've had a really good night, Milo. Hands down, this has been the best date I've ever been on. You make me feel...special. And safe. And I'm not used to either of those things."

"You are special, Beth." I gently graze her cheek. "And safe with me. Always. I won't ever intentionally do anything to hurt you or betray you. I'll never lie to you. And I'll take all the ribbing you direct at me. I swear."

"Stop being so charming."

"Can't help it." I grin, lifting my chin. "I've sought medical advice, but unfortunately, it looks like I'll have to live with this condition permanently."

She swats my chest, and I take the opportunity to latch onto her wrist. I raise her hand to my lips and softly kiss her knuckles one at a time.

I don't want Beth to have to settle for having some fictional book boyfriend, I want her to have the real thing. And in my one humble opinion, I believe I'm the best man for the job.

I'll always treat her right and respect her.

She can lead the way, and I'll follow.

I'm going to give her every reason to trust me, and maybe one day, when I tell her how beautiful she is, she'll believe me without any doubt or hesitation.

Unable to help myself, I ask, "So, does this mean you like me more than that Maverick Pebblerock or whatever his name is, guy?"

A soft smile lifts the corners of her mouth. "That depends."

"On?"

"On how you finish this date, mister. I'm still waiting for that kiss."

As soon as she's done talking, I lean down, curl my fingers around her neck, and put all the feelings I have for her into what I'm hoping will be the most unforgettable, magical end-of-first-date kiss she's ever had. Judging by the soft whimpers spilling out of her mouth, I'd say I'm in with a shot.

"So," I rasp, my lips hovering over hers. "How'd I do?"

"Maverick who?"

I grin. "'Atta girl."

19

Beth

"Come wif me, Daddy!"

"Uhhh..."

"Go on," I urge Milo, who's hesitating at Jonah's request.

"I'm not sure I'm going to fit," he says quietly to me before peeling off his shirt, and holy guacamole, that is one sight I can never get enough of.

Smooth skin, broad shoulders, muscular arms, a well-defined chest, and abs. So many abs. If Milo is looking for a post-hockey career, he would make a killing as a romance novel cover model.

Not that I'd want countless other women—and possibly some men—ogling him.

Okay. Scratch that.

If he wants to take up a new career, I'm sure something like hand modeling would be a great fit for him.

After I get in my obligatory ogling, I remind myself where I am—Milo's backyard.

Who I'm with—Milo, his kids, and Boden.

And what Jonah is asking—for Milo to join him in the temporary inflatable pool Milo bought since he was unable to find any contractors to build an actual pool until the fall.

"You'll be fine," I reassure him.

Josie and I are sitting on a blanket, enjoying the shade of a large California Sycamore. She looks up from her book and giggles. "But Daddy's too big."

I pick up my phone, knowing this is a moment worth capturing. "That's exactly the point," I say to her with a smile.

We watch as Milo carefully steps into the pool.

He was right. He barely fits as he awkwardly attempts to fold himself into the tiny pool. His knees are practically up to his ears, but Jonah couldn't be happier, splashing water everywhere and giggling.

It's the cutest thing ever.

I'm in awe.

Milo treats Jonah the way any father should treat his son. What does it matter if they're not connected by blood? They're joined by something much deeper—love.

Milo truly is Jonah's father.

I lift the phone. "Say cheese!"

"Don't you dare—"

"Excellent, thank you," I say, showing the photos I snapped to Josie, who lets out a delighted shriek. "Daddy's face. He looks like an ogre."

I cast my gaze to his oversized body in the undersized inflatable pool. "Yeah. That tracks," I say with a smile.

He smiles back at me, and I don't know if it's the cuteness of seeing him in the pool with Jonah, or the fact that he's shirtless, or if it's spending every day together since our first date at the fair two weeks ago, but in case there was any doubt, this anti-love girl is falling for Milo.

Big time.

And the crazy part?

I'm not scared.

Okay, let me rephrase that. I'm a *tiny bit* scared. But the fear bubbling up in me is residual pain from my past, it's got nothing to do with how I feel about Milo.

Because I have no doubt about my feelings for him. I know exactly what kind of man he is. He's demonstrated that time and time again.

And I think it was his nervousness on our date that completely won me over. His determination to get me that pink reading bear, him asking me to rate him, his fake jealousy

—at least, I think it was fake jealousy—over Maverick Pendleton, and then that kiss.

That. Kiss!

When a girl reads a few...thousand romance novels, it's easy to become jaded and have completely unrealistic expectations. I thought I'd have to rein my hopes in, settle for our usual amazing level of kisses, but nope, Milo blew it out of the water.

It was so much more than lips on lips. We were communicating to each other without saying a word.

I know I was.

And seeing as we haven't spent a day apart since then, I'd say Milo picked up what I was putting down.

We haven't made anything official, but it's clear our us-ship is going to become a relationship any day now.

"Want me to take the kids inside?" Boden suggests.

"That would be terrific. Thank you," Milo says, lifting a soaking wet Jonah into Boden's arms. He's got a towel ready to wrap him up in. Josie follows as Boden carries Jonah into the house, shutting the sliding door behind him with his foot.

It was a little odd at first, having a third person around all the time, but Boden is great, and he's got a sixth sense for knowing when Milo and I would like some alone time.

I keep meaning to ask him if he's single. I think he'd be a great match for Amiel. Not that I'd ever interfere in someone else's love life or anything.

Milo climbs out of the pool.

"What do you feel like for dinner?" he asks, drying off his hair, which is now so long it reaches way past his shoulders.

"Bold of you to assume I'm staying for dinner."

"You've stayed every night this week," he replies with a smirk.

A cocky smirk.

A cocky smirk that used to peeve me off but now turns me on.

"What can I say?" I reply nonchalantly. "I like free food."

He chuckles then leans down, the wet tips of his hair brushing against my shoulders as his mouth covers mine.

"What are you doing, Daddy?"

We break apart to see Josie staring at us.

I was so into the kiss I didn't hear the sliding door open.

Milo rubs the back of his neck. "Uh..."

"Sorry sorry sorry," Boden exclaims, chasing after her. "I was changing Jonah."

"It's all right," Milo says to him. "You're my nanny, not running clearance on my love life."

Jonah wanders out of the house, half-dressed. Boden attends to him as Josie looks between Milo and me and asks, "Is Beth your girlfriend?"

His eyes snap to mine. "Um, well..."

"Can you give us a minute?" I ask Boden.

"Of course."

He ushers the kids back inside.

I turn to face Milo. "Well, am I your girlfriend?"

"You'd make me the happiest man on earth if you were."

"So ask me."

He takes my hand in his. "Beth Anne Moore...will you be my girlfriend?"

"I will."

He pulls me into a tight hug, his strong arms wrapping around me like he never wants to let go. His skin is still slightly damp, and I can feel the steady thump of his heart. This is so right. I know it is.

"I should probably go inside," he says, moving back a few inches. "Explain things to the kids."

"You want some company?"

His eyebrows spring up. "Are you sure?"

"Of course."

"Okay. Great. That'd be wonderful. I...I have no idea what I'm going to say. There's no real roadmap for this."

"No. There isn't." I thread my fingers through his as we start walking toward the house. "So let's figure it out together."

∼

"Is she going to stay with us?"

"Can I visit her in her bookstore?"

"Is she our new mom?"

Okay, so maybe I slightly underestimated the grilling a six-year-old is capable of giving. Not that I'd expect anything less from Josie. She's not being mean or difficult about it, she's just inquisitive and genuinely wants to know.

I'm sitting quietly because Milo is handling all the questions she's throwing at him really well, including the last one. Talk about a toughie.

"No, sweetie, no one can ever replace your mommy," he answers, gently bouncing Jonah on his knee. "But Beth is someone who is very special to me."

"I wike her," Jonah chips in.

Milo smiles and continues, "I think you like her, too. Don't you, Josie?"

She nods. "I do."

"That's good," Milo says. "And over time, you'll get to know her even better and like her even more. But she's not here to be your mommy."

Josie takes a moment to think.

She looks at me, and I smile. She smiles back, but it's so hard to read what's going on in her head.

"Is that why you gave her a card with a love heart?" she asks.

Milo glances over at me. "Yeah. It was. I like Beth a lot." His eyes burn into mine. "That's why I asked her to be my girlfriend."

Jonah lets out an excited *Wee* even though he's a little too young to properly understand what's going on. Josie looks between Milo and me a few times, eventually saying, "Does this mean she can read me stories at bedtime?"

"It does. If Beth would like to."

I smile at Milo, then at Josie. "I'd love to."

And with that, Milo and I are a couple.

"We made it official," I tell Amiel and Courtland in the bookstore the day after Milo and I made the official, if not somewhat unexpected, announcement to Josie and Jonah.

It's a typical quiet summer afternoon in the store, and Amiel's dropped by after her shift at the bakery to stock up on our newest shipment of arrivals.

She lets out a squeal. "Tell. Us. Everything."

So I do, and when I'm done, they're both smiling at me. "The snarky bookworm and the grumpy goalie find their happily ever after in a classic enemies-to-lovers romcom," Courtland says, in his best voiceover voice.

"Whatever."

"Are you happy?" Amiel asks.

"Of course she's happy. Have you ever seen her smile so much?" Courtland answers for me.

"Let's not get too carried away," Amiel counters. "This is Beth. She's probably compiling a list of things Milo has said or done that's annoyed her."

I shake my head. "Nope. No list."

"What about the man bun?" she presses.

"I'm actually digging it. Plus, he's got the softest hair when he lets it out. It's so silky."

"Does he have any annoying habits?" Courtland presses. "Are the kids a nightmare?"

"Haven't stumbled upon any annoying habits yet. And the kids are great. I love hanging out with them."

"What about the nanny? Is he getting on your nerves?" Amiel asks.

"Nope." I shake my head. "Boden is a great guy. Awesome with the kids, and he reads the room to know when Milo and I need some space. Actually..." I shoot a look at Amiel and she immediately recoils.

"I just got chills. You're planning something evil."

"Me? Never?" I throw my head back and cackle. "But seriously, I think I may have found a guy for you."

"Who?"

"Boden."

"The nanny?"

"Yeah."

She scrunches up her face. "I'm not sure...Is he even single?"

"Yet to confirm. But once I do, you'll be the first to know."

"Yes, yes, yes, all riveting stuff, and we'll get around to the male nanny falling for the ginger-haired baker beauty at some stage, but let's get back to you," Courtland says, turning to face me. "There has to be something wrong with Milo or some impending conflict or something you guys should have talked about but have been neglecting. There always is in the majority of enemies-to-lovers stories."

"In that case, I guess we're the exception to the rule.

There's nothing wrong with Milo and nothing on the horizon that I'm worried about, either."

"So there's *nothing* you're freaking out about?" he asks, sounding exasperated.

"The only thing I'm freaking out about is that I'm not freaking out about anything. I really like Milo. He really likes me. He treats me with respect. We communicate openly. I feel good when I'm with him. Things are great."

"So, no third-act breakup in your future, then?" Amiel checks.

"I certainly hope not. Unless I happen to walk past the diner and see Milo talking to a beautiful woman. In which case, of course, I'll be obligated to fling myself in front of him, give him no chance to rationally explain it's someone he knows, make a huge scene, and proceed to fall into a two-week depression where I'm responsible for single-handedly lifting the Ben & Jerry's stock price." They're both grinning. "Seriously, guys. Everything is going well. Really well. Super duper well."

"I'm glad," Amiel says with a smile.

"Me, too," Courtland throws in. "And speaking of things going well..."

I roll my eyes.

Amiel looks between us. "What am I missing?"

"Lori Connors!" Courtland squeals, his voice rising an octave or two.

I groan.

"You'd think Taylor Swift was coming to town given how excited you are over my sister's book signing that isn't for a while yet," I say.

"Doesn't matter. I'm still marking off the days on my calendar, and you can't stop me."

I look at Amiel pleadingly. "See what I've been dealing with."

"He's allowed to be a fanboy." She scoops up her pile of books and smiles. "Just like you're allowed to be happy that you're in a relationship with a grumpy goalie."

I grin.

Well, when she puts it like that.

I sit on the edge of the couch, staring at the TV screen, my heart pounding in my chest. I take a big bite out of one of Amiel's delicious caramel cupcakes I bought on the way home and let out a moan. She is one seriously talented baker, and when a girl needs to comfort eat, you can't go wrong with one of her treats.

The sight of Milo standing at the podium, surrounded by cameras and microphones, fills the screen. He's so composed, every inch the professional athlete.

Not sure why he seems so calm and I'm not.

This is a good thing, I remind myself. *A really good thing.*

He begins to speak, his voice steady and strong. I already know what he's about to say—he's stepping back, leaving the game he's loved for so long, to spend more time with his children.

My heart swells with admiration for what he's doing, but there's also a sting of guilt. I know how much hockey means to him, how it's lifted him up in some of his darkest times, and the thought of him giving that up is a lot to take. Yes, he's giving that up for Josie and Jonah, but I factored into the decision as well. I hope he doesn't end up resenting me for it.

And then he finally drops the big news.

"I've decided that it's time to step away from the game I love."

I turn the volume up, my eyes glued to the screen, my mouth chomping down on the cupcake.

"Hockey has been my life for so many years. It's given me incredible opportunities, unforgettable memories, and the chance to compete at the highest level. I've shared the ice with amazing teammates, played for incredible fans, and been part of an organization that's supported me every step of the way. But as much as I love the game, my priorities have shifted."

He takes a breath and smiles, and I can tell he's thinking about Josie and Jonah. "My kids are growing up fast, and I don't want to miss out on any more moments with them. It's time for me to be there for them in the same way hockey has always been there for me."

He takes another breath and squares his shoulders. "There's also someone very special in my life, and I'm ready to focus on building a future together."

I almost choke on my cupcake. Whoa.

A wave of warmth rushes over me, and I can't help but smile. I was not expecting him to mention me. It feels a little surreal.

"This isn't goodbye to hockey completely. The sport will always be a part of who I am, and I'll continue to support the game in different ways. But for now, it's time to hang up my skates and focus on the most important team of all—my family and the person who means the world to me. Thank you to everyone who's been a part of this journey with me. I appreciate your understanding and support, and I'm excited for what the future holds."

I lean back on the sofa and let out a long breath.

I'm happy Milo made the announcement, and I definitely think he made the right decision, one made out of love.

I find myself daydreaming about the future, wondering what might come next.

20

Milo

Any fears I may have had that retirement would be boring—or that I'd start wearing velour tracksuits, take up golf, and be overcome by a sudden urge to move somewhere warmer and insist on having dinner at five—have not come to fruition.

Retired life is *the best*.

Why didn't I do this sooner?

Oh, I know.

Because I didn't have kids or a girl I am crazy, head over heels for.

But now I have both in my life...and I'm the happiest guy on the planet.

Although I'm not happy at how fast the summer is flying by. Josie will be starting school in a few weeks, and I'm not ready to not see her every day. What if she hates it? What if she struggles to make friends? What if the other kids tease her about the lunches I make for her?

I blow out a breath and try to rein in my mini-freakout. We've taken the kids to the beach. And by *we*, I mean Boden and I, not Beth and I, as I would have preferred, since unfortunately, one of us is not retired.

Since making it official last week, we've continued spending every spare moment we have together. For logistical reasons, Beth comes over to my place and we just hang out, play with the kids, make dinner, talk out in the backyard, and go for early morning walks.

I don't really care what we do, all that matters is that we're together, and that she's my girlfriend. Every time I think about it, I smile, and I think about it all the freaking time. I swear my cheek muscles are going to go on strike and demand a break.

I cherish every moment I get to spend with Beth, but I did comment yesterday that I hoped I wasn't taking up *too* much of her time, and that if she had other things to do, I wouldn't mind.

I *would* have minded, but I wasn't going to tell her that.

She simply shrugged and made an adorable noise, before rolling out her joke about how she only stays for the free food. Plus, she's too invested in the magical unicorn-themed puzzle she's doing with Josie and Jonah to stop coming over.

I love that she gets on so well with the kids, and they've really taken to her, too. Jonah, obviously, because he loves anyone after spending five minutes with them, but Josie as well, even if it's in her somewhat more reserved way.

I'm not placing any expectations on Beth when it comes to the kids. I'm just going to relax and see what happens. Everything's gone smoothly up to this point, and I hope it'll stay that way.

"Daddy, look!"

I'm sitting in the shallow water keeping a close eye on Josie who's in front of me, cautiously playing in the waves.

I raise my hands in the air. "You're doing great, sweetie."

She really is.

At the start of the summer, she'd barely venture into the water. Gradually, over time, she would only go in with me, sticking right by my side. Now, she's jumping and splashing about in the gentle waves all by herself.

I do the *let's swap kids* gesture to Boden who comes over to keep an eye on Josie while Jonah shows me the sandcastle he's building.

I had a fleeting thought that when I retired, I might not need a nanny, but that isn't happening. I have no idea how single parents manage, but I have all the respect in the world for them. I would not be able to cope on my own.

"Wike my castle?" Jonah asks, tapping his palm against my leg.

"I do. Good job, buddy."

I kneel in the sand, and he looks over at me and smiles. "Daddy, you watching?"

I nod. "I'm watching."

He takes a deep, solemn breath—something he's copying from the close up shots of the divers we've been watching at the national diving championships on TV every night—then he spins on his small heels and marches away from his sandcastles, arms winding up and down, counting out his paces until *eight,* which is where he gets confused and winds up at five again.

He turns back around with the most serious expression on his little face. And then, with all his strength and might, he races toward the sandcastle, flicking up sand everywhere, and stomps all over it, putting his whole body into it.

I cheer him on. "You show that sandcastle who's boss."

"Help me, Daddy," he says, kicking his leg out toward a section that hasn't crumbled yet.

"Want me to smash it?"

He squeals in delight. "Smash! Smash! Smash!"

I make a loud roaring sound, then lift my foot, slowly, menacingly.

Jonah is beside himself with giggles, eagerly anticipating what's to come.

I stomp my foot down, demolishing the last remaining part.

He hollers in glee and starts jumping up and down, using my shoulders for leverage. I roll over onto my back, grab him by his middle, and fly him over me.

He *loves* this, and I do, too.

I fell in love with the little guy immediately, but in the back of my mind, I had a fear I was too scared to even voice—that I would have a problem loving Jonah or that I wouldn't feel as connected to him as I would to Josie.

Those concerns haven't materialized. I feel so close to him. And it's not forced or something I try to make happen. It just is. He is one hundred percent my son, and no one can tell me otherwise.

"Let's go watch your sister in the water."

"Oh-tay."

I take his small hand in mine, and we walk over to Boden. "How's she doing?" I ask as Jonah splashes around in the shallow water beside me.

"Good. She's talking to some girls..." I look out and see the girls he means. There's three of them, and they look to be about the same age as Josie. "I think they're trying to get her to go out a little deeper so she can catch the waves like they are."

"Should I go out and see if she needs help?"

"And embarrass her in front of her new friends?" he asks with a friendly smile.

"Good point. I'll watch nervously from the sidelines, feeling completely helpless."

"Welcome to parenthood."

The next stretch of time is nerve wracking. For *me*. Jonah is having a great time running through the water, but in addition to watching him, I'm also keeping an eye on Josie, who is pushing herself out of her comfort zone—and into deeper water.

I keep telling myself that it's not that deep, and that in a pinch, I could reach her in a few seconds, but still, my brain is braining.

She's a strong swimmer, she's wearing a swim vest, and the conditions are relatively calm, but it's seeing her do something new for the first time. I want her to do well because if she doesn't, will that destroy her confidence and prevent her from trying new things again?

Children are fragile like that.

I glance over at Jonah, who has picked up his inflatable toy turtle, but instead of riding it, he's wrestling it.

Okay, so maybe children are fragile, toddlers not so much.

Josie goes out deeper and attempts to catch some waves. The first few times, her timing is off and she ends up in the churn.

The other girls come over to her after each attempt. I can't hear what they're telling her, but I assume it's something positive because she doesn't give up. She keeps trying, and after about five or six attempts, she finally succeeds and body surfs all the way to the shoreline.

Her new friends hug and high five her.

I'm filled with pride.

She runs over to us. "Did you see that?"

"I did, sweetie. You were awesome."

She practically jumps on top of me, wraps her arms around my shoulders, and says the four words I've been dying to hear her say all this time.

"I love you, Daddy."

My throat tightens with emotion. "I love you, too, Josie."

She gives me one final squeeze before returning to her friends.

I'm glad I'm wearing dark sunglasses to mask the tear that falls from my eye.

She finally said it.

It's taken a lot longer than I thought it would. So long I was beginning to doubt it would ever happen.

In addition to being cautious, she also takes her time to open up to people. Guess she gets that from me.

But now that she's said it, I know that she means it.

And there's no better feeling in the world than that.

I step into the bookstore and head toward the counter.

Once a week, I take Beth out on a lunch date. It's become a thing she lets me do—indulging her love of free food. That's what she likes to say, anyway, but I know she enjoys it as much as I do.

Hanging out at my house with the kids is great, but it's also nice to have a little alone time, too.

And we're going to have even more alone time this afternoon. I've cleared it with her boss, even though she probably doesn't remember what today is.

"Hey," she says, smiling warmly as I approach the counter.

"Hey, yourself."

She looks great. A fitted, burgundy blouse offsets her porcelain complexion beautifully, and a pair of high-waisted, dark wash jeans highlight her figure.

"I'll grab my purse and let Courtland know I'm going."

"Sure. No worries. You know where to find me."

She smiles knowingly as I make my way over to the thriller section. Despite retiring, I have absolutely zero time to read. But it's nice to see all the new releases I'm missing out on.

I really don't mind.

I'll take Josie telling me she loves me for the first time on the beach last week, or Jonah proudly trudging into my bedroom yesterday morning having dressed himself for the very first time, over the latest release from John Marrs, Harlan Coben, or Frieda McFadden.

Books aren't going anywhere. They'll still be there in twenty years when I may finally have some spare time.

But kids, they grow up way too fast, and I don't want to miss a thing. I want to be there for all of it.

"All right. You ready?" Beth asks when she reappears.

"Let's do it."

I take her hand in mine, but rather than turning right once we leave the store and head toward one of the nice restaurants by the marina, this time we turn left.

"Where are we going?" she asks.

"You'll find out in less than a minute."

Less than a minute later, I'm opening the door to Bear's diner for her. She looks at me with a curious look in her eye but doesn't say anything as Bear tips his head to the corner booth he's reserved for me.

We sit down.

"So..." As I steeple my fingers, a jolt of nervous energy crashes into me, much like the nerves I experienced before our first date.

Does Hokeyville need a new president? Because I have no idea how Beth is going to react to this.

I ran what I'm about to do past Boden yesterday, who assured me she'd love it and that it was just the right level of cutesy, so that's the reaction I'm hoping for from her.

"So?" Beth prompts when I don't follow up my opening with anything.

Right.

Talking.

One word followed by another.

Yep. I can do this.

"Do you know what today is?"

"Wednesday?"

"Uh-huh. And the date?"

"August tenth."

"Uh-huh. And do you remember what happened on August tenth last year?"

She shakes her head. "No. I can't say that I do."

"Here's a clue. You were a little mean to me."

"That doesn't really narrow it down, does it?"

I grin. "I suppose not. Okay, then. Spice Girls."

"Excuse me?"

"And Taylor Swift. Plus a few Bruno Mars tracks."

"Wait...Was that the night we went to karaoke?"

"Bingo." I pull out a rectangular box under the table where I asked Bear to stash it for me and slide it over to her. "Happy one year anniversary."

"Anniversary," she murmurs quietly, staring at the box before lifting her eyes to me. "You...you remembered?"

"Uh, yeah. I think I'd remember meeting my favorite person. Also, I do have the whole photographic memory thing."

"Right." She slowly shakes her head, looking a little dazed. "From what I recall—and I may have consumed a few too many glasses of wine that night, so my memory might be a little foggy—but I pretty much ignored you the whole time."

"You did."

"And as you pointed out, I was a little mean to you."

I shrug. "You were."

"So, how do I go from that to being your favorite person?"

"Firstly, I'll remind you that I'm a weirdo. And secondly...I honestly don't know. But I was intrigued by you from the moment you squinted at me from across the diner and muttered something I'm assuming was disparaging about me to your friends."

She drops her head. "Oh."

"And thirdly..." I reach across the table and take her hand in mine. "I'm a weirdo."

"You already said that."

"Weirdos have a tendency to repeat themselves."

She draws in a breath, and when she looks up at me, her hazel eyes are glistening. "I'm sorry."

"What are you sorry for?"

"For...for completely misjudging you and for acting like... Well, I won't say the word, but it rhymes with witch."

"A stitch?"

That brings a small smile to her lips. "Yeah. Sorry for being such a massive stitch."

"Well, thank you. But to be honest with you, I like it." I pause and take her in for a moment. "You've always been real with me, Beth. You've never hidden your feelings or been dishonest about what you want from me. I appreciate that. I respect that. I respect *you*."

"There's a difference between being open about your feelings and being downright mean and not nice."

"Eh, it's a fine line. I knew you'd come around eventually."

"You did?"

"Uh-huh."

"How?"

I've got two options here.

Option one, I make some crack about how my charming personality and good looks were bound to win her over. But that would set us off on another round of inevitable sparring, which, as much as I love, that's not what this moment calls for.

So I go with option two.

Honesty.

"Life is unexpected. I never thought I'd wind up with two kids. Or that I fall for someone snarky, who hates hockey and man buns, and teases me mercilessly. But both things have happened." I reach across the table and slide my gift out of the way for the moment. "May I?"

"Yes."

I wrap my fingers around hers and instantly feel my chest expand. "Something happened the night we met, Beth. I was struck with a feeling...I...I can't explain it very well. All I know is that it's the same feeling I got when I saw Josie and Jonah for the first time. It felt right even though I didn't know you. Maybe it's..."

I trail off.

There is no way I can say what I was about to say. Forget cutesy, this would be hurtling into cheesy territory at a thousand miles an hour.

"What? Say it?" She aims those hazel eyes I'm a sucker for at me and murmurs, "Please."

I take a breath. "Promise you won't tease me about it?"

"Never."

"That's what I thought." Okay, here goes my dignity. "I was going to say, maybe it's the feeling you get when you meet your soulmate. You see someone you've never met before but your soul *knows*. It knows they're a good person. It knows they're the right fit for you. It knows they're worth all the roadblocks and challenges they put up in your way."

She's not laughing at me, so I finish with, "I had that feeling when I met you, Beth. And it's only grown the more we've gotten to know each other."

"I'm...I don't know what to say."

"You don't have to say anything." I nudge my gift closer to her. "Here."

She delicately opens the rectangular jewelry box, her fingers trembling slightly. Inside, nestled on a soft velvet cushion, rests a gleaming necklace with multiple charms, including a book and a heart.

"Open the locket," I suggest, pointing to the heart-shaped locket.

She does, and she reads out the inscription. "MP."

"Maverick Pendleton. Your ultimate book boyfriend, remember?"

"But, wait...I never told you what he bought her."

"Yeah, well, I read the book. Okay, *skimmed* the book, found the grand gesture part, and took inspiration from it."

She keeps staring at the inscription for a while. A long while. And then she looks up, her expression unreadable. "MP?"

"Yeah. MP."

"And it's just a coincidence that MP happen to be your initials, too?"

"Oh. Are they? I hadn't even realized."

"You did so."

I grin. "Okay. So maybe I wasn't too mad at the universe for the fortunate coincidence."

She gets up out of the seat, sits next to me, and plants the biggest kiss on my lips.

When it ends, I mutter, "Note to self, buy Beth a necklace every day."

"That kiss wasn't for the necklace, even though I love it and will wear it all the time," she says, locking her earnest gaze on mine. "It's for you being you. You've always seen something in me, Milo, even when I didn't treat you well. And somehow, you managed to break through all the walls I've built up without applying any pressure or making me feel uncomfortable. You said we could do things on my timeframe, and you stayed true to your word. Only a strong man can manage a complicated woman, and believe me, I'm very complicated."

"Oh, I know," I murmur, tucking a loose strand behind her ear. "You're the most complicated, challenging, stubborn woman I've ever met."

Her breath hitches.

I mean it as a compliment. It takes her a few seconds to register that, and when she does, her shoulders visibly loosen.

"Yeah, well, that makes you the strongest man I've ever met."

I grin again. "Looks like we're a perfect match."

After we finish lunch, and I settle the bill—leaving Bear an extra-large tip for breaking his no-reservations-ever rule and saving me the best booth in the house—we step out of the diner, but instead of walking Beth back to the bookstore, I lead her in the opposite direction.

"Where are we going?"

"I have another surprise for you."

"But I have to get back to the shop."

"No you don't."

"Uh, yes I do. Courtland is a pretty chill boss, but he's not cool with me skipping out on work."

"Courtland knows you won't be back at work this afternoon."

Beth stops walking. "What are you talking about? You've prearranged this?"

"I have."

"Without telling me?"

"It wouldn't be a surprise if you knew."

I resume walking, and after a few moments, Beth catches up to me. "Am I going to like this surprise?"

My hand finds its way to hers.

She's been waiting for me to do this since the night she laid eyes on me at karaoke night last year.

"Yeah," I say, grinning big. "I think you're going to like the surprise."

21

Beth

For the umpteenth time, I'm at a loss for words.

I'm walking hand in hand with Milo, wearing the necklace he gave me as a nod to the grand gesture from my favorite romance ever, over an anniversary lunch I didn't even know we had, during which he basically told me he thought we were soulmates, and now he's leading me somewhere else for another surprise.

How is this happening?

I'm both elated and uneasy at the same time.

Elated because, hello, this sweet, sensitive side of Milo is one of my favorite things about him.

But uneasy because I was such a stitch to him that I didn't even think he would be capable of having a side like this.

I made assumptions about him because...what? He was a pro hockey player? He looked grumpy on the ice? He doesn't talk a lot in social settings?

When did I become so judgmental?

It's not a nice feeling when you discover something about yourself you're not proud of.

I will revisit this again later—one apology is nowhere near enough—but right now, I'm going to put that to the side and enjoy whatever Milo has in store.

As we walk hand in hand, I sneak a glance at him.

I stand by what I told him at the diner. He really is the strongest man I know. I haven't made any of this easy, and not once has he turned around and treated me badly. And he's stayed true to his word, not pressuring me into doing anything I'm not ready for physically. He really is a patient man.

Spending time together this past year has helped me

release a lot of the old stuff I was holding onto. In my mind, there's now a clear distinction between how I've been treated by guys before and how Milo treats me.

I guess that's what comes with being with a real man, a man who knows how to treat a woman right.

I have nothing to fear, no impending betrayal to anticipate, no heartbreak looming around the corner. So I've released it, determined not to let those things from the past stand in the way of the amazing thing Milo and I have.

We come to a stop in front of Miss Patty's salon.

"Here we are," he says with a broad smile.

"Aw, did you read an article online about how joint mani-pedis are a new trend? Because, let me assure you, they most definitely are not."

He chuckles. "We're not doing a joint mani-pedi."

"Then why are we here?"

He holds open the door for me. "All will be revealed shortly."

"Ah, Milo, doll." Miss Patty welcomes us as we enter. "And Beth, good to see you."

"Hey, Miss Patty."

"Come on over," she says, waving Milo over to a styling chair.

Milo smiles at me before following Miss Patty's lead. I stay close, still totally in the dark as to what is going on.

What could it be?

Why has Milo brought me to a hair—

No.

Noooo.

I think you're going to like this.

He's cutting off his man bun.

"Charlotte will be over in a sec, doll," Miss Patty says as

Milo takes a seat in the salon chair. "Can I get either of you anything while you wait?"

"I'm good," Milo replies.

"Same," I manage before Miss Patty totters away.

As soon as she's out of earshot, I lunge toward him. "Are you cutting your hair?"

"I sure am. Say sayonara to the man bun." He's smiling, but when he sees my face, the smile vanishes. "What's wrong? I thought you'd be jumping for joy. Wait. Are you sad you won't be able to tease me about it anymore?"

"That's not it." I slump into the empty chair beside him. "I was...kinda liking it."

"You serious?"

I nod. "Yeah."

"Oh. But I have to cut it."

"What do you mean you *have to* cut it?"

Before he can answer, Charlotte comes bouncing over. I know her, and she's really nice but way too cheery and upbeat for us to be close friends.

"Hey, Beth."

"Hi, Charlotte."

She turns her attention to Milo. "Hey, Milo. This is such an amazing thing you're doing."

He's cutting his hair. What's so amazing about that?

Something isn't adding up here, and I'm not just thinking that because I'm in shock and yes, even a little sad, that the man bun will be no more.

"What's going on?" I ask.

Charlotte spins around to me. "Milo is donating his hair to make a human wig for children going through chemotherapy."

"Oh."

Milo leans forward so I can see him behind Charlotte and smiles. "Surprise!"

Yeah, he can say that again.

Charlotte gets to work, and I sit next to him, watching in a stunned silence.

Just when I think I couldn't have made any more wrong assumptions about the guy, he goes ahead and does something amazing like this. The thing I didn't like and would tease him about so much is actually the nicest, sweetest thing he's doing for sick kids.

When Charlotte excuses herself to get something, I lean forward and ask, "Why didn't you tell me?"

"I wanted my haircut to be a surprise."

"I don't mean the haircut. I mean the reason why you grew your hair long in the first place."

"What? And risk you liking me? No way."

He smiles, and while I appreciate he's trying to make me feel better, it doesn't work. I feel bad, and I should feel bad. I deserve to.

"What made you do it?" I ask.

"Hockey teams visit sick kids in hospitals," he explains. "One day, I was speaking with a nurse who mentioned how expensive human hair wigs are. It got me thinking, since I have such wonderful hair, why not grow it out and put it to good use? This will be my third wig."

I almost topple out of the chair. "You've done this twice before?"

"I have." He pauses. "And stop looking at me like that?"

"Like what?"

"Like you're making this into a thing."

"It is a thing."

"It's not a thing. Or if it is, it's a tiny, minuscule thing. The kids who have to endure chemotherapy, *they're* the heroes. I'm just some guy whose hair grows quickly and can pull off— wait, sort of pull off—a man bun."

Charlotte returns, robbing me of the chance to correct him on both counts.

One, he can pull off a man bun.

And two, he's a hero, too, regardless of if he's willing to admit it or not.

Whether it's adapting to sudden and unexpected fatherhood, rushing into a crumbling building to save lives, or growing his hair out for sick children, Milo Payne is my hero.

And as I sit here, watching Charlotte transform him into a new man right before my eyes, something else dawns on me.

Something that should be scary...but isn't.

Something I can pass off as new...though it's not.

Something that I could try to deny...but won't.

I, Beth Moore, am head over hardcover in love with Milo Payne.

"You said I have the whole afternoon off, right?" I ask a newly short-haired Milo once we're on the sidewalk.

"That's right."

He glances at his reflection in the storefront window and plays with his hair. "You really think it looks okay?"

It looks way more than okay. "You look incredible."

"I think she left it a little too long at the top. I don't want it to be too stylish."

"It's not too stylish," I say, curling my hand around his arm and gently steering him away from the window. "It's just the right amount of stylish. Besides, I assume you're going to grow it out again?"

"I am."

"Then it's a good thing she left a little length."

"Yeah, I suppose you're right."

"I'm always right. Now, back to my question. Are we free this afternoon?"

"We are."

"Good. Because I'm ready."

We come to a sudden halt.

"Ready for...?"

"I think you know." I grin up at him. "Unless that's not amenable for you."

"Oh, no. It's amenable. It's incredibly amenable. It's more amenable than anything has ever been amenable in the entire history of human amenableness."

I giggle. "Good."

He looks at me with soft, caring eyes. "Are you sure?"

"I am." I exhale. "I feel safe with you, and I want to do this. I *want* you, Milo."

His eyes light up. "You are safe, Beth. I promise you."

I slide my hand over his solid chest. "I know. Now let's get moving."

We get moving.

"Uhhh..."

We get moving all the way to my house until we spot Boden and the kids playing out the front of Milo's place.

"Don't worry. I have a secret route," I say, grabbing him by the hand.

"Do I want to know why you need to have a secret route to your own house?" he asks as we sneak past the rose bushes by the side of my other neighbor, Mrs. Hinkley's house.

"You really don't."

We sneak through her backyard, and I lift the loose fence palings for Milo to go under. He goes first then spins around, holding them up for me.

We race through my yard and into my house through the back door for an afternoon I will never forget as long as I live.

I let out a startled noise as I'm sprayed with water from the tub.

"Jonah, no," Milo says firmly, and Jonah stops splashing immediately. "Here. Play with your new boat."

"Oh-tay."

Milo hands me a towel. "I'm so sorry. But I did warn you."

I start drying off. "You did. Several times. I just didn't believe one small kid could splash so much."

"Welcome to toddler bathtime."

I place the towel on the edge of the tub and stare up into Milo's eyes. "Thank you for letting me be a part of this."

He breaks out into a massive smile, and how could I have ever made jokes about scaring children away? A smiling Milo is one of my favorite Milos.

"I'm happy you wanted to be here," he says. "But keep the towel close. You'll never know when you might need it again."

I watch as he gently washes his son, his large hands somehow soft and careful, guiding Jonah through the bath with ease. There's something so tender and natural about the way he handles him, and it melts my heart to see this side of him.

It's been a week since we were intimate, and this is the first night I'm staying over. It's a big deal. Just like Milo inviting me to be part of the kids' nighttime routine. It means things are getting even more serious, becoming even more real.

And the really wild part? I'm still not freaking out.

This feels right, and that feeling is so strong it overpowers whatever fears I have from my past relationships. My head knows Milo won't ever treat me the way I've been treated before. And more importantly, so does my heart.

After finishing the bath, Milo hands Jonah over to me, and

I wrap him up in a fluffy white towel, his little face peeking out with a smile as he chats about his boats. Milo lifts him up and carries him to his bedroom where we're met by the soft glow of a nightlight casting gentle shadows on the walls.

I dry Jonah off as Milo picks up a bright-red fire pajamas set. It's adorable, the way he fumbles with the tiny pajama buttons, his hands too big for the task. He looks up and catches me gawking at him.

"These are his favorite," he explains with a bashful grin.

Jonah claps excitedly, his face lighting up. "Fave-wit! Fave-wit! Fave-wit!"

I hand Jonah over to him, and there's a tender sweetness in the way he carefully tugs the sleeves over Jonah's little arms.

"You're a natural," I say quietly.

"Months of practice," he quips back.

"Modesty doesn't suit you," I whisper into his ear, and he lets out a low chuckle.

"Noted."

Together, we help Jonah climb into his toddler bed, which is low to the ground and surrounded by an assortment of stuffed animals.

Milo tucks a blanket snugly around him as Jonah settles in, his small body wriggling for the perfect spot. He gives Jonah a goodnight kiss on the forehead, and I do the same, before he puts on soft lullaby music in the background. In seconds, Jonah's eyes start to droop.

"Wish I could fall asleep that fast," I whisper.

Milo grins, his eyes sparkling in the soft light as he looks at his son. "Same."

Jonah's soft breathing fills the room as he drifts off, and we quietly step out, leaving the door slightly ajar.

"One down, one to go," Milo says as we reach Josie's door.

"She usually goes to bed a little later, but after a day at her favorite bookstore, followed by the park, and an afternoon of arts and crafts—"

"Don't forget the puzzles."

"How could I?" Milo cups my face in his big hands. "The kids had fun today. Thank you."

I quirk a brow. "Just the kids had fun?"

He smiles. "I had fun, too. I always do when I'm with you."

I lift on my toes and press my lips to his. "Correct answer."

We step into Josie's room. She's already in bed, reading, and doesn't even notice us.

"Reminds me of someone else I know," Milo murmurs.

I shrug. "Sorry not sorry."

He chuckles. "Hey, sweetie."

"Hey, Dad."

Her eyes are still glued to the page. It so reminds me of myself at that age.

"Josie."

She looks up. "Sorry. Oh, Beth. Hi!"

"Hi yourself."

"Can you read me a story please?"

I glance at Milo, and he gives me a nod.

"Sure. I'd love to," I say, sitting down on the edge of the bed.

I expect Milo to join me on the other side, but instead, he says, "I might leave you ladies to it."

"Oh."

"If that's okay?"

"Yeah, of course." I glance at Josie and smile. "We don't need boys, do we?"

"Boys are the worst."

Milo laughs and gives us a wave before slipping out the door.

I start reading her a story and after a few minutes, her eyelids grow heavy. She lets out a yawn, and right before she falls asleep, she murmurs, "I love my daddy."

It's so sweet. I press a kiss on her forehead and think to myself, *Yeah, I love him, too.*

22

Milo

We're standing at the back of one very crowded bookstore. It seems as if half of Comfort Bay has come out to Beth's sister's book signing today.

I haven't seen her yet, but I'm nervous. Not because she's a hugely popular and bestselling author—although that would be intimidating enough on its own—but also because she's the first person from Beth's family that I'm meeting.

It's a big step.

But I'm ready, and more importantly, so is Beth. She's never introduced a boyfriend to her family before, and I'm honored to be the first.

Just like I'm honored to have been her first in another special, intimate way.

I honestly wasn't expecting to end our anniversary afternoon making love to Beth in her house last month, but I sure as heck ain't complaining.

It wasn't just a physical thing, our souls truly connected, and ever since, my feelings for her have only intensified.

I always thought that when you fell in love with someone, that was it. Your feelings were capped. But I'm learning that love is a bottomless cup, you can just keep filling it up and it never overflows. Just when I think I can't love her anymore, I do.

I have to keep reminding myself that our relationship is still so new. We may have known each other for over a year, but technically, we've only been together a short while.

But it doesn't feel new to me.

I was smitten with her the first night we met.

She intrigued me and frustrated me and lived rent-free in my head ever since.

We've survived a blizzard and an earthquake together.

I've opened up to her in ways I haven't to anyone else.

She's come into my home and into my kids' lives. They adore her.

And I love her. With everything I have in me, I love her.

And the only thing preventing me from telling her that is not wanting to scare her off or come across too strong.

I promised her that she was in charge, that we'd always do things on her timeframe.

This is one of those things. It has to be.

I continually tell myself this relationship isn't going anywhere, so there's no need to rush into anything. We have all the time in the world, and when the time is right, she'll say it. Just like Josie waited to tell me she loved me, and when she finally did, I knew she meant it.

Beth is worth the wait.

I smile when I see her making her way through the throng of people to us, but if I'd like to kiss my girlfriend, I need to form an orderly queue.

She crouches down and gives Josie a hug and manages to not get bulldozed by Jonah, who is on a banana oat cookie sugar high. She gets to her feet and says hi to Boden.

"Finally," I say with a wide grin on my face as she turns to me. "My turn."

"The best things in life are worth waiting for."

I slide my hands around her waist and lower my head until my lips are hovering just over hers. "They sure are," I murmur before kissing her.

"Sorry to interrupt," Courtland says, coming over. The guy looks frazzled, like he hasn't slept for days. Beth warned me that may actually be true. Apparently, he's been counting down until today for a long time. "I hate to break this up, but Beth, your sister asked for you, and she's on in five, so..."

"Yeah. That's fine. I'm coming." She pauses. "Why don't you join me?" she suggests. "Meet her now, and then you won't be so nervous."

"I'm not nervous."

Beth arches an eyebrow.

"Fine. So I'm a little nervous."

I scoop up the kids, and we walk over to a cordoned off section of the store. Schapelle looks nothing like Beth. She's tall with long brown hair and blue eyes.

"So you're the guy who managed to snag my anti-love bookworm sis?" she says, greeting me with a warm hug.

"I guess I am."

"You're tall," says a small voice.

Schapelle glances down at Jonah and smiles. "And you must be Jonah."

"I am," he says with a clap.

"And you're Josie."

Josie nods then tucks herself behind my leg.

"It's great to finally meet you," Schapelle says, looking straight at me. "I've heard a lot about you."

My eyebrows shoot up. "People often say, *Don't believe everything you hear*, but in this case...*definitely* don't believe everything you hear."

She laughs, but something catches in her throat. She covers her mouth to cough.

"It's a packed house out there," I say.

All of a sudden, color drains from her face. "That's great. I...Oh, no..." She lurches forward.

I manage to step in front of Josie and scoop Jonah in my arms, stopping them from seeing Schapelle hurl all over the floor.

"Oh my gosh, Schapelle. Are you okay?" Beth jumps into

protective sister mode, as Courtland and I back out of the space, giving them some privacy.

Boden walks up to me. "What's the matter?"

Courtland races over, frantically muttering something about getting Schapelle water. "Uh, nothing," I say to Boden, handing him Jonah. "Would you mind taking the kids for a bit?"

"No problem."

I watch as he leads them over to the children's section.

Beth's mentioned setting him up with Amiel, which I think is a great idea. I can see those two hitting it off. Not that this is the right time to bring that up, and not that I'm about to become like everyone else in Comfort Bay and start meddling in other people's lives.

This isn't meddling, it's helping, and I'm sure there's a world of difference between the two.

Boden doesn't talk a lot about himself, but I've managed to ascertain that he's single.

And that he has his eye on a certain local girl.

He wouldn't elaborate on *who* that local girl is, only that she works on Main Street, which isn't really helpful since the street is packed with stores and restaurants and clinics.

But Amiel works at the bakery on Main Street, so if the stars align...You know what, I think I might hand this one over to Beth and her girlfriends and leave it in their capable hands.

I'm about to go and check in on Beth and her sister when a firm hand lands on my shoulder, and I spin around. "Oh, hey, you guys."

"Milo. Is that you?" Fraser asks with a chuckle, standing next to a very different-looking Culver. "I almost didn't recognize you with that thing on your face."

"You mean his smile?" Culver supplies, completing their one-two joke comedy routine.

"How long did you guys have to work on that one?" I ask rhetorically as we exchange hugs.

It's been months since I've been with my old teammates, and seeing them now makes me happy. And smiley, apparently.

"Speaking of things on our faces." I look over at Culver and tap my cheeks.

"You like?" he asks, running his fingers through his thick, dark beard.

"I do. But aren't you worried about depriving the world of your world-famous dimples?" I ask, grinning.

"As long as I'm not depriving my girl, I couldn't care less about the rest of the world."

At the exact same moment, he and Fraser tilt their heads to where Hannah and Evie are standing with Summer and Amiel.

It's nice seeing them both in love...and it's nice being in the club along with them.

"Your hair looks good, man," Fraser says.

"Thanks."

"Where's Beth?" Culver asks, looking around.

"With her sister."

"Uh-huh."

"Uh-huh."

"Uh-huh, what?" I try to glare at their goofy, smiling faces, but I know I'm in for a ribbing, and honestly, I'm kinda looking forward to it.

It's about damn time.

"What's the deal with you guys?" Fraser asks. "I see she hasn't killed you yet."

I chuckle. "No. She hasn't."

"Does that mean things are serious?" Culver chips in.

I run a hand through my newly-cropped hair, still not used

to the feel of it. "Yeah. They are. I'm..." I can't tell these guys I'm in love with her before saying the words to Beth, so I go with, "I'm a goner."

"Awww. That's so sweet," Fraser says, and while there's a hint of teasing in his delivery, there's also genuine sincerity there as well.

"It's good to see you happy," Culver supplies. "You deserve it...*Daddy*."

There's a long beat of silence at how wrong that sounded coming out of this mouth.

And then...

The three of us burst out laughing.

"Don't ever call me that again."

"I'm sorry. I'm sorry. That came out even worse than I thought it would."

"So, what's been happening with you guys? How's the house hunting going, Culver?"

He and Hannah are back from six months in Italy and looking for their forever place.

"Yeah. Fine." Fraser and I exchange a look. "Okay. Not fine. Horribly."

He goes on to tell us how much of a nightmare Willow Wilkins has been to deal with, and I can totally relate.

"She's pretty intense," I say after Culver finishes filling us in.

"Can you find another agent?" Fraser suggests.

"Already on it. We're meeting with him tomorrow."

"And what about you, Fraser. Any wedding update?"

He shakes his head, his jaw tightening. "Staying engaged is the new getting married." Culver and I look at him with blank faces, so he explains, "Evie stuck that quote on the refrigerator in an attempt to convince herself that it's okay if we have the world's longest engagement, and before you ask, yes, I've told her repeatedly that plenty of people have had way longer engagements than us, but she's not buying it."

"You'll figure it out, man," Culver says, clapping him on the shoulder.

"Who's that woman?" I ask, discreetly tipping my head to an attractive woman who's walked up to Evie and her friends.

"That's Evie's sister, Harper," Fraser says.

"Hmm. She doesn't work on Main Street by any chance, does she?"

"No." Fraser eyes me suspiciously. "And why are you asking?"

I tell them about Boden, and that I'm sleuthing for clues without sleuthing for clues.

Culver laughs. "Looks like the Comfort Bay busybody gene has claimed another victim."

"I'm not sticking my nose into other people's business," I protest, even though I totally am.

Fraser smiles. "Your nanny wouldn't have much luck with Harper, anyway. I hear she has her heart set on someone else. Not that I'm gossiping or anything."

"Like who?" I ask. "Not that I'm gossiping or anything."

"My brother," he replies.

"Does it have anything to do with contract negotiations for the new reality TV show Harper is producing and trying to get your brother to join?" Culver asks. "Not that I'm gossiping or anything."

"Could've fooled me."

A deep voice from behind has all three of us turning around.

Fraser's eyes light up. "Clayton, what are you doing here?" He doesn't give the guy a chance to respond, giving him a massive hug before introducing his brother to Culver and me.

I've never watched a single episode of any of the countless

reality TV shows Clayton Rademacher has appeared in, but his mug has been on enough magazine covers for me to recognize him. He looks a lot like Fraser, slightly shorter with a thicker build, but their facial features are similar.

"Are you a fan of Lori Connors?" I ask, wondering why he's popped up unexpectedly.

"No."

"So why are you here?" Fraser asks. "Not that it's not great to see you, I just had no idea you were in town."

Clayton doesn't respond as he scans the room, a look of intense focus on his face. I follow his gaze. His eyes have landed on Harper.

She's engrossed in a conversation, but the second her eyes land on Clayton, she mouths an expletive I can read from all the way over here and goes white as a sheet.

"Clayton? What's going on?"

Clayton ignores Fraser and mutters something that sounds an awful lot like, "I'm here to see my new wife," before stomping over to Harper.

"Did he just say..." Culver trails off as I say, "New wife?"

"That makes no sense." Fraser shakes his head in disbelief. "I mean, how? When? *Why*?"

I stand next to him. "Good thing we're not the gossiping kind, right?"

We don't get the chance to speculate on Clayton's bombshell because Courtland steps up to the stand and introduces Schapelle, I mean, Lori Connors.

Thankfully, she looks a lot better than the last time I saw her, and it's a good thing, too, because she has a lot of books to sign.

I spot Beth in the corner of the room and leave a shell-shocked Fraser and Culver to make my way to her.

"I take it Schapelle's feeling better?"

"She is. Let's go out the back," Beth says quietly. "I've got something to tell you."

"You're not secretly married to one of the Rademachers, are you?"

"Huh?"

"Nothing. Forget it."

I follow her back to a tiny storage space that, by the looks of it, doubles as a staff lounge and admin office, too.

"Is something wrong? Is it to do with your sister?"

"Schapelle is fine. Well, pregnant, but fine."

"*Pregnant*?"

"Yeah. It's a long story. I'll explain later. That's not why I brought you back here, though."

I smirk. "Was it to make out with me?"

She swats me across the chest. "Stop it. No. It was to tell you this." She tips her head up until her eyes find mine. "I love you, Milo."

I blink rapidly.

Is my mind playing tricks on me, or did she really just say that?

Guess there's only one way to find out.

"Finally," I say, keeping my voice as steady as I can.

Her eyes narrow. "What do you mean, *finally*?"

I caress the side of her face with my fingers. "Finally you've caught up with me."

"Wait. Are you saying what I think you're saying in the most annoying way you could possibly say it?"

My deep booming laugh bounces off the walls around us. "If what you think I'm saying is that I'm in love with you, too, and have been for a *loooong* time, then yes, yes it is." I tug her in closer to me, our bodies connecting. "I love you, too, Beth."

We kiss, and when she makes her signature whimpering sounds I love so much, my heart nearly leaps out of my chest.

This feels so good, so right.

It may have taken us a while to get here, but I wouldn't change a single thing about it. Okay, maybe I could have done without the earthquake, but apart from that, every single step to get to where Beth and I are today has been worth it.

They say it's about the journey, not the destination. That may well be true. But with a woman like Beth, I have a feeling it's going to be both.

And I cannot wait to see what our future has in store.

EPILOGUE

Beth

4 months later...

"'Goodnight, little man," I say, planting a soft kiss on Jonah's forehead.

"'Nigh-nigh."

His eyes are closing before I turn on the lullaby music. I will never not marvel at how he's able to do that.

I get up and leave the door slightly open.

Milo and Josie are in the living room, but before I join them, I take a look around the house—our house. Because, yes, I've moved in. I was practically living here anyway, so it made sense, but it was nice when Milo asked me during one of our weekday dates.

I've kept my place, and we're discussing whether to rent it out or keep both houses, merge the blocks, and build a bigger home. I'm veering toward that option. I love Milo and the kids more than anything, but a girl's gotta have her bathroom space.

I join Milo and Josie on the couch, and we chill in front of the TV until it's her bedtime. It's amazing how such a simple act as sitting and watching something together can feel so good.

Reading as many romance novels as I do, it can skew your perception of love a little. It's not all grand gestures and moments of emotional intensity. Real love is just as much about the simple, even mundane, everyday moment as it is all the big stuff.

The best thing is that I know that I'm safe and loved with Milo. Underneath his slightly grumpy demeanor, he's warm and kind and funny and smart...all the things I've ever wanted in a guy.

All the things my exes never were.

It's taken being with a real man to help me heal the last of the damage they did. But I have. I refuse to let what happened to me in the past get in the way of the amazing future I have with Milo and the kids.

When Josie starts yawning, I take her to bed and read her a bedtime story. Milo and I take turns, and I love how naturally he's allowed me to blend in with the kids. Like he has with our entire relationship, he's let me take control and be in charge of the pace at which things happen.

Although, with how quickly I fell for Josie and Jonah, everything has felt so natural. I have no intention of ever replacing their mom, but I can love them with all my heart and be there for them whenever they need me.

When I leave Josie's room, Milo's already in the shower, so I get ready for bed.

Another simple, mundane thing that I love?

Spending hours reading in bed at night.

It's my favorite way to spend an evening, and I'm so glad I don't have to give it up, that I've found a guy who enjoys it as much as I do. There's nothing better than snuggling up with a good book with the man you love right by your side.

Milo enters the room and I glance up from my book. He's wearing only his pajama bottoms, his sexy chest and muscular arms on full display. He may have joked about dad bod being imminent, but I ain't seeing it yet.

His hair is growing out, and I look forward to the day it's long enough so that he can tie it into a man bun.

Yep. For real.

Wild that I'd ever think that, huh?

"What?" he says, when he notices me staring. "Why are you looking at me like that?"

"No reason," I say as he climbs into bed. "I was just thinking it'll be good once your hair is a little longer and you'll be able to tie it up."

He chuckles to himself as he reaches for his book off the nightstand. "And to think, it's one of the things you used to dislike about me."

"That's before I realized you're a real softie underneath."

"Well." His eyes meet mine, and I recognize the familiar fire burning in them. "I'm not entirely soft."

I let out a small giggle. "That's very true."

Okay. So maybe reading in bed has been relegated to my second favorite bedtime activity.

I *love* being intimate with Milo. He makes me feel so safe, so loved, so beautiful. For a girl who used to be chubby and insecure about her appearance, it's an intoxicating feeling I never want to give up.

A little while later, once we're back to reading again, I notice Milo resting his book in his lap. "I've been thinking," he says.

I put my book down, too, and give him my full attention. "What's up?"

He turns on an angle so he's facing me. "Well, since we're seeing your sister tomorrow..."

I smile. "And her growing bump."

"Exactly. It's got me thinking. You're so great with Josie and Jonah, and I know they absolutely adore you..."

I have no idea where he's going with this. "Yeah?"

He curls his fingers around mine. "I'm not saying we have to rush into anything, but I do want to put it out there."

"Put what out there?"

He pauses for a moment. "I'm open to...more."

I squint. "More what?"

"Kids. Down the track. Way down the track."

"Oh."

"Yeah. I just wanted you to know that." He studies my face for a moment. "You seem surprised."

"I guess I am a little. I...I love the kids so much that I guess...they're enough, you know? Like, I know they're not biologically mine, but my love for them is as real and strong as if they were."

"I know *exactly* what you mean." He squeezes my hand. "I don't feel any difference in how I love Josie and Jonah."

"So, I'm not saying no to more kids. It just wasn't something that's on my mind."

"Fair enough."

"To be honest, I'm looking forward to becoming an aunt."

After finding out Schapelle was pregnant at her book launch, she went up the mountain to stay with Mom and Dad while she figured stuff out. Her ex is a real jerk who dumped her the moment she told him she was pregnant and said he wanted nothing to do with her and the baby.

It turns out she's figured stuff out, even if it's one of the wildest stories I've ever heard. I can totally see her putting this in a book one day. Hers is a meet-cute for the ages, that's for sure.

"It'll be nice to see your sister," Milo says.

"And her mountain man *husband*," I say with a tone.

Schapelle may be five years older than me, but she's got *a lot* going on at the moment. My sisterly instincts are on high alert

"I thought you liked the guy."

"Give me more time, and I'll find something wrong with him. I'm sure I will."

Milo chuckles. "Give the man a chance."

"I suppose I should." I make a noncommittal sound. "I just don't get it. She's seven months pregnant. Now is the worst time to be starting a relationship. She's a romance author, she knows better than that."

Milo chuckles again. "I don't think that has anything to do with it. Love happens when it happens."

Our eyes meet, and I smile. "Yeah. I guess it does." Milo doesn't return to his book straight away, so I ask, "Anything else on your mind?"

"Nope."

His neck has turned red, so I know he's lying. "Come on. Spit it out."

"What? There's nothing to spit," he says. I make a slight throat-clearing noise that always gets Milo to talk. "Okay. Fine. I was just thinking that every time we drive up that mountain, something good happens to us."

"Like getting caught in a snowstorm on our first trip and then surviving an earthquake on our second?"

"Exactly," he says with a grin. "Both things brought us closer, right? It's like that mountain is our good luck charm or something."

I let out a giggle. "But Evie and Fraser aren't getting married this time, so even if I believed your crazy theory—which, for the record, I do not—maybe our good luck has run out?"

"Nah, babe." He leans over and gives me a quick kiss. "Our good luck is just beginning."

"What was that you said last night about our good luck just beginning?"

Milo brushes off my question, letting out a grunt as he crouches by the car. Our road trip up the mountain is currently delayed by a flat tire. Granted, it's not as bad as what we've encountered before, but if anything, I'm starting to think this mountain might be a *bad* luck charm.

I glance inside the car. Josie is engrossed in her book, and Jonah is happily watching "Bluey" on a tablet.

"Can I do anything to help?" I ask.

"Nope. I got this."

I watch him calmly handle the tire, every movement smooth and confident, like he's done this a hundred times before. There's something reassuring about the way he works, focused but relaxed, making me feel at ease even by the side of the road. He tightens the last lug nut, then hoists the spare, fitting it neatly into the back. He shuts the trunk with a satisfying thud.

I hand him a wipe, and he quickly cleans his hands.

"There. All done. Ready to keep going?" he asks.

"One thing."

"What?"

"This."

I step closer, feeling the cool mountain breeze as I rise onto my toes to meet his lips. My heart races a little as I lean in, wrapping my arms around his neck. His hands gently settle on my waist, and when our lips finally touch, everything feels so right.

When we pull apart, I realize we have an audience. Josie lowers the window. "Did you give Beth the ring, Dad?"

The ring?

Milo tries to disguise his panic—and fails—forcing a smile that takes me back in time to when his smiles were enough to scare small children.

"What ring?" I ask, looking up into his eyes.

"I had it all planned out," he mutters, shaking his head. "I've been in touch with Schapelle, and she helped me plan out a big romantic proposal in the mountains."

My heart stops.

I'm so overwhelmed I can't help the tears from falling down my face.

"What's wrong, Beth?" Josie asks.

I start wiping them away, not to worry her. "Nothing. I'm fine, sweetie. These are good tears. Happy tears."

"Like when Dad watches *The Lion King*?"

"Hey. That was meant to be our little secret." Milo frowns, pretending to be upset, but I can tell he's not.

At least not about the movie.

"The ring?" I hedge.

He lets out a deep breath. "Well, I suppose we are in the mountains. And I am doing this in front of the three people I love more than anything in the world. Wait here."

He goes to the car and when he returns a moment later, he drops down on one knee. Looking up at me, he says, "I don't know what it is about you, but you captivated me from the moment I met you. I've opened up to you more than I have to anyone else in my life. You bring out the best in me, and I hope I make you feel safe and protected and loved and cherished because you deserve that, Beth. You deserve to be treated like a queen."

He takes another deep breath. "Beth Anne Moore, will you do me the honor of being my wife?"

"Yes. Of course."

He slips the ring onto my finger, his hand a little shaky, and my heart feels like it might burst. The ring sparkles in the mountain sunlight, delicate and perfect, just like this moment. I glance over and see the kids watching from the car, their wide eyes making everything feel even more real, and all I can think is, this is my forever.

He rises from his bent knee, his eyes never leaving mine, and before I can catch my breath, his hands are on my waist, pulling me gently toward him. The kiss is soft at first but filled with so much emotion it makes my knees weak. The mountains, the kids watching—it all fades away as his lips meet mine.

"I just realized something," I pull back as it dawns on me.

"What?"

If I do the hyphenated thing and keep my maiden name, my new surname will be Moore-Payne."

He lets out a chuckle, skimming the backs of his fingers down the side of my face. "Fitting, wouldn't you say?"

I slap him across the chest and huff. "I hope it's not an omen."

"It isn't," he says, his voice deep and filled with emotion. "You make me happier than I've ever been, Beth. We're going to have a great life together."

"Can I come out and give you hugs?" Josie asks.

"Of course, sweetie," Milo answers.

The car door flies open, and Josie leaps into her father's arms before launching into mine. We go over to Jonah in the backseat to give him high-fives but he's more interested in "Bluey" than in joining our celebration.

It's funny. I've read thousands of romance novels with epic proposals on a beautiful beach at sunset, or in a historical castle, or during a hot air balloon ride. But nothing I've ever read comes close to the proposal I got. The one by the side of the road. It might not be the most romantic setting, but it sure is the perfect one.

Milo wraps his arms around me, and I have this incredible warmth and certainty wash over me. It's not shock, it's pure happiness. Everything feels so right, like this is exactly where I'm meant to be. My heart is so full, and I can't stop smiling, knowing we're starting something beautiful together.

The other funny thing about romance novels is that they

always end on the cusp of forever. The couple have all their setbacks—they go from being friends, or enemies, or just plain clueless to lovers—and then, after getting through all the obstacles thrown their way, they end up together and it's *The End*.

But the thing about Milo and me is, the happily-ever-after *isn't* the end—it's only the beginning.

THE END

ABOUT ASH KELLY

Ash writes sweet contemporary closed-door romances - think
lovable characters + *Gilmore Girls* vibes.

For more information about Ash,
please visit - **www.ashkellyauthor.com**

Made in the USA
Middletown, DE
19 March 2025

72954456R00171